C0-AYJ-598

FIVE LITTLE PEPPERS
AND HOW THEY GREW

To Robin

Her 9th birthday

From

Auntie Ruth

Five Little Peppers and How They Grew

(Complete Authorized Edition)

by
MARGARET SIDNEY

(Lothrop, Mrs. Harriet Mulford (Stone) 1844-1924)

GROSSET & DUNLAP

Publishers   NEW YORK

By arrangement with Houghton Mifflin Company

PZ7
L913
Fi7

COPYRIGHT, 1881, BY D. LOTHROP AND COMPANY
COPYRIGHT, 1909, BY HARRIETT M. LOTHROP
COPYRIGHT, 1936, BY HOUGHTON MIFFLIN COMPANY

ALL RIGHTS RESERVED INCLUDING THE RIGHT TO REPRODUCE
THIS BOOK OR PARTS THEREOF IN ANY FORM

PRINTED IN THE U.S.A.

TO THE MEMORY OF

MY MOTHER:

wise in counsel, tender in judgment and in all charity,

strong in Christian faith

and purpose,

I dedicate, with reverence, this simple book

CONTENTS

CONTENTS

FIVE LITTLE PEPPERS
AND HOW THEY GREW

FIVE LITTLE PEPPERS AND HOW THEY GREW

I

A HOME VIEW

THE little old kitchen had quieted down from the bustle and confusion of midday; and now, with its afternoon manners on, presented a holiday aspect that, as the principal room in the brown house, it was eminently proper it should have. It was just on the edge of the twilight; and the little Peppers, all except Ben, the oldest of the flock, were taking a "breathing spell" as their mother called it, which meant some quiet work suitable for the hour. It was all the "breathing spell" they could remember, however, poor things; for times were hard with them now. The father had died when Phronsie was a baby, and since then Mrs. Pepper had had hard work to scrape together money enough to put bread into her children's mouths, and to pay the rent of the Little Brown House.

But she had met life too bravely to be beaten down now. So with a stout heart and a cheery

11

face, she had worked away day after day at mak‹ ing coats, and tailoring and mending of all descriptions; and she had seen with pride that couldn't be concealed, her noisy, happy brood growing up around her, and filling her heart with comfort, and making the Little Brown House fairly ring with jollity and fun.

"Poor things!" she would say to herself, "they haven't had any bringing up; they've just scrambled up!" And then she would set her lips together tightly, and fly at her work faster than ever. "I must get learning for 'em someway, but I don't see *how!*"

Once or twice she had thought, "Now the time's coming!" but it never did: for winter shut in very cold, and it took so much more to feed and warm them that the money went faster than ever. And then, when the way seemed clear again, the store changed hands, so that for a long time she failed to get her usual supply of sacks and coats to make; and that made sad havoc in the quarters and half-dollars laid up as her nest-egg. But —— "Well, it'll come *some* time," she would say to herself; "because it *must!*" And so at it again she would fly, brisker than ever.

"To help mother," was the great ambition of

all the children, older and younger; but in Polly's and Ben's souls, the desire grew so overwhelmingly great as to absorb all lesser things. Many and vast were their secret plans, by which they were to astonish her at some future day, which they would only confide—as they did everything else—to one another. For this brother and sister were everything to each other, and stood loyally together through thick and thin.

Polly was ten, and Ben one year older; and the younger three of the "Five Little Peppers," as they were always called, looked up to them with the intensest admiration and love. What *they* failed to do, *couldn't* very well be done by *any* one!

"O dear!" exclaimed Polly, as she sat over in the corner by the window, helping her mother pull out basting threads from a coat she had just finished, and giving an impatient twitch to the sleeve, "I do wish we could ever have any light— just as much as we want!"

"You don't need any light to see these threads," said Mrs. Pepper, winding up hers carefully, as she spoke, on an old spool. "Take care, Polly, you broke that; thread's dear now."

"I couldn't help it," said Polly, vexedly; "it

snapped; everything's dear now, seems to me! I wish we could have—oh! ever an' ever so many candles; as many as we wanted! I'd light 'em all, so there! and have it light here *one* night, anyway! "

" Yes, and go dark all the rest of the year, like as anyway," observed Mrs. Pepper, stopping to untie a knot. " Folks who do so never have any candles," she added, sententiously.

" How many'd you have, Polly? " asked Joel, curiously, laying down his hammer, and regarding her with the utmost anxiety.

" Oh, two hundred! " said Polly, decidedly. " I'd have two hundred, all in a row! "

" *Two hundred candles!* " echoed Joel, in amazement. " My whockety! what a lot! "

" Don't say such dreadful words, Joel," put in Polly, nervously, stooping to pick up her spool of basting thread that was racing away all by itself; " 'tisn't nice."

" 'Tisn't worse 'n to wish you'd got things you haven't," retorted Joel. " I don't believe you'd light 'em all at once," he added, incredulously.

" Yes, I would, too! " replied Polly, recklessly; " two hundred of 'em, if I had a chance; all at once, so there, Joey Pepper! "

"Oh!" said little Davie, drawing a long sigh. "Why, 'twould be just like heaven, Polly! but wouldn't it cost money, though!"

"I don't care," said Polly, giving a flounce in her chair, which snapped another thread; "O dear me! I didn't mean to, mammy; well, I wouldn't care how much money it cost, we'd have as much light as we wanted for once; so!"

"Goodness!" said Mrs. Pepper, "you'd have the house afire! Two hundred candles! who ever heard of such a thing!"

"Would they burn?" asked Phronsie, anxiously, getting up from the floor where she was crouching with David, overseeing Joel nail on the cover of an old box; and going to Polly's side she awaited her answer patiently.

"Burn?" said Polly. "There, that's done now, mamsie dear!" And she put the coat, with a last little pat, into her mother's lap. "I guess they *would*, Phronsie, pet." And Polly caught up the little girl, and spun round and round the old kitchen till they were both glad to stop.

"Then," said Phronsie, as Polly put her down and stood breathless after her last glorious spin, "I do so wish we might, Polly; oh, just this very one minute! " And Phronsie clasped her fat little hands in rapture at the thought.

"Well," said Polly, giving a look up at the old clock in the corner; "goodness me! it's half-past five; and 'most time for Ben to come home! "

Away she flew to get supper. So for the next few moments nothing was heard but the pulling out of the old table into the middle of the floor, the laying of the cloth, and all the other bustle attendant upon the getting ready for Ben. Polly went skipping around, cutting the bread, and bringing dishes; only stopping long enough to fling some scraps of reassuring nonsense to the two boys, who were thoroughly dismayed at being obliged to remove their traps into a corner.

Phronsie still stood just where Polly left her *Two hundred candles!* oh! what *could* it mean! She gazed up to the old beams overhead, and around the dingy walls, and to the old black stove, with the fire nearly out, and then over everything the kitchen contained, trying to think how it would seem. To have it bright and winsome and warm! to suit Polly—"*Oh!*" she screamed.

"Goodness! " cried Polly, taking her head out of the old cupboard in the corner, "how you scared me. Phronsie! "

"Would they *never* go out?" asked the child, gravely, still standing where Polly left her.

"What?" asked Polly, stopping with a dish of cold potatoes in her hand. "What, Phronsie?"

"Why, the candles," said the child, "the ever-an'-ever so many pretty lights!"

"O my senses!" cried Polly, with a little laugh, "haven't you forgotten that! Yes—no, that is, Phronsie, if we could have 'em at all, we wouldn't *ever* let 'em go out!"

"Not once?" asked Phronsie, coming up to Polly with a little skip, and nearly upsetting her, potatoes and all—"not once, Polly, truly?"

"No, not forever-an'-ever," said Polly; "take care, Phronsie! there goes a potato; no, we'd keep 'em always!"

"No, you don't want to," said Mrs. Pepper, coming out of the bedroom in time to catch the last words; "they won't be good to-morrow; better have 'em to-night, Polly."

"Ma'am!" said Polly, setting down her potato-dish on the table, and staring at her mother with all her might—"have *what*, mother?"

"Why, the potatoes, to be sure," replied Mrs. Pepper; "didn't you say you better keep 'em child?"

" 'Twasn't potatoes—at all," said Polly, with a little gasp; " 'twas—O dear me! here's Ben!" for the door opened, and Phronsie, with a scream of delight, bounded into Ben's arms.

"It's just jolly," said Ben, coming in, his chubby face all aglow, and his big blue eyes shining so honest and true; "it's just jolly to get home! Supper ready, Polly?"

"Yes," said Polly; "that is—all but ——" and she dashed off for Phronsie's eating-apron.

"Sometime," said Phronsie, with her mouth half-full, when the meal was nearly over, "we're going to be *awful* rich; we are, Ben, truly!"

"No?" said Ben, affecting the most hearty astonishment; "you don't say so, Chick."

"Yes," said Phronsie, shaking her yellow head very wisely at him, and diving down into her cup of very weak milk and water to see if Polly *had* put any sugar in by mistake—a custom always expectantly observed. "Yes, we are really, Bensie, very dreadful rich!"

"I wish we could be rich now, then," said Ben, taking another generous slice of the brown bread; "in time for mamsie's birthday," and he cast a sorrowful glance at Polly.

"I know," said Polly; "O dear! if we only *could* celebrate it!"

"I don't want any other celebration," said Mrs. Pepper, beaming on them so that a little flash of sunshine seemed to hop right down on the table, "than to look around on you all; I'm rich now, and that's a fact!"

"Mamsie doesn't mind her five bothers," cried Polly, jumping up and running to hug her mother, thereby producing a like desire in all the others, who immediately left their seats and followed her example.

"Mother's rich enough," ejaculated Mrs. Pepper, her bright, black eyes glistening with delight, as the noisy troop filed back to their bread and potatoes; "if we can only keep together, dears, and grow up good, so that the Little Brown House won't be ashamed of us, that's all I ask."

"Well," said Polly, in a burst of confidence to Ben, after the table had been pushed back against the wall, the dishes nicely washed, wiped, and set up neatly in the cupboard, and all traces of the meal cleared away; "I don't care; let's *try* to get a celebration, somehow, for mamsie!"

"How are you going to do it?" asked Ben, who was of a decidedly practical turn of mind, and thus couldn't always follow Polly in her flights of imagination.

"I don't know," said Polly; "but we *must* some way."

"Phoh! that's no good," said Ben, disdainfully; then seeing Polly's face, he added, kindly, "let's think, though; and p'raps there'll be some way."

"Oh, I know," cried Polly, in delight; "I know the very thing, Ben! let's make her a cake; a big one, you know, and ——"

"She'll see you bake it," said Ben; "or else she'll smell it, and that'd be just as bad."

"No, she won't, either," replied Polly. "Don't you know she's going to help Mrs. Henderson to-morrow; so there!"

"So she is," said Ben; "good for you, Polly, you always think of everything!"

"And then," said Polly, with a comfortable little feeling in her heart at Ben's praise, "why, we can have it all out of the way perfectly splendid when she comes home—and besides, Grandma Bascom'll tell me how. You know we've only got brown flour, Ben; I mean to go right over and ask her now."

"Oh, no, you mustn't," cried Ben, catching hold of her arm as she was preparing to fly off. "Mammy'll find it out; better wait till to-morrow; and besides, Polly ——" and Ben stopped, unwilling to dampen this propitious beginning. " The stove'll act like everything, to-morrow! I know 'twill; then what'll you do! "

" It *sha'n't!* " said Polly, running up to look it in the face; " if it does, I'll shake it; the mean old thing! "

The idea of Polly's shaking the lumbering old black affair, sent Ben into such a peal of laughter that it brought all the other children running to the spot; and nothing would do, but they must one and all be told the reason. So Polly and Ben took them into confidence, which so elated them that half an hour after, when long past her bed-time, Phronsie declared, " I'm not going to bed! I want to sit up like Polly! "

" Don't tease her," whispered Polly to Ben, who thought she ought to go; so she sat straight up on her little stool, winking like everything to keep awake.

At last, as Polly was in the midst of one of her liveliest sallies, over tumbled Phronsie, a sleepy little heap, right on to the floor.

" I want—to go—to bed! " she said; " take me —Polly! "

" I thought so," laughed Polly, and bundled her off into the bedroom.

II

MAKING HAPPINESS FOR MAMSIE

AND so the minute her mother had departed for the minister's house next morning, and Ben had gone to his day's work, chopping wood for Deacon Blodgett, Polly assembled her forces around the old stove, and proceeded to business. She and the children had been up betimes that morning to get through with the work; and now, as they glanced around with a look of pride on the neatly swept floor, the dishes all done, and everything in order, the moment their mother's back was turned they began to implore Polly to hurry and begin.

"It's 'most 'leven o'clock," said Joel, who, having no work to do outside, that day, was prancing around, wild to help along the festivities; "it's 'most 'leven o'clock, Polly Pepper! you won't have it done."

"Oh, no; 'tisn't either, Joe," said Polly, with a very flushed face, and her arms full of kindlings,

22

glancing up at the old clock as she spoke; " 'tisn't but quarter of nine; there, take care, Phronsie! you can't lift off the cover; do help her, Davie."

"No; let me! " cried Joel, springing forward; " it's my turn; Dave got the kindlings; it's my turn, Polly."

"So 'tis," said Polly; "I forgot; there," as she flung in the wood, and poked it all up in a nice little heap, coaxingly. " It can't help but burn; *what* a cake we'll have for mamsie! "

"It'll be so big," cried Phronsie, hopping around on one toe, "that mamsie won't know what to do, will she, Polly? "

"No, I don't believe she will," said Polly, gaily, stuffing in more wood; "O *dear!* there goes Ben's putty; it's all fallen out! "

"So it has," said Joel, going around back of the stove to explore; and then he added, cheerfully, "it's bigger'n ever; oh! it's an awful big hole, Polly! "

"Now, whatever *shall* we do! " said Polly, in great distress; "that hateful old crack! and Ben's clear off to Deacon Blodgett's! "

"I'll run an' get him," cried Joel, briskly; "I'll bring him right home in ten minutes."

"Oh, no, you must not, Joe," cried Polly, in

alarm; " it wouldn't ever be right to take him from his work; mamsie wouldn't like it."

" What *will* you do then? " asked Joel, pausing on his way to the door.

" I'm sure I don't know," said Polly, getting down on her knees to examine the crack; " I shall have to stuff it with paper, I s'pose."

" 'Twon't stay in," said Joel, scornfully; " don't you know you stuffed it before, last week? "

" I know," said Polly, with a small sigh; and sitting down on the floor, she remained quite still for a minute, with her two black hands stuck out straight before her.

" Can't you fix it? " asked Davie, soberly, coming up; " then we can't have the cake."

" O dear me! " exclaimed Polly, springing up quickly; " don't be afraid; we're going to *have* that cake! There, you ugly old thing, you! (this to the stove) see what you've done! " as two big tears flew out of Phronsie's brown eyes, at the direful prospect; and the sorrowful faces of the two boys looked up into Polly's own, for comfort. " I can fix it, I 'most know; do get some paper, Joe, as quick as you can."

" Don't know where there is any," said Joel,

rummaging around; " it's all torn up; 'xcept the almanac; can't I take that? "

" Oh, mercy, no! " cried Polly; " put it right back, Joe; I guess there's some in the wood-shed."

" There isn't, either," said little Davie, quickly; " Joel and me took it to make kites with."

" O dear! " groaned Polly; " I don't know what we *shall* do; unless," as a bright thought struck her, " you let me have the kites, boys."

" Can't," said Joel; " they all flew away; or got tore up."

" Well, now, children," said Polly, turning round impressively upon them, the effect of which was heightened by the extremely crocky appearance she had gained in her explorations, " we *must* have some paper, or something to stop up that old hole with—some way, *there!* "

" I know," said little Davie, " where we'll get it! it's up-stairs; " and without another word he flew out of the room, and the next minute he put into Polly's hand an old leather boot-top, one of his most treasured possessions. " You can chip it," he said, " real fine, and then 'twill go in."

" So we can," said Polly; " and you're a real good boy, Davie, to give it; that's a splendid present to help celebrate for mamsie! "

"I'd give a boot-top," said Joel, looking grimly at the precious bit of leather which Polly was rapidly stripping into little bits, "if I had it; I don't have anything!"

"I know you would, Joey," said Polly, kindly; "there, now, you'll stay, I guess!" as with the united efforts of the two boys, cheered on by Phronsie's enthusiastic little crow of delight, the leather was crammed into place, and the fire began to burn.

"Now, boys," said Polly, getting up, and drawing a long breath, "I'm going over to Grandma Bascom's to get her to tell me how to make the cake; and you must stay and keep house."

"I'm going to nail," said Joel; "I've got lots to do."

"All right," said Polly, tying on her hood; "Phronsie'll love to watch you; I won't be gone long," and she was off.

"Grandma Bascom" wasn't really the children's grandmother; only everybody in the village called her so by courtesy. Her cottage was over across the lane, and just a bit around the corner; and Polly flew along and up to the door, knowing that now she would be helped out of her difficulty. She didn't stop to knock, as the old lady was so

deaf she knew she wouldn't hear her, but opened
the door and walked in. Grandma was sweeping
up the floor, already as neat as a pin; when she
saw Polly coming, she stopped, and leaned on her
broom.

" How's your ma? " she asked, when Polly had
said " good morning," and then hesitated.

" Oh, mammy's pretty well," shouted Polly into
the old lady's ear; " and to-morrow's her birthday! "

" To-morrow'll be a bad day! " said grandma.
" Oh, don't never say that. You mustn't borrow
trouble, child."

" I didn't," said Polly; " I mean—it's her
birthday, grandma! " this last so loud that
grandma's cap-border vibrated perceptibly.

" The land's sakes 'tis! " cried Mrs. Bascom, delightedly; " you don't say so! "

" Yes," said Polly, skipping around the old
lady, and giving her a small hug; " and we're going to give her a surprise."

" What is the matter with her eyes? " asked
grandma, sharply, turning around and facing her;
" she's been a-sewin' too stiddy, hain't she? "

" A *surprise!* " shouted Polly, standing upon

tiptoe, to bring her mouth on a level with the old lady's ear; " a *cake,* grandma, a big one! "

" A *cake!* " exclaimed grandma, dropping the broom to settle her cap, which Polly, in her extreme endeavors to carry on the conversation, had knocked slightly awry; " well, that'll be fine."

" Yes," said Polly, picking up the broom, and flinging off her hood at the same time; " and, oh! won't you please tell me how to make it, grandma! "

" To be sure; to be sure; " cried the old lady, delighted beyond measure to give advice; " I've got splendid receets; I'll go get 'em right off," and she ambled to the door of the pantry.

" And I'll finish sweeping up," said Polly, which grandma didn't hear; so she took up the broom, and sent it energetically and merrily flying away to the tune of her own happy thoughts.

" Yes, they're right in here," said grandma, waddling back with an old tin teapot in her hand; —" goodness, child! what a dust you've kicked up! that ain't the way to sweep," and she took the broom out of Polly's hand, who stood stock still in mortification. " There," she said, drawing it mildly over the few bits she could scrape together, and gently coaxing them into a little heap; " that's the way; and then they don't go all over the room."

" I'm sorry," began poor Polly.

" 'Tain't any matter," said Mrs. Bascom, kindly, catching sight of Polly's discomfited face; " 'tain't a mite of matter; you'll sweep better next time; now let's go to the cake; " and putting the broom into the corner, she waddled back again to the table, followed by Polly, and proceeded to turn out the contents of the teapot, in search of just the right " receet."

But the right one didn't seem to appear; not even after the teapot was turned upside down and shaken by both grandma's and Polly's anxious hands. Every other " receet " seemed to tumble out gladly, and stare them in the face,—little dingy rolls of yellow paper, with an ancient odor of spice still clinging to them; but all efforts to find this particular one failed utterly.

" Won't some other one do? " asked Polly, in the interval of fruitless searching, when grandma bewailed and lamented, and wondered, " where I could 'a' put it! "

" No, no, child," answered the old lady; " now, where *do* you s'pose 'tis! " and she clapped both hands to her head, to see if she could possibly remember; "no, no, child," she repeated. "Why, they had it down to my niece Mirandy's weddin' —'twas just elegant! light as a feather; and 'twa'n't rich, either," she added; "no eggs, nor——"

"Oh! I couldn't have *eggs!*" cried Polly, in amazement at the thought of such luxury; "and we've only brown flour, grandma, you know."

"Well, you can make it of brown," said Mrs. Bascom, kindly; "when the raisins is in 'twill look quite nice."

"Oh! we haven't any raisins," answered Polly.

"*Haven't any raisins!*" echoed grandma, looking at her over her spectacles; "what *are* you goin' to put in?"

"Oh—cinnamon," said Polly, briskly; "we've got plenty of that, and—it'll be good, I guess, grandma! " she finished, anxiously; "anyway, we *must* have a cake; there isn't any other way to celebrate mamsie's birthday."

"Well, now," said grandma, bustling around; "I shouldn't be surprised if you had real good luck, Polly! and your ma'll set ever so much by it; now, if we only could find that receet! " And returning to the charge she commenced to fumble among her bits of paper again; " I never shall forget how they eat on it; why, there wasn't a crumb left, Polly! "

" O dear! " said Polly, to whom " Mirandy's wedding-cake " now became the height of her desires; " if you only *can* find it! can't I climb up and look on the pantry shelves?."

" Maybe 'tis there," said Mrs. Bascom, slowly; " you might try; sometimes I do put things away, so's to have 'em safe."

So Polly got an old wooden chair, mounted up on it, and with grandma below to direct, she handed down bowl after bowl, interspersed at the right intervals with cracked teacups and handleless pitchers. But at the end of these explorations, " Mirandy's wedding-cake " was farther off than ever!

" 'Tain't a mite o' use," at last said the old lady, sinking down in despair, while Polly perched on the top of the chair and looked at her; " I must 'a' give it away."

" Can't I have the next best one, then? " asked Polly, despairingly, feeling sure that " Mirandy's wedding-cake " would have celebrated the day just right; " and I must hurry right home, please," she added, getting down from the chair.

and tying on her hood; " or Phronsie won't know what to do."

So another " receet " was looked over, and selected; and with many charges, and bits of advice not to let the oven get too hot, etc., Polly took the precious scrap of paper in her hand, and flew over home.

" Now, we've got to ——" she began, bounding in merrily, with dancing eyes; but her delight had a sudden stop, as she brought up so suddenly at the sight within, that she couldn't utter another word. Phronsie was crouching, a miserable little heap of woe, in one corner of the mother's big calico-covered rocking-chair, and crying bitterly, while Joel hung over her in the utmost concern.

" *What's the matter?* " gasped Polly. Flinging the " receet " on the table, she rushed up to the old chair and was down on her knees before it, her arms around the little figure. Phronsie turned, and threw herself into Polly's protecting arms, who gathered her up, and sitting down in the depths of the chair, comforted her as only she could.

" What is it? " she asked of Joel, who was nervously begging Phronsie not to cry; " now. tell me all that's happened."

" I was a-nailing," began Joel; " O dear! Don't cry, Phronsie! do stop her, Polly."

" *Go on,*" said Polly, hoarsely.

" I was a-nailing," began Joel, slowly, " and— and—Davie's gone to get the peppermint," he added, brightening up.

" Tell me, Joe," said Polly, " all that's been going on! " and she looked sternly into his face; " or I'll get Davie to," as little Davie came running back, with a bottle of castor oil, which in his flurry he had mistaken for peppermint. This he presented with a flourish to Polly, who was too excited to see it.

" Oh, no! " cried Joel, in intense alarm; " Davie ain't going to! I'll tell, Polly; I will, truly."

" Go on, then," said Polly; " tell at *once;* " feeling that if somebody didn't tell pretty soon, she should tumble over.

" Well," said Joel, gathering himself up with a fresh effort, " the old hammer was shaking, and Phronsie stuck her foot in the way—and—I couldn't help it, Polly—no, I just couldn't, Polly."

Quick as a flash, Polly tore off the little old shoe, and well-worn stocking, and brought to light Phronsie's fat little foot. Tenderly taking hold of the white toes, the boys clustering around in the greatest anxiety, she worked them back and forth, and up and down. " There isn't anything broken," she said at last, and drew a long breath.

" It's there," said Phronsie, through a rain of tears; " and it hurts, Polly; " and she began to wiggle the big toe, where around the nail was settling a small, black spot.

" Poor little toe," began Polly, cuddling up the suffering foot. Just then, a small and peculiar noise struck her ear; and looking up she saw Joel, with a very distorted face, making violent efforts to keep from bursting out into a loud cry. All his attempts, however, failed; and he flung himself into Polly's lap in a perfect torrent of tears. " I didn't—mean to—Polly," he cried; " 'twas the— ugly old hammer! *O dear!*"

" There, there, Joey, dear," said Polly, gathering him up in the other corner of the old chair, close to her side; " don't feel bad; I know you didn't mean to," and she dropped a kiss on his stubby brown head.

When Phronsie saw that anybody else *could* cry, she stopped immediately, and leaning over Polly, put one little fat hand on Joel's neck. " Don't cry," she said; " does *your* toe ache? "

At this, Joel screamed louder than ever; and Polly was at her wit's end to know what to do, for the boy's heart was almost broken. That he should have hurt Phronsie! the baby, and pet of the whole house, upon whom all their hearts centred—it was too much. So for the next few moments, Polly had all she could do in the way of comforting and consoling him. Just as she had succeeded, the door opened, and Grandma Bascom walked in.

"Settin' down?" said she; "I hope your cake ain't in, Polly," looking anxiously at the stove, "for I've found it;" and she waved a small piece of paper triumphantly towards the rocking-chair as she spoke.

"Do tell her," said Polly to little David, "what's happened; for I can't get up."

So little Davie went up to the old lady, and standing on tiptoe, screamed into her ear all the particulars he could think of, concerning the accident that had just happened.

"Hey?" said grandma, in a perfect bewilderment; "what's he a-sayin', Polly?—I can't make it out."

"You'll have to go all over it again, David,"

said Polly, despairingly; "I don't believe she heard one word."

So David tried again; this time with better success. And then he got down from his tiptoes, and escorted grandma to Phronsie, in flushed triumph.

"Land alive!" said the old lady, sitting down in the chair which he brought her; "you got pounded, did you?" looking at Phronsie, as she took the little foot in her ample hand.

"Yes'm," said Polly, quickly; "it wasn't any one's fault; what'll we do for it, grandma?"

"Wormwood," said the old lady, adjusting her spectacles with extreme deliberation, and then examining the little black-and-blue spot, which was spreading rapidly—"wormwood is the very best thing; and I've got some to home—you run right over," she said, turning round on David, quickly, "an' get it; it's a-hangin' by the chimbley."

"Let me! let me!" cried Joel, springing out of the old chair, so suddenly that grandma's spectacles nearly dropped off in fright. "Oh! I want to do it for Phronsie!"

"Yes, let Joel, please," put in Polly; "he'll find it, grandma."

So Joel departed with great speed; and presently returned, with a bunch of dry herbs, which dangled comfortingly by his side, as he came in.

"Now I'll fix it," said Mrs. Bascom, getting up and taking off her shawl; "there's a few raisins for you, Polly; I don't want 'em, and they'll make your cake go better," and she placed a little parcel on the table as she spoke. "Yes, I'll put it to steep; an' after it's put on real strong, and tied up in an old cloth, Phronsie won't know as she's got *any* toes! " and grandma broke up a generous supply of the herb, and put it into an old tin cup, which she covered up with a saucer, and placed on the stove.

"Oh! " said Polly; " I *can't* thank you! for the raisins and all—you're *so* good! "

"They're awful hard," said Joel, investigating the bundle with Davie, which, however, the old lady luckily didn't hear.

"There, don't cry," she said, cheerily; "an' I found Cousin Mirandy's weddin'-cake receet, for ——"

"*Did* you? " cried Polly; " oh! I'm *so* glad! " feeling as if that were comfort enough for a good deal.

"Yes, 'twas in my Bible," said Mrs. Bascom;

" I remember now; I put it there to be ready to give John's folks when they come in; they wanted it; so you'll go all straight now; and I must get home, for I left some meat a-b'ilin'." So grandma put on her shawl, and waddled off, leaving a great deal of comfort behind her.

" Now, says I," said Polly to Phronsie, when the little foot was snugly tied up in the wet wormwood, " you've got to have on one of mamsie's old slippers."

" Oh, ho! " laughed Phronsie; " won't that be funny, Polly! "

" I should think it *would*," laughed Polly, back again, pulling on the big black cloth slipper, which Joel produced from the bedroom, the two boys joining uproariously, as the old black thing flapped dismally up and down, and showed strong symptoms of flying off. " We shall have to tie it on."

" It looks like a pudding-bag," said Joel, as Polly tied it securely round the middle with a bit of twine; " an old black pudding-bag! " he finished.

" Old black pudding-bag! " echoed Phronsie, with a merry little crow; and then all of a sudden she grew very sober, and looked intently at the foot stuck out straight before her, as she still sat in the chair.

"What is it, Phronsie?" asked Polly, who was bustling around, making preparations for the cake-making.

"Can I *ever* wear my new shoes again?" asked the child, gravely, looking dismally at the black bundle before her.

"Oh, yes; my goodness, yes!" cried Polly, "as quick again as ever; you'll be around again as smart as a cricket in a week—see if you are not!"

"Will it go on?" asked Phronsie, still looking incredulously at the bundle, "and button up?"

"Yes, indeed!" cried Polly, again; "button into every one of the little holes, Phronsie Pepper; just as elegant as ever!"

"Oh!" said Phronsie; and then she gave a sigh of relief, and thought no more of it, because Polly said so.

III

MAMSIE'S BIRTHDAY

"Run down and get the cinnamon, will you, Joey!" said Polly; "it's in the 'Provision Room.'"

The "Provision Room" was a little shed that was tacked on to the main house, and reached by a short flight of rickety steps; so called, because Polly said, "It's a good place to *keep* provisions, even if we haven't any; and besides," she always finished, "it sounds nice!"

"Come on, Dave! then we'll get something to eat!"

So the cinnamon was handed up, and then Joel flew back to Davie.

And now, Polly's cake was done, and ready for the oven. With many admiring glances from herself and Phronsie, who with Seraphina, an extremely old but greatly revered doll, tightly hugged in her arms, was watching everything with the biggest of eyes from the depths of the old chair, it was placed in the oven, the door shut to with a happy little bang, and then Polly gathered Phronsie up in her arms, and sat down in the chair to have a good time with her and to watch the process of cooking.

There was a bumping noise coming from the "Provision Room" that sounded ominous, and then a smothered sound of words, followed by a scuffling over the old floor.

"*Boys!*" called Polly. No answer; everything was just as still as a mouse. "*Joel and David!*" called Polly, again, in her loudest tones.

"Yes," came up the crooked stairs, in Davie's voice.

"Come up here, right away!" went back again from Polly. So up the stairs trudged the two boys, and presented themselves rather sheepishly before the big chair.

"What was that noise?" she asked; "what have you been doing?"

"Warn't nothing but the pail," answered Joel, not looking at her.

"We had something to eat," said Davie, by way of explanation; "you always let us."

"I know," said Polly; "that's right, you can have as much bread as you want to; but what have you been doing with the pail?"

"Nothing," said Joel; "'twouldn't hang up, that's all."

"And you've been bumping it," said Polly; "oh! Joel, how *could* you! You might have broken it; and then what would mamsie say?"

"I didn't bump it worse'n Davie, so there!" said Joel, stoutly, with his hands in his pockets.

"Why, Davie," said Polly, turning to him sorrowfully, "I shouldn't have thought *you* would!"

"Well, I'm tired of hanging it up," said little Davie, vehemently; "and I said I wasn't a-going to; Joel *always* makes me; I've done it for two million times, I guess!"

"O dear!" said Polly, sinking back into the chair, "I don't know what I ever *shall* do; here's Phronsie hurt; and we want to celebrate to-morrow; and you two boys are bumping and banging out the bread pail, and——"

"Oh! we won't!" cried both of the children, perfectly overwhelmed with remorse; "we'll hang it right up."

"*I'll* hang it," said Davie, clattering off down the stairs with a will.

"No, *I* will!" shouted Joel, going after him at double pace; and presently both came up with shining faces, and reported it nicely done.

" And now," said Polly, after they had all sat around the stove another half-hour, watching and sniffing expectantly, " the cake's done!—oh! dreadful!   it's turning *black!*" and quick as a wink Polly twitched it out with energy, and set it on the table.

O dear! of all things in the world!   The beautiful cake over which so many hopes had been formed, that was to have given so much happiness on the morrow to the dear mother, presented a forlorn appearance as it stood there in anything but holiday attire.   It was quite black on the top, in the centre of which was a depressing little dump, as if to say, " My feelings wouldn't allow me to rise to the occasion! "

" *Now,*" said Polly, turning away with a little fling, and looking at the stove, " I hope you're satisfied, you old thing!   You've spoiled our mamsie's birthday! " and without a bit of warning, she sat right down in the middle of the floor and began to cry as hard as she could!

" Well, I never! " said a cheery voice, that made the children skip.

" It's Mrs. Beebe; oh, it's Mrs. Beebe! " cried Davie; " see, Polly."

Polly scrambled up to her feet, ashamed to be

caught thus, and whisked away the tears; the others explaining to their new visitor the sad disappointment that had befallen them; and she was soon oh-ing and ah-ing to suit even their distressed little souls.

"You poor creeters, you!" she exclaimed at last, for about the fiftieth time. "Here, Polly, here's some posies for you, and ——"

"Oh, thank you!" cried Polly, with a radiant face, and burying her nose in the bunch for a good sniff; "why, Mrs. Beebe, we can put them in here, can't we? the very thing!" And she set the little knot of flowers in the hollow of the cake, and there they stood and nodded away, to the delighted children, like brave little comforters, as they were!

"The very thing!" echoed Mrs. Beebe, tickled to death to see their delight; "it looks beautiful, I declare! and now, I must run right along, or pa'll be worrying;" and so the good woman trotted out to her waiting husband, who was impatient to be off. Mr. Beebe kept a little shoe-shop in town; and always being of the impression if he left it for ten minutes that crowds of customers would visit it, he was the most restless of companions on any pleasure excursion.

"And Phronsie's got hurt," said Mrs. Beebe, telling him the news, as he finished tucking her up, and started the old horse.

"Ho? you don't say so!" he cried; "*whoa!*"

"Mercy!" said Mrs. Beebe; "how you scared me, pa! What's the matter?"

"What?—the little girl that bought the shoes?" asked her husband.

"Yes," replied his wife, "she's hurt her foot."

"Sho, now," said the old gentleman; "that's too bad," and he began to feel in all his pockets industriously; "there, can you get out again, and take her that?" and he laid a small piece of peppermint candy, thick and white, in his wife's lap.

"Oh, yes," cried Mrs. Beebe, good-naturedly, beginning to clamber over the wheel.

So the candy was handed in to Phronsie, who insisted that Polly should hold her up to the window to thank Mr. Beebe. So amid nods and shakings of hands, the Beebes drove off, and quiet settled down over the Little Brown House again.

"Now, children," said Polly, after Phronsie had made them take a bite of her candy all around, "let's get the cake put away safe, for mamsie may come home early."

"Where'll you put it?" asked Joel, wishing the world were all peppermint candy.

"Oh—in the cupboard," said Polly, taking it up; "there, Joe, you can climb up, and put it clear back in the corner; oh! wait; I must take the posies off, and keep them fresh in water;" so the cake was finally deposited in a place of safety, followed by the eyes of all the children.

"Now," said Polly, as they shut the door tight, "don't you go to looking at the cupboard, Joey, or mammy'll guess something."

"Can't I just open it a little crack, and take one smell when she ain't looking?" asked Joel; "I should think you might, Polly; just *one*."

"No," said Polly, firmly; "not *one*, Joe; she'll guess if you do."

But Mrs. Pepper was so utterly engrossed with her baby when she came home and heard the account of the accident, that she wouldn't have guessed if there had been a dozen cakes in the cupboard. Joel was consoled, as his mother assured him in a satisfactory way that she never should think of blaming him; and Phronsie was comforted and coddled to her heart's content. And so the evening passed rapidly and happily away, Ben smuggling Phronsie off into a corner, where she told him all the doings of the day—the disappointment of the cake, and how it was finally crowned with flowers; all of which Phronsie, with no small pride in being the narrator, related gravely to her absorbed listener. " And don't you think, Bensie," she said, clasping her little hand in a convincing way over his two bigger, stronger ones, " that Polly's stove was *very* naughty to make poor Polly cry? "

" Yes, I do," said Ben, and he shut his lips tightly together. To have Polly cry hurt him more than he cared to have Phronsie see.

" What *are* you staring at, Joe? " asked Polly, a few minutes later, as her eyes fell upon Joel, who sat with his back to the cupboard, persistently gazing at the opposite wall.

" Why, you told me yourself not to look at the cupboard," said Joel, in the loudest of stage whispers.

" O dear me! that'll make mammy suspect worse'n anything else if you look like *that*," said Polly.

" What did you say about the cupboard? " asked Mrs. Pepper, who caught Joe's last word.

" We can't tell," said Phronsie, shaking her head at her mother; " 'cause there's a ca——"

"*Ugh!*" and Polly clapped her hand on the child's mouth; "don't you want Ben to tell us a story?"

"Oh, yes!" cried the little one, in which all the others joined with a whoop of delight; so a most wonderful story, drawn up in Ben's best style, followed till bedtime.

The first thing Polly did in the morning was to run to the old cupboard, followed by all the others, to see if the cake was safe; and then it had to be drawn out, and dressed anew with the flowers, for they had decided to have it on the breakfast-table.

"It looks better," whispered Polly to Ben, "than it did yesterday; and aren't the flowers pretty?"

"It looks good enough to eat, anyway," said Ben, smacking his lips.

"Well, we *tried*," said Polly, stifling a sigh; "now, boys, call mamsie; everything's ready."

Oh! how surprised their mother appeared when she was ushered out to the feast, and the full glory of the table burst upon her! Her delight in the cake was fully enough to satisfy the most exacting mind. She admired and admired it on every side, protesting that she shouldn't have sup-

posed Polly could possibly have baked it so well
in the old stove; and then she cut it, and gave a
piece to every child, with a little posy on top.
Wasn't it good, though! Like many other things,
the cake proved to be better on trial than it
looked, and so turned out to be really quite a
good surprise all around.

"Why can't I ever have a birthday?" asked
Joel, finishing the last crumb of his piece; "I
should think I might," he added, reflectively.

"Why, you have, Joe," said Ben; "eight of
'em."

"What a story!" ejaculated Joel; "when did
I have 'em? I *never* had a cake; did I, Polly?"

"Not a cake-birthday, Joel," said his mother;
"you haven't got to that yet."

"When's it a-coming?" asked Joel, who was
decidedly of a matter-of-fact turn of mind.

"I don't know," said Mrs. Pepper, laughing;
"but there's plenty of time ahead."

IV

"OH, I do wish," said Joel, a few mornings after, pushing back his chair and looking discontentedly at his bowl of mush and molasses, " that we could ever have something new besides this everlasting old breakfast! Why can't we, mammy?"

"Better be glad you've got that, Joe," said Mrs. Pepper, taking another cold potato, and sprinkling on a little salt; "folks shouldn't complain so long as they've got *anything* to eat."

"But I'm so tired of it—same old thing!" growled Joel; "seems as if I sh'd turn into a meal-bag or a molasses jug!"

"Well, hand it over, then," proposed Ben, who was unusually hungry, and had a hard day's work before him.

"No," said Joel, alarmed at the prospect, and putting in an enormous mouthful; "it's better than nothing."

"O dear!" said little Phronsie, catching Joel's

50

tone, "it isn't nice; no, it isn't!" and she put down her spoon so suddenly that the molasses spun away in a big drop, that trailed off the corner of the table, and made Polly jump up and run for the floor-cloth.

"Oh, Phronsie," she said, reprovingly, "how could you? Never mind, pet," as she caught sight of two big tears trying to make a path in the little molasses-streaked face, "Polly'll wipe it up."

"Sha'n't we ever have anything else to eat, Polly?" asked the child, gravely, getting down from her high chair to watch the operation of cleaning the floor.

"Oh, yes," said Polly, cheerfully, "lots and lots —when our ship comes in."

"What'll they be?" asked Phronsie, in the greatest delight, prepared for anything.

"Oh, I don't know," said Polly; "ice-cream for one thing, Phronsie, and maybe, little cakes."

"With pink on top?" interrupted Phronsie, getting down by Polly's side.

"Oh, yes," said Polly, warming with her subject; "ever an' ever so much pink, Phronsie Pepper; more'n you could eat!"

Phronsie just clasped her hands and sighed. More than she could eat was beyond her!

"Hoh!" said Joel, who caught the imaginary bill of fare, "that's nothing, Polly! *I'd* speak for a plum pudding."

"Like the one mother made us for Thanksgiving?" asked Polly, getting up and waiting a minute, cloth in hand, for the answer.

"Yes, *sir*," said Joel, shutting one eye and looking up at the ceiling, musingly, while he smacked his lips in remembrance; "wasn't that *prime*, though!"

"Yes," said Polly, thoughtfully; "would you have 'em *all* like that, Joe?"

"Every one," replied Joe, promptly; "I'd have seventy-five of 'em."

"Seventy-five what?" asked Mrs. Pepper, who had gone into the bedroom, and now came out, a coat in her hand, to sit down in the west window, where she began to sew rapidly. "Better clear up the dishes, Polly, an' set the table back—seventy-five what, Joel?"

"Plum puddings," said Joel, kissing Phronsie.

"Goodness!" ejaculated Mrs. Pepper; "you don't know what you're saying, Joel Pepper; the house couldn't hold 'em!"

"Wouldn't long," responded Joel; "we'd eat 'em."

" That'd be foolish," interposed Ben; " I'd have roast beef and fixings—and oysters—and huckleberry pie."

" O dear! " cried Polly; " how nice, Ben! you always do think of the very best things."

But Joel phoohed and declared he wouldn't waste his time " over old beef; I'd have something like! " And then he cried: " Come on, Dave, what'd *you* choose? "

Little Davie had been quietly eating his breakfast amid all this chatter, and somehow thinking it might make the mother feel badly, he had refrained from saying just how tiresome he had really found this " everlasting breakfast," as Joel called it. But now he looked up eagerly, his answer all ready. " Oh, I know," he cried, " what'd be most beautiful! toasted bread—white bread— and *candy*."

" What's candy? " asked Phronsie.

" Oh, don't you know, Phronsie? " cried Polly, " what Mrs. Beebe gave you the day you got your shoes—the pink sticks; and ——"

" And the peppermint stick Mr. Beebe gave you," finished Joel, his mouth watering at the remembrance.

" That day, when you got your toe pounded," added Davie, looking at Joel.

" *Oh!* " cried Phronsie; " I want some now, I *do!* "

" Well, Davie," said Polly, " you shall have that for breakfast when our ship comes in then."

" Your ships aren't ever coming," broke in Mrs. Pepper, wisely, " if you sit there talking—folks don't ever make any fortunes a-wishing."

" True enough," laughed Ben, jumping up and setting back his chair. " Come on, Joe; you've got to pile to-day."

" O dear! " said Joel, dismally; " I wish Mr. Blodgett's wood was all afire."

" Never say that, Joe," said Mrs. Pepper, looking up sternly; " it's biting your own nose off to wish that wood was afire—and besides it's dreadfully wicked."

Joel hung his head, for his mother never spoke in that way, unless she was strongly moved; but he soon recovered, and hastened off for his jacket.

" I'm sorry I can't help you do the dishes, Polly," said David, running after Joel.

" I'm going to help her," said Phronsie; " I *am.*"

So Polly got the little wooden tub that she always used, gave Phronsie the well-worn cup-napkin, and allowed her to wipe the handleless cups and cracked saucers, which afforded the little one intense delight.

"Don't you wish, Polly," said little Phronsie, bustling around with a very important air, nearly smothered in the depths of a big brown apron which Polly had carefully tied under her chin, "that you didn't ever-an'-ever have so many dishes to do?"

"Um—maybe," said Polly, thoughtlessly. She was thinking of something else besides cups and saucers just then; of how nice it would be to go off for just one day, and do *exactly* as she had a mind to in everything! She even envied Ben and the boys who were going to work hard at Deacon Blodgett's wood-pile.

"Well, I tell you," said Phronsie, confidentially, settling down a cup that she had polished with great care, "I'm going to do 'em all to-morrow, for you, Polly—I can truly; let me now, Polly, *do*."

"Nonsense!" said Polly, giving a great splash with her mop in the tub, ashamed of her inward repinings. "Phronsie, you're no bigger than a mouse!"

"Yes, I am," retorted Phronsie, very indignantly; her face began to get very red, and she straightened up so suddenly to show Polly just how very big she was that her little head came up against the edge of the tub—over it went! a pile of saucers followed.

"There now," cried Polly, "see what you've done!"

"Ow!" whimpered Phronsie, breaking into a subdued roar; "oh, Polly! it's all running down my back."

"Is it?" said Polly, bursting out into a laugh; "never mind, Phronsie, I'll dry you."

"Goodness me, Polly!" said Mrs. Pepper, who had looked up in time to see the tub racing along by itself towards the "Provision-Room" door, a stream of dish-water following in its wake, "she's wetter'n a rat! do get off her things, quick."

"Yes'm," cried Polly, picking up the tub, and giving two or three quick sops to the floor. "Here you are, Pussy," grasping Phronsie, crying as she was, and carrying her into the bedroom.

"O dear!" wailed the child, still holding the wet dish-towel; "I won't ever do it again, if you'll *only* let me do 'em all to-morrow."

"When you're big and strong," said Polly, giving her a hug, "you shall do 'em *every* day."

" May I *really?* " said little Phronsie, blinking through the tears, and looking radiant.

" Yes, truly—*every* day."

" Then I'll grow right away, I will," said Phronsie, bursting out merrily; and she sat down and pulled off the well-worn shoes, into which little puddles of dish-water had run, while Polly went for dry stockings.

" So you shall," said Polly, coming back, a big piece of gingerbread in her hand; " and this'll make you grow, Phronsie."

" *O-o-h!* " and Phronsie's little white teeth shut down quickly on the comforting morsel. Gingerbread didn't come often enough into the Pepper household to be lightly esteemed.

" Now," said Mrs. Pepper, when order was restored, the floor washed up brightly, and every cup and platter in place, hobnobbing away to themselves on the shelves of the old corner cupboard, and Polly had come as usual with needle and thread to help mother—Polly was getting so that she could do the plain parts on the coats and jackets, which filled her with pride at the very thought—" now," said Mrs. Pepper, " you needn't help me this morning, Polly; I'm getting on pretty smart; but you may just run down to the parson's, and see how he is."

" Is he sick? " asked Polly, in awe.

To have the parson sick was something quite different from an ordinary person's illness.

" He was taken with a chill," said Mrs. Pepper, biting off a thread, " so Miss Huldy Folsom told me last night, and I'm afraid he's going to have a fever."

" O dear! " said Polly, in dire distress; " whatever'd we do, mammy! "

" Don't know, I'm sure," replied Mrs. Pepper, setting her stitches firmly; " the Lord'll provide. So you run along, child, and see how he is."

" Can't Phronsie go? " asked Polly, pausing half-way to the bedroom door.

" Well, yes, I suppose she might," said Mrs. Pepper, assentingly.

" No, she can't, either," said Polly, coming back with her sunbonnet in her hand, and shutting the door carefully after her, " 'cause she's fast asleep on the floor."

" Is she? " said Mrs. Pepper; " well, she's been a-running so this morning, she's tired out, I s'pose."

" And her face is dreadful red," continued

Polly, tying on her bonnet; " now, what'll I say, mammy? "

" Well, I should think 'twould be," said Mrs. Pepper, replying to the first half of Polly's speech; " she cried so. Well, you just tell Mrs. Henderson your ma wants to know how Mr. Henderson is this morning, and if *'twas* a chill he had yesterday, and how he slept last night, and ——"

" Oh, ma," said Polly, " I can't ever remember all *that*."

" Oh, yes, you can," said Mrs. Pepper, encouragingly; " just put your mind on it, Polly; 'tisn't anything to what I used to have to remember—when I was a little girl, no bigger'n you are."

Polly sighed, and feeling sure that something must be the matter with her mind, gave her whole attention to the errand; till at last after a multiplicity of messages and charges not to forget any one of them, Mrs. Pepper let her depart.

Up to the old-fashioned green door, with its brass knocker, Polly went, running over in her mind just which of the messages she ought to give first. She couldn't for her life think whether " if *'twas* a chill he had yesterday? " ought to come before " how he slept? " She knocked timidly, hoping Mrs. Henderson would help her out of her difficulty by telling her without the asking. All other front doors in Badgertown were just for ornament, and were only opened on grand occasions, like a wedding or a funeral. But the minister's was accessible at all times. So Polly let fall the knocker, and awaited the answer.

A scuffling noise sounded along the passage; and then Polly's soul sank down in dire dismay. It was the minister's sister, and not gentle little Mrs. Henderson. She never could get on with Miss Jerusha in the least. She told her mother once: "Miss Jerusha makes me feel as if I don't know what my name is." And here she was; and all those messages!

Miss Jerusha unbolted the door, slid back the great bar, opened the upper half, and stood there. She was a big woman, with sharp black eyes, and spectacles—over which she looked—which to Polly was much worse, for that gave her four eyes.

"Well, and what do you want?" she asked.

"I came to see—I mean my ma sent me," stammered poor Polly.

"And who *is* your ma?" demanded Miss Jerusha, as much like a policeman as anything; "and where do you live?"

"I live in Primrose Lane," replied Polly, wishing very much that she was back there.

"I don't want to know where you live, before I know who you *are*," said Miss Jerusha; "you should answer the question I asked first; always remember that."

"My ma's Mrs. Pepper," said Polly.

"Mrs. who?" repeated Miss Jerusha.

By this time Polly was so worn that she came very near turning and fleeing, but she thought of her mother's disappointment in her, and the loss of the news.

"What is it, Jerusha?" a gentle voice here broke upon Polly's ear.

"I don't know," responded Miss Jerusha, tartly, still holding the door much as if Polly were a robber; "it's a little girl, and I can't make out what she wants."

"Why, it's Polly Pepper!" exclaimed Mrs. Henderson, pleasantly. "Come in, child." She opened the other half of the big door, and led the way through the wide hall into a big, old-fashioned room, with painted floor, and high, old sideboard, and some stiff-backed rocking-chairs.

Miss Jerusha stalked in also and seated herself by the window, and began to knit. Polly had just opened her mouth to tell her errand, when the door also opened suddenly, and Mr. Henderson walked in.

"*Oh!*" said Polly, and then she stopped, and the color flushed up into her face.

"What is it, my dear?" and the minister took her hand kindly, and looked down into her flushed face.

"You are not going to have a fever, and be sick and die!" she cried.

"I hope not, my little girl," he smiled back, encouragingly; and then Polly gave her messages, which she managed easily enough now.

"There!" broke in Miss Jerusha, "a cat can't sneeze in this town but everybody'll know it in a quarter of an hour!"

And then Mrs. Henderson took Polly out to see a brood of new little chicks, that had just popped their heads out into the world; and to Polly, down on her knees, admiring, the time passed very swiftly indeed.

"Now I must go, ma'am," she said at last, looking up into the lady's face regretfully, "for mammy didn't say I was to stay."

"Very well, dear; do you think you could carry a little pat of butter? I have some very nice my sister sent me, and I want your mother to share it."

"Oh, thank you, ma'am!" cried Polly, thinking, "how glad Davie'll be, for he does so love butter! only——"

"Wait a bit, then," said Mrs. Henderson, who didn't seem to notice the objection. So she went into the house, and Polly went down again in admiration before the fascinating little puff-balls of chickens.

But she was soon on the way, with a little pat of butter in a blue bowl, tied over with a clean cloth, happy in her gift for mammy, and in the knowledge of the minister being all well.

"I wonder if Phronsie's awake," she thought to herself, turning in at the little brown gate; "if she is, she shall have a piece of bread with lots of butter."

"*Hush!*" said Mrs. Pepper, from the rocking-chair in the middle of the floor. She had something in her arms. Polly stopped suddenly, almost letting the bowl fall.

"It's Phronsie," said the mother, "and I don't know what the matter is with her; you'll have to go for the doctor, Polly, and just as fast as you can."

Polly still stood, holding the bowl, and staring with all her might. *Phronsie sick!*

" Don't wake her," said Mrs. Pepper.

Poor Polly couldn't have stirred to save her life, for a minute; then she said, " Where shall I go, mammy? "

" Oh, run to Doctor Fisher's; and don't be gone long."

Polly set down the bowl of butter, and sped on the wings of the wind for the doctor. Something dreadful was the matter, she felt, for never had a physician been summoned to the hearty Pepper family since she could remember, only when the father died. Fear lent speed to her feet; and soon the doctor came, and bent over poor little Phronsie, who still lay in her mother's arms, in a burning fever.

" It's measles," he pronounced, " that's all; no cause for alarm; you ever had it? " he asked, turning suddenly around on Polly, who was watching with wide-open eyes for the verdict.

" No, sir," answered Polly, not knowing in the least what " measles " was.

" What *shall* we do! " said Mrs. Pepper; " there hasn't any of 'em had it."

The doctor was over by the little old table under the window, mixing up some black-looking stuff in a tumbler, and he didn't hear her.

"There," he said, putting a spoonful into Phronsie's mouth, " she'll get along well enough; only keep her out of the cold." Then he pulled out a big silver watch. He was a little thin man, and the watch was immense. Polly for her life couldn't keep her eyes away from it; if Ben could only have one so fine!

" Polly," whispered Mrs. Pepper, "run and get my purse; it's in the top bureau drawer."

" Yes'm," said Polly, taking her eyes off from the fascinating watch by a violent wrench; and she ran quickly and got the little old stocking-leg, where the hard earnings, that stayed long enough to be put anywhere, always found refuge. She put it into her mother's lap, and watched while Mrs. Pepper counted out slowly one dollar in small pieces.

"Here, sir," said Mrs. Pepper, holding them out towards the doctor ; "and thank you for coming."

"Hey!" said the little man, spinning round; "that dollar's the Lord's!"

Mrs. Pepper looked bewildered, and still sat holding it out.

" And the Lord has given it to you to take care
of these children with; see that you do it! " and
without another word he was gone.

" Wasn't he good, mammy? " asked Polly, after
the first surprise was over.

" I'm sure he was," said Mrs. Pepper. " Well,
tie it up again, Polly, tie it up tight; we shall
want it, I'm sure," sighing at her little sick girl.

" Mayn't I take Phronsie, ma? " asked Polly.

" No, *no*," said Phronsie. She had mammy,
and she meant to improve the privilege.

" What *is* ' measles ' anyway, mammy? " asked
Polly, sitting down on the floor at their feet.

" Oh, 'tis something children always have," replied Mrs. Pepper; " but I'm sure I hoped it
wouldn't come just yet."

" *I* sha'n't have it," said Polly, decisively; " I
know I sha'n't! nor Ben—nor Joe—nor—nor
Davie—I *guess*," she added, hesitatingly, for
Davie was the delicate one of the family; at least
not nearly so strong as the others.

Mrs. Pepper looked at her anxiously; but Polly
seemed as bright and healthy as ever, as she
jumped up and ran to put the kettle on.

" What'll the boys say, I wonder! " she thought
to herself, feeling quite important that they really

had sickness in the house. As long as Phronsie wasn't dangerously sick, it seemed quite like rich folks; and she forgot the toil and the grind of poverty. She looked out from time to time as she passed the window, but no boys came.

"I'll put her in bed, Polly," said Mrs. Pepper, in a whisper, as Phronsie closed her eyes and breathed regularly.

"And then will you have your dinner, ma?"

"Yes," said Mrs. Pepper, "I don't care—if the boys come."

"The boys'll *never* come," said Polly, impatiently; "I don't believe—why! here they are now!"

"O dear!" said Joel, coming in crossly, "I'm so hungry—*oh—butter!* where'd you get it? I thought we never *should* get here!"

"I thought so, too," said Polly. "*Hush!* why, where's Ben?"

"He's just back," began Joel, commencing to eat, "and Davie; something's the matter with Ben—he says he feels funny."

"*Something the matter with Ben!*" repeated Polly. She dropped the cup she held, which broke in a dozen pieces.

" Oh, whocky! " cried Joel; " see what you've done, Polly Pepper! "

But Polly didn't hear; over the big, flat doorstone she sped, and met Ben with little David, coming in the gate. His face was just like Phronsie's! And with a cold, heavy feeling at her heart, Polly realized that this was no play.

" Oh, Ben! " she cried, flinging her arms around his neck, and bursting into tears; " *don't!* please —I wish you wouldn'i, Phronsie's got 'em, and that's enough! "

" Got *what?* " asked Ben, while Davie's eyes grew to their widest proportions.

" Oh, measles! " cried Polly, bursting out afresh; " the *hatefullest, horridest measles!* and now you're taken."

" Oh, no, I ain't," responded Ben, cheerfully, who knew what measles were; " wipe up, Polly; I'm all right, only my head aches, and my eyes feel funny."

But Polly. only half-reassured, gulped down her sobs; and the sorrowful trio repaired to mother.

" O dear me! " exclaimed Mrs. Pepper, sinking in a chair in dismay, at sight of Ben's red face; " whatever'll we do *now!* "

The prop and stay of her life would be taken.

away if Ben should be laid aside. No more stray half or quarter dollars would come to help her out when she didn't know where to turn.

Polly cleared off the deserted table—for once Joel had all the bread and butter he wanted. Ben took some of Phronsie's medicine, and crawled up into the loft, to bed; and quiet settled down on the little household.

"Polly," whispered Ben, as she tucked him in, "it'll be hard buckling-to now for ycu, but I guess you'll do it."

V

MORE TROUBLE

" O DEAR! " said Polly to herself, the next morning, trying to get a breakfast for the sick ones out
of the inevitable mush; " everything's just as bad
as it *can* be! they can't ever eat this; I wish I
had something nice."

" Toast some of the bread in the pail, Polly,"
said Mrs. Pepper.

She looked worn and worried; she had been up
nearly all night, back and forth from Ben's bed in
the loft to restless, fretful little Phronsie in the
big four-poster in the bedroom; for Phronsie
wouldn't get into the crib. Polly had tried her
best to help her, and had rubbed her eyes dili-
gently to keep awake, but she was wholly unaccustomed to it, and her healthy, tired little body
succumbed—and then when she awoke, shame
and remorse filled her very heart.

" That isn't nice, ma," she said, glancing at
the poor old pail, which she had brought out of

70

the "Provision Room." "Old brown bread! I want to fix 'em something nice."

"Well, you can't, you know," said Mrs. Pepper, with a sigh; "but you've got butter now; that'll be splendid! "

"I know it," said Polly, running to the corner cupboard where the precious morsel in the blue bowl remained; "whatever should we do without it, mammy? "

"Do *without* it! " said Mrs. Pepper; "same's we have done."

"Well, 'twas splendid in Mrs. Henderson to give it to us, anyway," said Polly, longing for just one taste; "seems as if 'twas a year since I was thoro oh, ma! " and here Polly took up the thread that had been so rudely snapped; "don't you think, she's got ten of the prettiest—yes, the sweetest little chickens you ever saw! Why can't we have some, mammy?"

"Costs money," replied Mrs. Pepper. "We've got too many chickens in the house to have any outside."

"O dear! " said Polly, with a red face that was toasting about as much as the bread she was hold-ing on the point of an old fork; "we never have had anything. There," she added at last; "that's the best I can do; now I'll put the butter on this little blue plate; isn't that cunning, ma?"

"Yes," said Mrs. Pepper, approvingly; "it takes you, Polly, to fix things nicely."

So Polly trotted first to Ben, up the crooked, low stairs to the loft; and while she regaled him with the brown toast and butter, she kept her tongue flying on the subject of the little chicks, and all that she saw on the famous Henderson visit. Poor Ben pretended hard to eat, but ate nothing really; and Polly saw it all, and it cut her to the heart—so she talked faster than ever.

"Now," she said, starting to go back to Phronsie, "Ben Pepper, just as soon as you get well, *we'll* have some chickens—so there!"

"Guess we sha'n't get 'em very soon," said Ben, despondently, "if I've got to lie here; and, besides, Polly, you know every bit we can save has got to go for the new stove."

"O dear!" said Polly, "I forgot that; so it has; seems to me everything's giving out!"

"You can't bake any longer in the old thing," said Ben, turning over and looking at her; "poor girl, I don't see how you've stood it so long."

"And we've been stuffing it," cried Polly, merrily, "till 'twon't stuff any more."

"No," said Ben, turning back again, "that's all worn out."

"Well, you must go to sleep," said Polly, "or mammy'll be up here; and Phronsie hasn't had her breakfast either."

Phronsie was wailing away dismally, sitting up in the middle of the old bed. Her face pricked, she said, and she was rubbing it vigorously with both fat little hands, and then crying worse than ever.

"O me! O my!" cried Polly; "how you look, Phronsie!"

"I want my mammy!" cried poor Phronsie.

"Mammy can't come now, Phronsie, dear; she's sewing. See what Polly's got for you—butter; isn't that *splendid!*"

Phronsie stopped for just one moment, and took a mouthful; but the toast was hard and dry, and she cried harder than before.

"Now," said Polly, curling up on the bed beside her, "if you'll stop crying, Phronsie Pepper, I'll tell you about the cunningest, yes, the *very* cunningest little chickens you ever saw. One was white, and he looked just like this," said Polly, tumbling over on the bed in a heap; "he couldn't stand up straight, he was so fat."

" Did he *bite?* " asked Phronsie, full of interest.

" No, he didn't bite me," said Polly; " but his mother put a bug in his mouth—just as I'm doing, you know," and she broke off a small piece of the toast, put on a generous bit of butter, and held it over Phronsie's mouth.

" Did he swallow it? " asked the child, obediently opening her little red lips.

" Oh, *snapped* it," answered Polly, " quick as ever he could, I tell you; but it wasn't good like this, Phronsie."

" Did he have *two* bugs? " asked Phronsie, eyeing suspiciously the second morsel of dry toast that Polly was conveying to her mouth.

" Well, he would have had," replied Polly, " if there'd been bugs enough; but there were nine other chicks, Phronsie."

" Poor chickies," said Phronsie, and looked lovingly at the rest of the toast and butter on the plate; and while Polly fed it to her, listened with absorbed interest to all the particulars concerning each and every chick in the Henderson hen-coop.

" Mother," said Polly, towards evening, " I'm going to sit up with Ben to-night; say I may; do, mother."

" Oh, no, you can't," replied Mrs. Pepper;

" you'll be worn out, and then what shall I do? Joel can hand him his medicine."

" Oh, Joe would tumble to sleep, mammy," said Polly, " the first thing—let me."

" Perhaps Phronsie'll let me go to-night," said Mrs. Pepper, reflectively.

" Oh, no, she won't, I know," replied Polly, decisively; " she wants you all the time."

" *I* will, Polly," said Davie, coming in with an armful of wood, in time to hear the conversation. " I'll give him his medicine, mayn't I, mammy? " and David let down his load, and came over where his mother and Polly sat sewing, to urge his rights.

"I don't know," said his mother, smiling on him. "Can you, do you think?"

"Yes, *ma'am!*" said Davie, straightening himself up.

When they told Ben, he said he knew a better way than for Davie to watch; he'd have a string tied to Davie's arm, and the end he'd hold in bed, and when it was time for medicine he'd pull the string, and that would wake Davie up!

Polly didn't sleep much more on her shake-down on the floor than if she had watched with Ben; for Phronsie cried and moaned, and wanted a drink of water every two minutes, it seemed to her. As she went back into her nest after one of these travels, Polly thought: "Well, I don't care, if nobody else gets sick, if Ben'll only get well. To-morrow I'm going to do mammy's sack she's begun for Mr. Jackson; it's all plain sewing, just like a bag, and I can do it, I know ——" and so she fell into a troubled sleep, only to be awakened by Phronsie's fretful little voice: " I want a drink of water, Polly, I *do*."

"Doesn't she drink awfully, mammy?" asked Polly, after one of these excursions out to the kitchen after the necessary draught.

"Yes," said Mrs. Pepper, "and she mustn't have any more; 'twill hurt her." But Phronsie fell into a delicious sleep after that, and didn't want any more, luckily.

"Here, Joe," said Mrs. Pepper, the next morning, "take this coat up to Mr. Peters; and be sure you get the money for it."

"How'll I get it?" asked Joe, who didn't relish the long, hot walk.

"Why, tell 'em we're sick—Ben's sick," added Mrs. Pepper, as the most decisive thing; "and we must have it: and then wait for it."

" 'Tisn't pleasant up at the Peters's," grumbled Joel, taking the parcel and moving slowly off.

"No, no, Polly," said Mrs. Pepper, "you needn't do that," seeing Polly take up some sewing after doing up the room and finishing the semi-weekly bake; "you're all beat out with that tussle over the stove; that sack'll have to go till next week."

"It can't, mammy," said Polly, snipping off a basting thread; "we've got to have the money; how much'll he give you for it?"

"Thirty cents," replied Mrs. Pepper.

"Well," said Polly, "we've got to get all the thirty centses we can, mammy dear, and I know I can do it, truly—try me once," she implored.

"Well," Mrs. Pepper relented, slowly.

"Don't feel bad, mammy dear," comforted Polly, sewing away briskly; "Ben'll get well pretty soon, and then we'll be all right."

"Maybe," said Mrs. Pepper; and went back to Phronsie, who could scarcely let her out of her sight.

Polly stitched away bravely. "Now if I do this good, mammy'll let me do it other times," she said to herself.

Davie, too, worked patiently out-of-doors, try-

ing to do Ben's chores. The little fellow blun-
dered over things that Ben would have accom-
plished in half the time, and he had to sit down
often on the steps of the little old shed where the
tools were kept, to wipe his hot face and rest.

"Polly," said Mrs. Pepper, "hadn't you better
stop a little? Dear me! how fast you sew, child!"

Polly gave a delighted little hum at her
mother's evident approval.

"I'm going to do 'em all next week, mammy,"
she said; "then Mr. Atkins won't take 'em away
from us, I guess."

Mr. Atkins kept the store, and gave out coats
and sacks of coarse linen and homespun to Mrs.
Pepper to make; and it was the fear of losing the
work that had made the mother's heart sink.

"I don't believe anybody's got such children as
I have," she said; and she gave Polly a motherly
little pat that the little daughter felt clear to the
tips of her toes with a thrill of delight.

About half-past two, long after dinner, Joe
came walking in, hungry as a bear, but flushed
and triumphant.

"Why, where have you been all this time?"
asked his mother.

"Oh, Joe, you didn't stop to play?" asked Polly, from her perch where she sat sewing, giving him a reproachful glance.

"Stop to play!" retorted Joe, indignantly; "no, I guess I didn't! I've been to old Peters's."

"*Not all this time!*" exclaimed Mrs. Pepper.

"Yes, I have, too," replied Joel, sturdily marching up to her. "And there's your money, mother;" and he counted out a quarter of a dollar in silver pieces and pennies, which he took from a dingy wad of paper, stowed away in the depths of his pocket.

"Oh, Joe," said Mrs. Pepper, sinking back in her chair and looking at him, "what do you mean?"

Polly put her work in her lap, and waited to hear.

"Where's my dinner, Polly?" asked Joel; "I hope it's a big one."

"Yes, 'tis," said Polly; "you've got lots to-day; it's in the corner of the cupboard, covered up with the plate—so go on, Joe."

"That's elegant!" said Joel, coming back with the well-filled plate, Ben's and his own share.

"Do tell us, Joey," implored Polly; "mother's waiting."

"Well," said Joel, his mouth half-full, "I waited—and he said the coat was all right;—and —and—Mrs. Peters said 'twas all right;—and Mirandy Peters said 'twas all right; but they didn't none of 'em say anything about payin', so I didn't think 'twas all right—and—and—can't I have some more butter, Polly?"

"No," said Polly, sorry to refuse him, he'd been so good about the money; "the butter's got to be saved for Ben and Phronsie."

"Oh!" said Joe, "I wish Mrs. Henderson would send us some more, I *do!* I think she might!"

"For shame, Joe!" said Mrs. Pepper; "she was very good to send this, I think; now what else did you say?" she asked.

"Well," said Joel, taking another mouthful of bread, "so I waited; you told me to, mother, you know—and they all went to work; and they didn't mind me at all, and—there wasn't any-thing to look at, so I sat—and sat—Polly, can't I have some gingerbread?"

"No," said Polly, "it's all gone; I gave the last piece to Phronsie the day she was taken sick."

"O dear!" said Joel, "everything's gone."

"Well, do go on, Joe, *do.*"

" And—then they had dinner; and Mr. Peters said, ' Hain't that boy gone home yet? ' and Mrs. Peters said, ' No,'—and he called me in, and asked me why I didn't run along home; and I said, Phronsie was sick, and Ben had the squeezles——"

" The *what?* " said Polly.

" The *squeezles,*" repeated Joel, irritably; " that's what you said."

" It's measles, Joey," corrected Mrs. Pepper; " never mind, I wouldn't feel bad."

" Well, they all laughed, and laughed, and then I said you told me to wait till I *did* get the money."

" Oh, Joe," began Mrs. Pepper, " you shouldn't have told 'em so—what did he say? "

" Well, he laughed, and said I was a smart boy, and he'd see; and Mirandy said, ' Do pay him, pa; he must be tired to death '—and don't you think, he went to a big desk in the corner, and took out a box, and 'twas full, 'most, of money— *lots!* oh! and he gave me mine—and—that's all; and I'm tired to death." And Joel flung himself down on the floor, expanded his legs as only Joel could, and took a comfortable roll.

" So you must be," said Polly, pityingly, " waiting at those Peters's."

"Don't ever want to *see* any more Peters's," said Joel; "never, never, *never!*"

"O dear!" thought Polly, as she sewed on into the afternoon, "I wonder what does ail my eyes! feels just like sand in 'em;" and she rubbed and rubbed to thread her needle. But she was afraid her mother would see, so she kept at her sewing. Once in a while the bad feeling would go away, and then she would forget all about it. "There now, who says I can't do it! that's 'most done," she cried, jumping up, and spinning across the room, to stretch herself a bit, "and to-morrow I'll finish it."

"Well," said Mrs. Pepper, "if you can do that, Polly, you'll be the greatest help I've had yet."

So Polly tucked herself into the old shakedown with a thankful heart that night, hoping for morning.

Alas! when morning did come, Polly could hardly move. The measles! what should she do! A faint hope of driving them off made her tumble out of bed, and stagger across the room to look in the old cracked looking-glass. All hope was gone as the red reflection met her gaze. Polly was on the sick-list now!

"I *won't* be sick," she said; "at any rate, I'll

keep around." An awful feeling made her clutch the back of a chair, but she managed somehow to get into her clothes, and go groping blindly into the kitchen. Somehow, Polly couldn't see very well. She tried to set the table, but it was no use. "O dear!" she thought, "whatever'll mammy do?"

"Hello!" said Joel, coming in, "what's the matter, Polly?"

Polly started at his sudden entrance, and, wavering a minute, fell over in a heap.

"Oh, ma! Ma!" screamed Joel, running to the foot of the stairs leading to the loft, where Mrs. Pepper was with Ben; "something's the matter with Polly! and she's fell; and I guess she's in the wood-box!"

VI

HARD DAYS FOR POLLY

"Ma," said David, coming softly into the bed-room, where poor Polly lay on the bed with Phronsie, her eyes bandaged with a soft old hand-kerchief, "I'll set the table."

"There isn't any table to set," said Mrs. Pepper, sadly; "you and Joel can get something out of the cupboard."

"Can we get whatever we've a mind to, ma?" cried Joel, who followed Davie, rubbing his face with a towel after his morning ablutions.

"Yes," replied his mother, absently.

"Come on, Dave!" cried Joel; "we'll have a breakfast!"

"We mustn't," said little Davie, doubtfully, "eat the *whole*, Joey."

But that individual already had his head in the cupboard, which soon engrossed them both.

Doctor Fisher was called in the middle of the morning to see what was the matter with Polly's

84

eyes. The little man looked at her keenly over his spectacles; then he said, "When were you taken?"

"This morning," answered Polly, her eyes smarting.

"Didn't you feel badly before?" questioned the doctor.

Polly thought back, and then she remembered that she had felt very badly; that when she was baking over the old stove the day before, her back had ached dreadfully; and that, somehow, when she sat down to sew, it didn't stop; only her eyes had bothered her so, she didn't mind her back so much.

"I thought so," said the doctor, when Polly answered. "And those eyes of yours have been used too much; what has she been doing, ma'am?" He turned around sharply on Mrs. Pepper as he asked this.

"Sewing," said Mrs. Pepper, "and everything. Polly does everything, sir."

"Humph!" said the doctor; "well, she won't again in one spell; her eyes are very bad."

At this a whoop, small but terrible to hear, came from the middle of the bed; and Phronsie sat bolt upright. Everybody started, while Phronsie broke out, " Don't make my Polly sick! oh, *please* don't! "

" Hey! " said the doctor; and he looked kindly at the small object with a very red face in the middle of the bed. Then he added, gently, " We're going to make Polly well, little girl; so that she can see splendidly."

" Will you, *really?* " asked the child, doubtfully.

" Yes," said the doctor; " we'll try hard; and you mustn't cry; 'cause then Polly'll cry, and that will make her eyes very bad; *very* bad indeed," he repeated, impressively.

" I won't cry," said Phronsie; " no, not one bit." And she wiped off the last tear with her fat little hand, and watched to see what next was to be done.

And Polly was left, very rebellious indeed, in the big bed, with a cooling lotion on the poor eyes, that somehow didn't cool them one bit.

" If 'twas anything but my eyes, mammy, I could stand it," she bewailed, flouncing over and over in her impatience; " and who'll do all the work now? "

" Don't think of the work, Polly," said Mrs. Pepper.

"I can't do anything *but* think," said poor Polly.

Just at that moment a queer noise out in the kitchen was heard.

"Do go out, mother, and see what 'tis," said Polly.

"I've come," said a cracked voice, close up by the bedroom door, followed by a big black cap, which could belong to no other than Grandma Bascom, "to set by you a spell; what's the matter?" she asked, and stopped, amazed to see Polly in bed.

"Oh, Polly's taken," screamed Mrs. Pepper in her ear.

"*Taken!*" repeated the old lady; "what is it—a fit?"

"No," said Mrs. Pepper; "the same as Ben's got; and Phronsie; the *measles*."

"The measles, has she?" said grandma; "well, that's bad; and Ben's away, you say?"

"No, he isn't, either," screamed Mrs. Pepper, "he's got 'em, too!"

"Got two *what?*" asked grandma.

"*Measles!* he's got the measles, too," repeated Mrs. Pepper, putting her mouth close to the old lady's cap-border.

"O the dreadful!" said grandma; "and this girl, too?" laying her hand on Phronsie's head.

"Yes," said Mrs. Pepper, feeling it a little relief to tell over her miseries; "all three of 'em."

"*I* hain't," said Joel, coming in hoping that grandma had a stray peppermint or two in her pocket, as she sometimes did; "and I ain't a-going to, either."

"O dear!" groaned his mother; "that's what Polly said; and she's got 'em bad. It's her eyes," she screamed to grandma, who looked inquiringly.

"Her eyes, is it?" asked Mrs. Bascom; "well, I've got a receet that Cousin Samanthy's folks had when John's children had 'em; and I'll run right along home and get it," and she started to go.

"No, you needn't," screamed Mrs. Pepper; "thank you, Mrs. Bascom; but Doctor Fisher's been here; and he put something on Polly's eyes; and he said they mustn't be touched."

"Hey?" said the old lady; so Mrs. Pepper had to go all over it again, till at last she made her understand that Polly's eyes were taken care of, and they must wait for time to do the rest.

"You come along of me," whispered grandma, when at last her call was done, to Joel who stood by the door. "I've got some peppermints to home; I forgot to bring 'em."

"Yes'm," said Joel, brightening up.

"Where are you going, Joe?" asked Mrs. Pepper, seeing him move off with Mrs. Bascom; "I may want you."

"Oh, I've got to go over to grandma's," said Joel, briskly; "she wants me."

"Well, don't be gone long, then," replied his mother.

"There," said grandma, going into her "keeping-room" to an old-fashioned chest of drawers; and opening one, she took therefrom a paper, from which she shook out before Joe's delighted eyes some red and white peppermint drops. "There, now, you take these home; you may have some, but be sure you give the most to the sick ones; and Polly—let Polly have the biggest."

"She won't take 'em," said Joel, wishing he had the measles.

"Well, you try her," said grandma; "run along, now." But it was useless to tell Joel that, for he was half-way home already. He carried out grandma's wishes, and distributed conscientiously the precious drops. But when he came to Polly, she didn't answer; and looking at her in surprise he saw two big tears rolling out under the bandage and wetting the pillow.

"I don't want 'em, Joe," said Polly, when he made her understand that " 'twas peppermints, real peppermints; " "you may have 'em."

"Try one, Polly; they're real good," said Joel, who had an undefined wish to comfort; "there, open your mouth."

So Polly opened her mouth, and Joel put one in with satisfaction.

"Ain't it good?" he asked, watching her crunch it.

"Yes," said Polly, "real good; where'd you get 'em?"

"Over to Grandma Bascom's," said Joel; "she gave me lots for all of us; have another, Polly?"

"No," said Polly, "not yet; you put two on my pillow where I can reach 'em; and then you keep the rest, Joel."

"I'll put three," said Joel, counting out one red and two white ones, and laying them on the pillow; "there! "

"And I want another, Joey, I *do*," said Phronsie, from the other side of the bed.

"Well, you may have one," said Joel; "a red one, Phronsie; yes, you may have two. Now come on, Dave; we'll have the rest out by the wood-pile."

How they ever got through that day, I don't know. But late in the afternoon, carriage wheels were heard; and then they stopped right at the Peppers' little brown gate.

"Polly," said Mrs. Pepper, running to the bed-room door, "it's Mrs. Henderson!"

"Is it?" said Polly, from the darkened room, "oh! I'm so glad! Is Miss Jerushy with her?" she asked, fearfully.

"No," said Mrs. Pepper, going back to ascertain; "why, it's the parson himself! Dear me! how we look!"

"Never mind, mammy," called back Polly, longing to spring out of bed and fix up a bit.

"I'm sorry to hear the children are sick," said Mrs. Henderson, coming in, in her sweet, gentle way.

"We didn't know it," said the minister, "until this morning—can we see them?"

"Oh, yes, sir," said Mrs. Pepper; "Ben's up-stairs; and Polly and Phronsie are in here."

"Poor little things!" said Mrs. Henderson, compassionately; "hadn't you better," turning to

the minister, " go up and see Ben first, while 1
visit the little girls? "

So the minister mounted the crooked stairs;
and Mrs. Henderson went straight up to Polly's
side; and the first thing Polly knew, a cool, gentle
hand was laid on her hot head, and a voice said,
" I've come to see *my* little chicken now! "

" Oh, ma'am," said Polly, bursting into a sob,
" I don't care about my eyes—only mammy——"
and she broke right down.

" I know," said the minister's wife, soothingly;
" but it's for you to bear patiently, Polly—what
do you suppose the chicks were doing when I
came away? "   And Mrs. Henderson, while she
held Polly's hand, smiled and nodded encouragingly to Phronsie, who was staring at her from
the other side of the bed.

" I don't know, ma'am," said Polly; " please
tell us."

" Well, they were all fighting over a grass-
hopper—yes, ten of them."

" Which one got it? " asked Polly, in intense
interest; " oh! I hope the white one did! "

" Well, he looked as much like winning as any
of them," said the lady, laughing.

" Bless her! " thought Mrs. Pepper to herself

out in the kitchen, finishing the sack Polly had
left; " *she's* a parson's wife, *I* say! "

And then the minister came down from Ben's
room, and to go into the bedroom; and Mrs. Henderson went up-stairs into the loft.

" So," he said, kindly, as after patting Phronsie's head he came over and sat down by Polly,
" this is the little girl who came to see if I were
sick? "

" Oh, sir," said Polly, " I'm *so* glad you
wasn't! "

" Well, when I come again," said Mr. Henderson, rising after a merry chat, " I see I shall have
to slip a book into my pocket, and read for those
poor eyes."

" Oh, thank you! " cried Polly; and then she
stopped and blushed.

" Well, what is it? " asked the minister, encouragingly.

" Ben loves to hear reading," said Polly.

" Does he? well, by that time, my little girl,
I guess Ben will be down-stairs; he's all right,
Polly; don't you worry about him—and I'll sit in
the kitchen, by the bedroom door, and you can
hear nicely."

So the Hendersons went away; but somehow.

before they went, a good many things found their way out of the old-fashioned chaise into the Peppers' little kitchen.

But Polly's eyes didn't get any better, with all the care; and the lines of worry on Mrs. Pepper's face grew deeper and deeper. At last, she just confronted Doctor Fisher in the kitchen, one day after his visit to Polly, and boldly asked him if they ever could be cured. "I know she's—and there isn't any use keeping it from me," said the poor woman—" she's going to be stone-blind!"

"My good woman"—Doctor Fisher's voice was very gentle; and he took the hard, brown hand in his own—" your little girl will *not* be blind; I tell you the truth; but it will take some time to make her eyes quite strong—time, and rest. She has strained them in some way, but she will come out of it."

"Praise the Lord!" cried Mrs. Pepper, throwing her apron over her head; and then she sobbed on, "and you, sir—I can't ever thank you—for—for—if Polly was blind, we might as well give up!"

The next day, Phronsie, who had the doctor's permission to sit up, only she was to be kept from taking cold, scampered around in stocking-feet in search of her shoes, which she hadn't seen since she was first taken sick.

" Oh, I want on my very *best* shoes," she cried; " can't I, mammy? "

" Oh, no, Phronsie; you must keep them nice," remonstrated her mother; " you can't wear 'em every day, you know."

" 'Tisn't every day," said Phronsie, slowly; " it's only *one* day."

" Well, and then you'll want 'em on again to-morrow," said her mother.

" Oh, no, I won't! " cried Phronsie; " never, no more to-morrow, if I can have 'em to-day; *please*, mammy, dear! "

Mrs. Pepper went to the lowest drawer in the high bureau, and took therefrom a small parcel done up in white tissue-paper. Slowly unrolling this before the delighted eyes of the child, who stood patiently waiting, she disclosed the precious red-topped shoes which Phronsie immediately clasped to her bosom.

" My own, *very* own shoes! *Whole* mine! " she cried, and trudged out into the kitchen to put them on herself.

" Hello! " cried Doctor Fisher, coming in about a quarter of an hour later to find her tugging laboriously at the buttons—"*new* shoes! I declare!"

"My own!" cried Phronsie, sticking out one foot for inspection where every button was in the wrong buttonhole, "and they've got red tops, too!"

"So they have," said the doctor, getting down on the floor beside her; "beautiful red tops, aren't they?"

"Be-*you-ti*-ful," sang the child, delightedly.

"Does Polly have new shoes every day?" asked the doctor in a low voice, pretending to examine the other foot.

Phronsie opened her eyes very wide at this.

"Oh, no, she doesn't have anything, Polly doesn't."

"And what does Polly want most of all—do you know? See if you can tell me." And the doctor put on the most alluring expression that he could muster.

"Oh, I know!" cried Phronsie, with a very wise look.

"There now," cried the doctor, "you're the girl for me! to think you know! so, what is it?"

Phronsie got up very gravely, and with one

shoe half on, she leaned over and whispered in the doctor's ear:

" A *stove!* "

"A *what?* " said the doctor, looking at her, and then at the old, black thing in the corner, that looked as if it were ashamed of itself; " why, she's got one."

" Oh," said the child, " it won't burn; and sometimes Polly cries, she does, when she's all alone—and I see her."

" Now," said the doctor, very sympathetically, " that's too bad; that is! and then what does she do? "

" Oh, Ben stuffs it up," said the child, laughing; " and so does Polly, too, with paper; and then it all tumbles out quick; oh! just as quick! " And Phronsie shook her yellow head at the dismal remembrance.

" Do you suppose," said the doctor, getting up, " that you know of any smart little girl around here, about four years old, that knows how to button on her own red-topped shoes, who would like to go to ride to-morrow morning in my carriage with me? "

" Oh, I do! " cried Phronsie, hopping on one toe; " it's *me!* "

"Very well, then," said Doctor Fisher, going to the bedroom door, "we'll look out for to-morrow, then."

To poor Polly, lying in the darkened room, or sitting up in the big rocking-chair—for Polly wasn't really very sick in other respects, the disease having all gone into the merry brown eyes— the time seemed interminable. Not to *do* anything! The very idea at any time would have filled her active, wide-awake little body with horror; and now, here she was!

"O dear! I *can't* bear it!" she said, when she knew by the noise in the kitchen that everybody was out there; so nobody heard, except a fat, old black spider in the corner, and he didn't tell any one!

"I *know* it's a week," she said, "since dinner-time! If Ben was only well, to talk to me."

"Oh, I say, Polly," screamed Joel at that moment, running in, "Ben's a-coming down the stairs!"

"Stop, Joe," said Mrs. Pepper; "you shouldn't have told; he wanted to surprise Polly."

"Oh, is he!" cried Polly, clasping her hands in rapture; "mammy, can't I take off this horrid bandage, and *see* him?"

"Goodness, no!" said Mrs. Pepper, springing forward; "not for the world, Polly! Doctor Fisher'd have our ears off!"

"Well, I can hear, anyway," said Polly, resigning herself to the remaining comfort; "here he is! oh, Ben!"

"There," said Ben, grasping Polly, bandage and all; "now we're all right; and I say, Polly, you're a brick!"

"Mammy told me not to say that the other day," said Joel, with a very virtuous air.

"Can't help it," said Ben, who was a little wild over Polly, and besides, he had been sick himself, and had borne a good deal, too.

"Now," said Mrs. Pepper, after the first excitement was over, "you're so comfortable together, and Phronsie doesn't want me now, I'll go to the store; I must get some more work if Mr. Atkins'll give it to me."

"I'll be all right mammy, now that Ben's here," cried Polly, settling back into her chair, with Phronsie on the stool at her feet.

"I'm going to tell her stories, ma," cried Ben, "so you needn't worry about us."

"Isn't it funny, Ben," said Polly, as the gate

clicked after the mother, " to be sitting still, and telling stories in the daytime? "

" Rather funny! " replied Ben.

" Well, do go on," said Joel, as usual, rolling on the floor, in a dreadful hurry for the story to begin.   Little David looked up quietly, as he sat on Ben's other side, his hands clasped tight together, just as eager, though he said nothing.

" Well; once upon a time," began Ben, delightfully, and launched into one of the stories that the children thought perfectly lovely.

" Oh, Bensie," cried Polly, entranced, as they listened with bated breath, " however do you think of such nice things! "

" I've had time enough to think, the last week," said Ben, laughing, " to last a lifetime! "

" Do go *on!* " put in Joel, impatient at the delay.

" Don't hurry him so," said Polly, reprovingly; " he isn't strong."

" Ben," said David, drawing a long breath, his eyes very big—" did he *really* see a bear? "

" No," said Ben; " oh! where was I? "

" Why, you said Tommy heard a noise," said Polly, " and he *thought* it was a bear."

"Oh, yes," said Ben; "I remember; 'twasn't a ——"

"Oh, *make* it a bear, Ben!" cried Joel, terribly disappointed; "don't let it be not a bear."

"Why, I can't," said Ben; "'twouldn't sound true."

"Never mind, *make* it sound true," insisted Joel; "you can make anything true."

"Very well," said Ben, laughing; "I suppose I must."

"Make it *two* bears, Ben," begged little Phronsie.

"Oh, no, Phronsie, that's too much," cried Joel; "that'll spoil it; but make it a *big* bear, do, Ben, and have him bite him somewhere, and 'most kill him."

"Oh, Joel!" cried Polly, while David's eyes got bigger than ever.

So Ben drew upon his powers as story-teller, to suit his exacting audience, and was making his bear work havoc upon poor Tommy in a way captivating to all, even Joel, when ——

"Well, I declare," sounded Mrs. Pepper's cheery voice, coming in upon them, "if this isn't comfortable!"

"Oh, mammy!" cried Phronsie, jumping **out**

of Polly's arms, whither she had taken refuge during the thrilling tale, and running to her mother who gathered her baby up, " we've had a bear! a *real, live bear,* we *have!* Ben made him! "

" Have you! " said Mrs. Pepper, taking off her shawl, and laying her parcel of work down on the table, " now, that's nice! "

" Oh, mammy! " cried Polly, " it does seem so good to be all together again! "

" And I thank the Lord! " said Mrs. Pepper, looking down on her happy little group; and the tears were in her eyes—" and children, we ought to be very good and please Him, for He's been so good to us."

VII

THE CLOUD OVER THE LITTLE BROWN HOUSE

WHEN Phronsie, with many crows of delight, and much chattering, had gotten fairly started the following morning on her much-anticipated drive with the doctor, the whole family excepting Polly drawn up around the door to see them off, Mrs. Pepper resolved to snatch the time and run down for an hour or two to one of her customers, who had long been waiting for a little " tailoring " to be done for her boys.

" Now, Joel," she said, putting on her bonnet before the cracked looking-glass, " you stay with Polly; Ben must go up to bed, the doctor said; and Davie's going to the store for some molasses; so you and Polly must keep house."

" Yes'm," said Joel; " may I have something to eat, ma? "

" Yes," said Mrs. Pepper; " but don't you eat the new bread; you may have as much as you want of the old."

" Ain't there *any* molasses, mammy? " asked

Joel, as she bade Polly good-by! and gave her numberless charges " to be careful of your eyes," and " not to let a crack of light in through the curtain," as the old green paper shade was called.

" No; if you're very hungry, you can eat bread," said Mrs. Pepper, sensibly.

" Joel," said Polly, after the mother had gone, " I do wish you could read to me."

" Well, I can't," said Joel, glad he didn't know how; " I thought the minister was coming."

" Well, he was," said Polly, " but mammy said he had to go out of town to a consequence."

" A *what!* " asked Joel, very much impressed.

" A con——" repeated Polly. " Well, it began with a *con*—and I am sure—yes, *very* sure it was consequence."

" That must be splendid," said Joel, coming up to her chair, and slowly drawing a string he held in his hand back and forth, " to go to consequences, and everything! When I'm a man, Polly Pepper, *I'm* going to be a minister, and have a nice time, and go—just everywhere! "

" Oh, Joel! " exclaimed Polly, quite shocked; " you couldn't be one; you aren't good enough."

" I don't care," said Joel, not at all dashed by her plainness, " I'll be good then—when I'm a big man; don't you suppose, Polly," as a new idea struck him, "that Mr. Henderson *ever* is naughty?"

"No," said Polly, very decidedly; "never, *never*, NEVER!"

"Then, I don't want to be one," said Joel, veering round with a sigh of relief, "and besides I'd rather have a pair of horses like Mr. Slocum's, and *then* I could go everywheres, I guess!"

"And sell tin?" asked Polly, "just like Mr. Slocum?"

"Yes," said Joel; "this is the way I'd go— Gee-*whop!* gee-*whoa!*" and Joel pranced with his imaginary steeds all around the room, making about as much noise as any other four boys, as he brought up occasionally against the four-poster or the high old bureau.

"Well!" said a voice, close up by Polly's chair, that made her skip with apprehension, it was so like Miss Jerushy Henderson's—Joel was whooping away behind the bedstead to his horses that had become seriously entangled, so he didn't hear anything. But when Polly said, bashfully, "I can't see anything, ma'am," he came up red and shining to the surface, and stared with all his might.

"I came to see you, little girl," said Miss Jerushy, severely, seating herself stiffly by Polly's side.

"Thank you, ma'am," said Polly, faintly.

"Who's this boy?" asked the lady, turning around squarely on Joel, and eyeing him from head to foot.

"He's my brother Joel," said Polly.

Joel still stared.

"Which brother?" pursued Miss Jerushy, like a census-taker.

"He is next to me," said Polly, wishing her mother was home; "he's nine, Joel is."

"He's big enough to do something to help his mother," said Miss Jerushy, looking him through and through. "Don't you think you might do something, when the others are sick, and your poor mother is working so hard?" she continued, in a cold voice.

"I *do* do something," blurted out Joel, sturdily; "lots and lots!"

"You shouldn't say 'lots,'" reproved Miss Jerushy, with a sharp look over her spectacles, "'tisn't proper for boys to talk so; what do you do all day long?" she asked, turning back to

Polly, after a withering glance at Joel, who still stared.

"I can't do anything, ma'am," replied Polly, sadly, "I can't see to do anything."

"Well, you might knit, I should think," said her visitor, "it's dreadful for a girl as big as you are to sit all day idle; I had sore eyes once when I was a little girl—how old are you?" she asked, abruptly.

"Eleven last month," said Polly.

"Well, I wasn't only nine when I knit a stocking; and I had sore eyes, too; you see I was a very little girl, and——"

"Were you ever little?" interrupted Joel, in extreme incredulity, drawing near, and looking over the big square figure.

"Hey?" said Miss Jerushy; so Joel repeated his question before Polly could stop him.

"Of course," answered Miss Jerushy; and then she added, tartly, "little boys shouldn't speak unless they're spoken to. Now," and she turned back to Polly again, "didn't you ever knit a stocking?"

"No, ma'am," said Polly, "not a *whole* one."

"Mercy!" exclaimed Miss Jerushy; "did I ever!" And she raised her black mitts in intense disdain. "A big girl like you never to knit a stocking! to think your mother should bring you up so! and ——"

"She didn't bring us up," screamed Joel, in indignation, facing her with blazing eyes.

"Joel," said Polly, "be still."

"And you're very impertinent, too," said Miss Jerushy; "a good child *never* is impertinent."

Polly sat quite still; and Miss Jerushy continued:

"Now, I hope you will learn to be industrious; and when I come again I will see what you have done."

"You ain't ever coming again," said Joel, defiantly; "no, *never!*"

"Joel!" implored Polly, and in her distress she pulled up her bandage as she looked at him; "you know mamma'll be so sorry. Oh, ma'am," and she turned to Miss Jerushy, who was now thoroughly aroused to the duty she saw before her of doing these children good, "I don't know what is the reason, ma'am; Joel never talks so; he's real good; and ——"

"It only shows," said the lady, seeing her way quite clear for a little exhortation, "that you've all had your own way from infancy; and that you don't do what you might to make your mother's life a happy one."

" Oh, ma'am," cried Polly, and she burst into a perfect flood of tears, " please, *please* don't say that! "

" And I say," screamed Joel, stamping his small foot, " if you make Polly cry you'll *kill* her! Don't, Polly, *don't!* " and the boy put both arms around her neck, and soothed and comforted her in every way he could think of. And Miss Jerusha, seeing no way to make herself heard, disappeared, feeling pity for children who would turn away from good advice.

But still Polly cried on; all the pent-up feelings that had been so long controlled had free vent now. She really couldn't stop! Joel, frightened to death, at last said, " I'm going to wake up Ben."

That brought Polly to; and she sobbed out, " Oh, no, Jo—ey—I'll stop."

" I will," said Joel, seeing his advantage; " I'm going, Polly," and he started to the foot of the stairs.

" No, I'm done now, Joe," said Polly, wiping her eyes, and choking back her thoughts——

"Oh, Joe! I *must* scream! my eyes ache so! " and poor Polly fairly writhed all over the chair.

"What'll I do? " said Joel, at his wits' end, running back, "do you want some water? "

"Oh, no," gasped Polly; "doctor wouldn't let me; oh! I wish mammy'd come! "

"I'll go and look for her," suggested Joel, feeling as if he must do something; and he'd rather be out at the gate, than to see Polly suffer.

"That won't bring her," said Polly, trying to keep still; "I'll try to wait."

"Here she is now! " cried Joel, peeping out of the window; "O goody! "

VIII

JOEL'S TURN

"WELL"—Mrs. Pepper's tone was unusually blithe as she stepped into the kitchen—"you've had a nice time, I suppose—what in the world!" and she stopped at the bedroom door.

"Oh, mammy, if you'd been here!" said Joel, while Polly sat still, only holding on to her eyes as if they were going to fly out; "there's been a big woman here; she came right in—and she talked awful! and Polly's been a-crying, and her eyes ache dreadful—and——"

"Been crying!" repeated Mrs. Pepper, coming up to poor Polly. "Polly been crying!" she still repeated.

"Oh, mammy, I couldn't help it," said Polly; "she said——" and in spite of all she could do, the rain of tears began again, which bade fair to be as uncontrolled as before. But Mrs. Pepper took her up firmly in her arms, as if she were Phronsie, and sat down in the old rocking-chair and just patted her back.

111

" There, there," she whispered, soothingly, " don't think of it, Polly; mother's got home."

" Oh, mammy," said Polly, crawling up to the comfortable neck for protection, " I oughtn't to have minded; but 'twas Miss Jerushy Henderson, and she said ——"

" What did she say? " asked Mrs. Pepper, thinking perhaps that it would be the wiser thing to let Polly free her mind.

" Oh! she said that we ought to be doing something; and I ought to knit, and ——"

" Go on," said her mother.

" And then Joel got naughty; oh, mammy, he never did so before; and I couldn't stop him," cried Polly, in great distress; " I really couldn't, mammy—and he talked to her; and he told her she wasn't ever coming here again."

" Joel shouldn't have said that," said Mrs. Pepper; and under her breath something was added that Polly even failed to hear—" but all the same, she isn't! "

" And, mammy," cried Polly—and she flung her arms around her mother's neck and gave her a grasp that nearly choked Mrs. Pepper, " ain't I helping you *some,* mammy? Oh! I wish I could

do something big for you? Aren't you happy,
mammy?"

"O dear me—*happy!*" cried Mrs. Pepper,
straining Polly to her heart, "whatever has that
woman—whatever *could* she have said to you?
Such a girl as you are, too!" cried Mrs. Pepper,
hugging Polly, and covering her with kisses so
tender, that Polly, warmed and cuddled up to her
heart's content, was comforted to the full.

"Well," said Mrs. Pepper, when at last she
thought she had formed between Polly and Joel
about the right idea of the visit, "well, now we
won't think of it any more; 'tisn't worth it, Polly,
you know."

But poor Polly! and poor mother! They both
were obliged to think of it. Nothing could avert
the suffering of the next few days, caused by that
long flow of burning tears.

"Nothing feels good on 'em, mammy," said
Polly, at last, twisting her hands in the vain at-
tempt to keep from rubbing the aching, inflamed
eyes that drove her nearly wild with their itch-
ing, "there isn't any use in trying anything."

"There *will* be use," energetically protested
Mrs. Pepper, bringing another cool bandage, "as

long as you've got an eye in your head, Polly Pepper! "

Doctor Fisher's face, when he first saw the change that the fateful visit had wrought, and heard the accounts, was very grave indeed. Everything had been so encouraging on his last visit, that he had come very near promising Polly speedy freedom from the hateful bandage.

But the little Pepper household soon had something else to think of more important even than Polly's eyes, for now the heartiest, the jolliest of all the little group was down,—Joel. How he fell sick, they scarcely knew, it all came so suddenly. The poor, bewildered family had hardly time to think, before delirium and, perhaps, death stared them in the face.

When Polly first heard it, by Phronsie's pattering down-stairs and screaming: " Oh, Polly, Joey's dre-ad-ful sick, he *is!* " she jumped right up, and tore off the bandage.

" Now, I *will* help mother! I *will,* so *there!* " and in another minute she would have been up in the sick-room. But the first thing she knew, a gentle but firm hand was laid upon hers; and she found herself back again in the old rocking-chair, and listening to the doctor's words, which were quite stern and decisive.

"Now, I tell you," he said, "you must *not* take off that bandage again; do you know the consequences? You will be blind! and then you will be a care to your mother all your life!"

"I shall be blind, anyway," said Polly, despairingly, "so 'twon't make any difference."

"No, your eyes will come out of it all right, only I did hope"—and the good doctor's face fell —"that the other two boys would escape; but " —and he brightened up at sight of Polly's forlorn visage—"see you do *your* part by keeping still."

But there came a day soon when everything was still around the once happy Little Brown House —when only whispers were heard from white lips; and thoughts were fearfully left unuttered.

On the morning of one of these days, when Mrs. Pepper felt she could not exist an hour longer without sleep, kind Mrs. Beebe came to stay until things were either better or worse.

Still the cloud hovered, dark and forbidding. At last, one afternoon, when Polly was all alone, she could endure it no longer. She flung herself down by the side of the old bed, and buried her face in the gay patched bed-quilt.

"Dear God," she said, "*make* me willing to have anything"—she hesitated—"yes, *anything* happen; to be blind forever, and to have Joey sick, only make me good."

How long she stayed there she never knew; for she fell asleep—the first sleep she had had since Joey was taken sick. And little Mrs. Beebe coming in found her thus.

"Polly," the good woman said, leaning over her, "you poor, pretty creeter, you; I'm goin' to tell you somethin'—there, there, just to think! Joel's goin' to get well!"

"Oh, Mrs. Beebe!" cried Polly, tumbling over in a heap on the floor, her face, as much as could be seen under the bandage, in a perfect glow, "Is he, *really?*"

"Yes, to be sure; the danger's all over now," said the little old lady, inwardly thinking—"if I hadn't a-come!"

"Well, then, the Lord wants him to," cried Polly, in rapture; "doesn't He, Mrs. Beebe?"

"To be sure—to be sure," repeated the kind friend, only half understanding.

"Well, I don't care about my eyes, then," cried Polly; and to Mrs. Beebe's intense astonishment and dismay, she spun round and round in the middle of the floor.

"Oh, Polly, *Polly!*" the little old lady cried, running up to her, "*do* stop! the doctor wouldn't let you! he wouldn't really, you know! it'll all go to your eyes."

"I don't care," repeated Polly, in the middle of a spin; but she stopped obediently; "seems as if I just as soon be blind as not; it's *so* beautiful Joey's going to get well!"

IX

SUNSHINE AGAIN

But as Joel was smitten down suddenly, so he came up quickly, and his hearty nature asserted itself by rapid strides towards returning health; and one morning he astonished them all by turning over suddenly and exclaiming:

"I want something to eat!"

"Bless the Lord!" cried Mrs. Pepper, "now he's going to live!"

"But he *mustn't* eat," protested Mrs. Beebe, in great alarm, trotting for the cup of gruel. "Here, you pretty creeter you, here's something nice." And she temptingly held the spoon over Joel's mouth; but with a grimace he turned away.

"Oh, I want something to *eat!* some gingerbread or some bread and butter."

"Mercy!" ejaculated Mrs. Beebe. "Gingerbread!"

Poor Mrs. Pepper saw the hardest part of her trouble now before her, as she realized that the returning appetite must be fed only on strength-ening food; for where it was to come from she couldn't tell.

"The Lord only knows where we'll get it," she groaned within herself.

Yes, He knew. A rap at the door, and little David ran down to find the cause.

"Oh, mammy," he said, "Mrs. Henderson sent it—see! see!"

And in the greatest excitement he placed in her lap a basket that smelt savory and nice even before it was opened. When it was opened, there lay a little bird delicately roasted, and folded in a clean napkin; also a glass of jelly, crimson and clear.

"Oh, Joey," cried Mrs. Pepper, almost overwhelmed with joy, "see what Mrs. Henderson sent you! Now you can eat fit for a king!"

That little bird certainly performed its mission in life; for, as Mrs. Beebe said, "It just touched the spot!" and from that very moment Joel improved so rapidly they could hardly believe their eyes.

"Hoh! I haven't been sick!" he cried, on the third day, true to his nature. "Mammy, I want to get up."

"O goodness, no! You mustn't, Joel!" cried

Mrs. Pepper, in a fright, running up to him as he was preparing to give the bedclothes a lusty kick; " you'll send 'em in."

" Send *what* in? " asked Joel, looking up at his mother in terror, as the dreadful thought made him pause.

" Why, the measles, Joey; they'll all go in if you get out."

" How they going to get in again, I'd like to know? " asked Joel, looking at the little red spots on his hands in incredulity; " say, ma! "

" Well, they *will*," said his mother, " as you'll find to your sorrow if you get out of bed."

" O dear! " said Joel, beginning to whimper, as he drew into bed again, " when *can* I get up, mammy? "

" Oh, in a day or two," responded Mrs. Pepper, cheerfully; " you're getting on so finely you'll be as smart as a cricket! Shouldn't you say he might get up in a day or two, Mrs. Beebe? " she appealed to that individual, who was knitting away cheerily in the corner.

" Well, if he keeps on as he's begun, I shouldn't know *what* to think," replied Mrs. Beebe. " It beats all how quick he's picked up. I never see anything like it. I'm sure! "

And as Mrs. Beebe was a great authority in sickness, the old, sunny cheeriness began to creep into the Little Brown House once more, and to bubble over as of yore.

"Seems as if 'twas just good to *live*," said Mrs. Pepper, thankfully once, when her thoughts were too much for her. "I don't believe I shall ever care how poor we are," she continued, "as long as we're together."

"And that's just what the Lord meant, maybe," replied good Mrs. Beebe, who was preparing to go home.

Joel kept the house in a perfect uproar all through his getting well. Mrs. Pepper observed one day, when he had been more turbulent than usual, that she was "almost worn to a thread."

"It wasn't anything to take care of you, Joe," she added, "when you were real sick, because then I knew where you were; but—well, you won't ever have the measles again, I s'pose, and that's some comfort!"

Little David, who had been nearly stunned by the sickness that had laid aside his almost constant companion, could express his satisfaction and joy in no other way than by running every third minute and begging to do something for him. And Joel, who loved dearly to be waited on, improved every opportunity that offered; which Mrs. Pepper observing, soon put a stop to.

"You'll run his legs off, Joel," she said at last, when he had sent David the third time down to the wood-pile for a stick of just the exact thickness, which the little messenger declared wasn't to be found. "Haven't you any mercy? You've kept him going all day, too," she added, glancing at David's pale face.

"Oh, mammy," panted David, "don't; I love to go. Here, Joe, is the best I could find," handing him a nice smooth stick.

"I know you do," said his mother; "but Joe's getting better now, and he must learn to spare you."

"I don't want to spare folks," grumbled Joel, whittling away with energy; "I've been sick— *real* sick," he added, lifting his chubby face to his mother to impress the fact.

"I know you have," she cried, running to kiss her boy; "but now, Joe, you're 'most well. To-morrow I'm going to let you go down-stairs; what do you think of *that!*"

"*Hooray!*" screamed Joel, throwing away the

stick and clapping his hands, forgetting all about his serious illness, "that'll be *prime!*"

"Aren't you too sick to go, Joey?" asked Mrs. Pepper, mischievously.

"No, I ain't sick," cried Joel, in the greatest alarm, fearful his mother meant to take back the promise; "I've never been sick. Oh, mammy! you *know* you'll let me go, won't you?"

"I guess so," laughed his mother.

"Come on, Phron," cried Joe, giving her a whirl.

David, who was too tired for active sport, sat on the floor and watched them frolic in great delight.

"Mammy," said he, edging up to her side as the sport went on, "do you know, I think it's just good—it's—oh, it's so *frisky* since Joe got well, ain't it, mammy?"

"Yes, indeed," said Mrs. Pepper, giving him a radiant look in return for his; "and when Polly's around again with her two eyes all right—well, I don't know what we *shall* do, I declare!"

"*Boo!*" cried a voice, next morning, close to Polly's elbow, unmistakably Joel's.

"Oh, Joel Pepper!" she cried, whirling around, "is that really *you!*"

"Ye-up," cried that individual, confidently "it's me; oh, I say, Polly, I've had fun up-stairs, I tell you! "

"Poor boy! " said Polly, compassionately.

"I wasn't a poor boy," cried Joel, indignantly; "I had splendid things to eat; O my! " and he closed one eye and smacked his lips in the delightful memory.

"I know it," said Polly, "and I'm so glad, Joel."

"I don't suppose I'll ever get so many again," observed Joel, reflectively, after a minute's pause, as one and another of the wondrous delicacies rose before his mind's eye; "not unless I have the measles again—say, Polly, can't I have 'em again? "

"Dear me, no! " cried Polly, in intense alarm, "I hope not."

"Well, I don't," said Joel, "I wish I could have 'em sixty—no—two hundred times, so there! "

"Well, mammy couldn't take care of you," said Ben; "you don't know what you're saying, Joe."

"Well, then, I wish I could have the things *without* the measles," said Joel, willing to accommodate; "only folks won't send 'em," he added. in an injured tone.

" Polly's had the hardest time of all," said her mother, affectionately patting the bandage.

" I think so, too," put in Ben; " if my eyes were hurt, I'd give up."

" So would I," said Davie; and Joel, to be in the fashion, cried also, " I know *I* would;" while little Phronsie said, squeezing up to Polly's side, " And *I*, too."

" Would what, Puss? " asked Ben, tossing her up high.

" Have good things," cried the child, in delight at understanding the others, " I would really, Ben," she cried, gravely, when they all screamed.

" Well, I hope so," said Ben, tossing her higher yet.

" Don't laugh at her, boys," put in Polly; " we're all going to have good times now, Phronsie, now we've got well."

" Yes," laughed the child from her high perch; " we ain't ever going to be sick again, never—no more," she added, impressively.

The good times were coming for Polly—coming pretty near, and she didn't know it! All the children were in the secret; for, as Mrs. Pepper declared, " They'd have to know it; and if they were let into the secret they'd keep it better."

So they had individually and collectively been entrusted with the precious secret, and charged with the extreme importance of " never letting any one know," and they had been nearly bursting ever since with the wild desire to impart their knowledge.

" I'm afraid I *shall* tell," said David, running to his mother at last; " oh, mammy, I don't dare stay near Polly, I do want to tell *so bad*."

" Oh, no, you won't, David," said his mother, encouragingly, " when you know mother don't want you to; and besides, think how Polly'll look when she sees it."

" I know," cried David, in the greatest rapture, " I wouldn't tell for all the world! I guess she'll look nice, don't you, mother? " and he laughed in glee at the thought.

" Poor child! I guess she will! " and then Mrs. Pepper laughed too, till the little old kitchen rang with delight at the accustomed sound.

The children all had to play " Clap in and clap out " in the bedroom while *it* came; and " Stage-coach," too—" Anything to make a noise," Ben said. And then after they got nicely started in the game, he would be missing to help about the mysterious thing in the kitchen, which was safe since Polly couldn't see him go on account of her bandage. So she didn't suspect in the least. And although the rest were almost dying to be out in the kitchen, they conscientiously stuck to their bargain to keep Polly occupied. Only Joel *would* open the door and peep once; and then Phronsie behind him began—" Oh, I see the sto ——" but David swooped down on her in a twinkling, and smothered the rest by tickling her.

Once they came very near having the whole thing pop out.

" Whatever is that noise in the kitchen? " asked Polly, as they all stopped to take breath after the scuffle of " Stage-coach." " It sounds just like grating."

" I'll go and see," cried Joel, promptly; and then he flew out where his mother and Ben and two men were at work on a big, black thing in the corner. The old stove, strange to say, was nowhere to be seen! Something else stood in its place, a shiny, black affair, with a generous supply of oven doors, and altogether such a comfortable, homelike look about it, as if it would say, " I'm going to make sunshine in this house! "

" Oh, Joel," cried his mother, turning around on him with very black hands, " you *haven't* told! "

"No," said Joel, "but she's hearing the noise, Polly's hearing it."

"*Hush!*" said Ben, to one of the men.

"We can't put it up without some noise," the man replied, "but we'll be as still as we can."

"Ain't it a big one, ma?" asked Joel, in the loudest of stage whispers, that Polly on the other side of the door couldn't have failed to hear if Phronsie hadn't laughed just then.

"Go back, Joe, do," said Ben, "play tag—*anything*," he implored, "we'll be through in a few minutes."

"It takes forever!" said Joel, disappearing within the bedroom door. Luckily for the secret, Phronsie just then ran a pin sticking up on the arm of the old chair into her finger; and Polly, while comforting her, forgot to question Joel. And then the mother came in, and though she had ill-concealed hilarity in her voice, she kept chattering and bustling around with Polly's supper to such an extent that there was no chance for a word to be got in.

Next morning it seemed as if the Little Brown House would turn inside out with joy.

"Oh, mammy!" cried Polly, jumping into her arms the first thing, as Doctor Fisher untied the bandage, "my eyes are *new!* just the same as if

I'd just got 'em!   Don't they *look* different? " she asked, earnestly, running to the cracked glass to see for herself.

" No," said Ben, " I hope not; the same brown ones, Polly."

" Well," said Polly, hugging first one and then another, " everybody looks different through 'em, anyway."

" Oh," cried Joel, " come out into the kitchen, Polly; it's a great deal better out there! "

" May I? " asked Polly, who was in such a twitter looking at everything that she didn't know which way to turn.

" Yes," said the doctor, smiling at her.

" Well, then," sang Polly, " come, mammy, we'll go first; isn't it just lovely—oh, MAMMY! " —and Polly turned so very pale, and looked as if she were going to tumble right over, that Mrs. Pepper grasped her arm in dismay.

" *What is it?* " she asked, pointing to the corner, while all the children stood around in the greatest excitement.

" Why," cried Phronsie, " it's a *stove*—don't you know, Polly? "

But Polly gave one plunge across the room, and before anybody could think, she was down on her knees with her arms flung right around the big, black thing, and laughing and crying over it, all in the same breath!

And then they all took hold of hands and danced around it like wild little things; while Doctor Fisher stole out silently—and Mrs. Pepper laughed till she wiped her eyes to see them go.

"We are never going to have any more burnt bread," sang Polly, all out of breath.

"And your back isn't going to break any more," panted Ben, with a very red face.

"Hooray!" screamed Joel and David, to fill any pause that might occur, while Phronsie gurgled and laughed at everything just as it came along. And then they all danced and capered again; all but Polly, who was down before the precious stove examining and exploring into ovens and everything that belonged to it.

"Oh, ma," she announced, coming up to Mrs. Pepper, who had been obliged to fly to her sewing again, and exhibiting a very crocky face and a pair of extremely smutty hands, "it's 'most all ovens, and it's just splendid!"

"I know it," answered her mother, delighted in the joy of her child. "My! how black you are, Polly!"

"Oh, I wish," cried Polly, as the thought struck

her, "that Doctor Fisher could have seen it! Where did he go to, ma?"

"I guess Doctor Fisher has seen it before," said Mrs. Pepper, and then she began to laugh. "You haven't ever asked where the stove came from, Polly."

And to be sure, Polly had been so overwhelmed that if the stove had really dropped from the clouds it would have been small matter of astonishment to her, as long as it had *come;* that was the main thing!

"Mammy," said Polly, turning around slowly, with the stove-lifter in her hand, "did Doctor Fisher bring that stove?"

"He didn't exactly *bring* it," answered her mother, "but I guess he knew something about it."

"Oh, he's the splendidest, *goodest* man!" cried Polly, "that ever breathed! Did he *really* get us that stove?"

"Yes," said Mrs. Pepper, "he would; I couldn't stop him. I don't know how he found out you wanted one so bad; but he said it must be kept as a surprise when your eyes got well."

"And he saved my eyes!" cried Polly, full of gratitude. "I've got a stove and two new eyes, mammy, just to think!"

"We ought to be good after all our mercies," said Mrs. Pepper, thankfully, looking around on her little group. Joel was engaged in the pleasing occupation of seeing how far he could run his head into the biggest oven, and then pulling it out to exhibit its blackness, thus engrossing the others in a perfect hubbub.

"I'm going to bake my doctor some little cakes," declared Polly, when there was comparative quiet.

"Do, Polly," cried Joel, "and then leave one or two over."

"No," said Polly; "we can't have any, because these must be very nice. Mammy, can't I have some white on top, just once?" she pleaded.

"I don't know," dubiously replied Mrs. Pepper; "eggs are dreadfully dear, and——"

"I don't care," said Polly, recklessly; "I must just once for Doctor Fisher."

"I tell you, Polly," said Mrs. Pepper, "what you might do; you might make him some little apple tarts—'most every one likes them, you know."

"Well," said Polly, with a sigh, "I s'pose they'll *have* to do; but *sometime,* mammy, I'm going to bake him a big cake, so there! "

X

A THREATENED BLOW

ONE day, a few weeks after, Mrs. Pepper and Polly were busy in the kitchen. Phronsie was out in the "orchard," as the one scraggy apple-tree was called by courtesy, singing her rag doll to sleep under its sheltering branches. But "Baby" was cross and wouldn't go to sleep, and Phronsie was on the point of giving up, and returning to the house, when a strain of music made her pause with dolly in her apron. There she stood with her finger in her mouth, in utter astonishment, wondering where the sweet sounds came from.

"Oh, Phronsie!" screamed Polly, from the back door, "where are—oh, here, come quick! it's the beau-ti-fullest!"

"What is it?" eagerly asked the little one, hopping over the stubby grass, leaving poor, discarded "Baby" on its snubby nose where it dropped in her hurry.

"Oh, a monkey!" cried Polly; "do hurry! the sweetest little monkey you ever saw!"

"What is a monkey?" asked Phronsie, skurrying after Polly to the gate where her mother was waiting for them.

"Why, a monkey's—a—monkey," explained Polly, "I don't know any better'n that. Here he is! Isn't he splendid!" and she lifted Phronsie up to the big post where she could see finely.

"O-oh! ow!" screamed little Phronsie, "see him, Polly! just see him!"

A man with an organ was standing in the middle of the road playing away with all his might, and at the end of a long rope was a lively little monkey in a bright red coat and a smart cocked hat. The little creature pulled off his hat, and with one long jump coming on the fence, he made Phronsie a most magnificent bow. Strange to say, the child wasn't in the least frightened, but put out her little fat hand, speaking in gentle tones, "Poor little monkey! come here, poor little monkey!"

Turning up his little wrinkled face, and glancing fearfully at his master, Jocko began to grimace and beg for something to eat. The man pulled the string and struck up a merry tune, and in a minute the monkey spun around and around at such a lively pace, and put in so many queer antics that the little audience was fairly convulsed with laughter.

"I can't pay you," said Mrs. Pepper, wiping her eyes, when at last the man pulled up the strap whistling to Jocko to jump up, "but I'll give you something to eat; and the monkey, too, he shall have something for his pains in amusing my children."

The man looked very cross when she brought him out only brown bread and two cold potatoes.

"Haven't you got nothin' better'n *that?*"

"It's as good as we have," answered Mrs. Pepper.

The man threw down the bread in the road. But Jocko thankfully ate his share, Polly and Phronsie busily feeding him; and then he turned and snapped up the portion his master had left in the dusty road.

Then they moved on, Mrs. Pepper and Polly going back to their work in the kitchen. A little down the road the man struck up another tune. Phronsie, who had started merrily to tell "Baby" all about it, stopped a minute to hear, and—she didn't go back to the orchard!

About two hours after, Polly said, merrily:

"I'm going to call Phronsie in, mammy; she must be awfully tired and hungry by this time."

She sang gaily on the way, "I'm coming, Phronsie, coming—why, where!—" peeping under the tree.

"Baby" lay on its face disconsolately on the ground—and the orchard was empty! Phronsie was gone!

"It's no use," said Ben, to the distracted household and such of the neighbors as the news had brought hurriedly to the scene, "to look any more around here—but somebody must go towards Hingham; he'd be likely to go that way."

"No one could tell where he *would* go," cried Polly, wringing her hands.

"But he'd change, Ben, if he thought folks would think he'd gone there," said Mrs. Pepper.

"We must go *all* roads," said Ben, firmly; "one must take the stage to Boxville, and I'll take Deacon Brown's wagon on the Hingham road, and somebody else must go to Toad Hollow."

"I'll go in the stage," screamed Joel, who could scarcely see out of his eyes, he had cried so; "I'll find—find her—I know."

"Be spry, then, Joe, and catch it at the corner!"

Everybody soon knew that little Phronsie Pepper had gone off with " a cross organ man and an awful monkey! " and in the course of an hour dozens of people were out on the hot, dusty roads in search.

" What's the matter? " asked a testy old gentleman in the stage of Joel, who, in his anxiety to see both sides of the road at once, bobbed the old gentleman in the face so often as the stage lurched, that at last he knocked his hat over his eyes.

" My sister's gone off with a monkey," explained Joel, bobbing over to the other side, as he thought he caught sight of something pink that he felt sure must be Phronsie's apron. " Stop! stop! there she is! " he roared, and the driver, who had his instructions and was fully in sympathy, pulled up so suddenly that the old gentleman flew over into the opposite seat.

" Where? "

But when they got up to it Joel saw that it was only a bit of pink calico flapping on a clothesline; so he climbed back and away they rumbled again.

The others were having the same luck. No trace could be found of the child. To Ben, who took the Hingham road, the minutes seemed like hours.

"I *won't* go back," he muttered, "until I take her. I *can't* see mother's face!"

But the ten miles were nearly traversed; almost the last hope was gone. Into every thicket and lurking-place by the roadside had he peered—but no Phronsie! Deacon Brown's horse began to lag.

"*Go on!*" said Ben, hoarsely; "O dear Lord, *make* me find her!"

The hot sun poured down on the boy's face, and he had no cap. What cared he for that? On and on he went. Suddenly the horse stopped. Ben doubled up the reins to give him a cut, when "Whoa!" he roared so loud that the horse in very astonishment gave a bounce that nearly flung him headlong. But he was over the wheel in a twinkling, and up with a bound to a small thicket of scrubby bushes on a high hill by the roadside. Here lay a little bundle on the ground, and close by it a big black dog; and over the whole, standing guard, was a boy a little bigger than Ben, with honest gray eyes. And the bundle was Phronsie!

"Don't wake her up," said the boy, warningly,

as Ben, with a hungry look in his eyes, leaped up the hill, "she's tired to death!"

"She's my sister!" cried Ben, "*our Phronsie!*"

"I know it," said the boy, kindly; "but I wouldn't wake her up yet if I were you. I'll tell you all about it," and he took Ben's hand, which was as cold as ice.

XI

" IT's all right, Prince," the boy added, encouragingly, to the big dog that, lifting his noble head, had turned two big eyes steadily on Ben. " He's all right; lie down again! "

Then, flinging himself down on the grass, he told Ben how he came to rescue Phronsie.

" Prince and I were out for a stroll," said he. " I live over in Hingham," pointing to the pretty little town just a short distance before them in the hollow; " that is," laughing, " I do this summer. Well, we were out strolling along about a mile below here on the cross-roads; and all of a sudden, just as if they sprung right up out of the ground, I saw a man with an organ, and a monkey, and a little girl, coming along the road. She was crying, and as soon as Prince saw that, he gave a growl, and then the man saw us, and he looked so mean and cringing I knew there must be something wrong, and I inquired of him what he was doing with that little girl, and then she looked up and begged so with her eyes, and all of a sudden broke away from him and ran towards me screaming, ' I want Polly! ' Well, the man sprang after her; then I tell you "—here the boy forgot his caution about waking Phronsie—" we went for him, Prince and I! Prince is a noble fellow " (here the dog's ears twitched very perceptibly), " and he kept at that man; oh! how he bit him! till he had to run for fear the monkey would get killed."

" Was Phronsie frightened? " asked Ben; " she's never seen strangers."

" Not a bit," said the boy, cheerily; " she just clung to me like everything—I only wish she was my sister," he added, impulsively.

" What were you going to do with her if I hadn't come along? " asked Ben.

" Well, I got out on the main road," said the boy, " because I thought anybody who had lost her would probably come through this way; but if somebody hadn't come, I was going to carry her in to Hingham; and then father and I'd have contrived some way to do."

" Well," said Ben, as the boy finished and fastened his bright eyes on him, " somebody did come along; and now I must get her home about as fast as I can for poor mammy—and Polly! "

"Yes," said the boy, "I'll help you lift her; perhaps she won't wake up."

The big dog moved away a step or two, but still kept his eye on Phronsie.

"There," said the boy, brightly, as they laid the child on the wagon seat; "now when you get in you can hold her head; that's it," he added, seeing them both fixed to his satisfaction. But still Ben lingered.

"Thank you," he tried to say.

"I know," laughed the boy; "only it's Prince instead of me," and he pulled forward the big black creature, who had followed faithfully down the hill to see the last of it. "To the front, sir, there! We're coming to see you," he continued, "if you will let us—where do you live?"

"Do come," said Ben, lighting up, for he was just feeling he couldn't bear to look his last on the merry, honest face; "anybody'll tell you where Mrs. Pepper lives."

"Is she a Pepper?" asked the boy, laughing, and pointing to the unconscious little heap in the wagon; "and are you a Pepper?"

"Yes," said Ben, laughing, too. "There are five of us besides mother."

"Jolly!   that's something like!   Good-by!
Come on, Prince! "

Then away home to mother! Phronsie never
woke up nor turned over once till she was put, a
little pink sleepy heap, into her mother's arms.
Joel was there, crying bitterly at his forlorn
search. The testy old gentleman in the seat opposite had relented and ordered the coach about
and brought him home in an outburst of grief
when all hope was gone. And one after another
they all had come back, disheartened, to the distracted mother. Polly alone clung to hope.

"Ben *will* bring her, mammy; I *know* God will
let him," she whispered.

But when Ben *did* bring her, Polly, for the
second time in her life, tumbled over with a gasp,
into old Mrs. Bascom's lap.

Home and mother! Little Phronsie slept all
that night straight through. The neighbors came
in softly, and with awestruck visages stole into
the bedroom to look at the child; and as they
crept out again, thoughts of their own little ones
tugging at their hearts, the tears would drop un-
heeded. ·

XII

NEW FRIENDS

Up the stairs of the hotel, two steps at a time, ran a boy with a big black dog at his heels. "Come on, Prince; soft, *now*," as they neared a door at the end of the corridor.

It opened into a corner room overlooking "the Park," as the small open space in front of the hotel was called. Within the room there was sunshine and comfort, it being the most luxurious one in the house, which the proprietor had placed at the disposal of this most exacting guest. He didn't look very happy, however—the gentleman who sat in an easy chair by the window; a large, handsome old gentleman, whose whole bearing showed plainly that personal comfort had always been his, and was, therefore, neither a matter of surprise nor thankfulness.

"Where have you been?" he asked, turning around to greet the boy who came in, followed by Prince.

144

" Oh, such a long story, father! " he cried, flushed, his eyes sparkling as he flung back the dark hair from his forehead. " You can't even guess! "

" Never mind now," said the old gentleman, testily; " your stories are always long; the paper hasn't come—strange, indeed, that one must needs be so annoyed! Do ring that bell again."

So the bell was pulled; and a porter popped in his head.

" What is it, sir? "

" The *paper*," said the old gentleman, irritably; " hasn't it come yet? "

" No, sir," said the man; and then he repeated, " 'Tain't in yet, sir."

" Very well—you said so once; that's all," waving his hand; then as the door closed, he said to his son, " That pays one for coming to such an out-of-the-way country place as this, away from papers—I never will do it again."

As the old gentleman, against the advice of many friends who knew his dependence on externals, had determined to come to this very place, the boy was not much startled at the decisive words. He stood very quietly, however, until his father finished. Then he said:

"It's too bad, father! Supposing I tell you my story? Perhaps you'll enjoy hearing it while you wait—it's really quite newspaperish."

"Well, you might as well tell it now, I suppose," said the old gentleman; "but it is a great shame about that paper! to advertise that morning papers are to be obtained—it's a swindle, Jasper! a complete swindle!" and the old gentleman looked so very irate that the boy exerted himself to soothe him.

"I know," he said; "but they can't help the trains being late."

"They shouldn't *have* the trains late," said his father, unreasonably. "There's no necessity for all this prating about 'trains late.' I'm convinced it's because they forgot to send down for the papers till they were all sold."

"I don't believe that's it, father," said the boy, trying to change the subject; "but you don't know how splendid Prince has been, nor ——"

"And then *such* a breakfast!" continued the old gentleman. "My liver certainly will be in a dreadful state if these things continue!" And he got up, and going to the corner of the room, opened his medicine-chest, and taking a box of pills therefrom, he swallowed two, which done,

he came back with a somewhat easier expression
to his favorite chair.

"He was just *splendid*, father," began the boy;
"he went for him, I tell you!"

"I hope, Jasper, your dog has not been doing
anything violent," said the old gentleman. "I
must caution you; he'll get you into trouble some
day; and then there'll be a heavy bill to pay; he
grows more irritable every day."

"*Irritable!*" cried the boy, flinging his arms
around the dog's neck, who was looking up at the
old gentleman in high disdain. "He's done the
most splendid thing you ever saw! Why, he
saved a little girl, father, from a cross old organ-
man, and he drove that man—oh! you ought to
have seen him run!"

And now that it was over, Jasper put back his
head and laughed long and loud, as he remembered the rapid transit of the musical pair.

"Well, how do you know she wasn't the man's
daughter?" asked his father, determined to find
fault some way. "You haven't any business to
go around the country setting your dog on people. I shall have an awful bill to pay some day,
Jasper—an awful bill!" he continued, getting out

of his chair and commencing to pace up and down the floor in extreme irritation.

"Father," cried the boy, half-laughing, half-vexed, springing to his side, and keeping step with him, "we found her brother; he came along when we were by the side of the road. We couldn't go any farther, for the poor little thing was all tired out. And don't you think they live over in Badgertown, and ——"

"Well," said the old gentleman, pausing in his walk, and taking out his watch to wonder if that paper would ever come, "she had probably followed the organ-man; so it served her right, after all."

"Well, but, father," and the boy's dark eyes glowed, "she was such a cunning little thing! she wasn't more than four years old; and she had such a pretty little yellow head; and she said so funnily, 'I want Polly.'"

"Did she?" said the old gentleman, getting interested in spite of himself; "what then?"

"Why, then, sir," said Jasper, delighted at his success in diverting his thoughts, "Prince and I waited—and waited; and I was just going to bring her here to ask you what we should do, when ——"

" Goodness! " exclaimed the old gentleman, instinctively starting back as if he actually saw the forlorn little damsel, "you needn't ever bring such people here, Jasper! I shouldn't know what to do with them, I'm sure! "

" Well," said the boy, laughing, "we didn't have to, did we, Prince? " stroking the big head of the dog, who was slowly following the two as they paced up and down, but keeping carefully on the side of his master; " for just as we really didn't know what to do, don't you think there was a big wagon came along, drawn by the ricketiest old horse, and a boy in the wagon looking both sides of the road, and into every bush, just as wild as he could be, and before I could think, hardly, he spied us, and if he didn't jump! I thought he'd broken his leg——"

" And I suppose he just abused you for what you had done," observed the old gentleman, petulantly; " that's about all the gratitude there is in this world."

" He didn't seem to see *me* at all," said the boy. " I thought he'd eat the little girl up."

" Ought to have looked out for her better then," grumbled the old gentleman, determined to find fault with somebody.

" And he's a splendid fellow, I just know," cried
Jasper, waxing enthusiastic; " and his name is
Pepper."

" Pepper! " repeated his father; " no nice family ever had the name of *Pepper!* "

" Well, I don't care," and Jasper's laugh was
loud and merry; " *he's* nice, anyway—*I know;*
and the little thing's nice; and I'm going to see
them—can't I, father? "

" Dear me! " said his father; " how can you,
Jasper? You do have the strangest tastes I ever
heard of! "

" It's dreadfully dull here," pleaded the boy,
touching the right string; " you know that yourself, father, and I don't know any boys around
here; and Prince and I are *so* lonely on our walks
—do let me, father! "

The old gentleman, who really cared very little about it, turned away, muttering, " Well, I'm
sure I don't care; go where you like," when a
knock was heard at the door, and the paper was
handed in, which broke up the conversation, and
restored good humor.

The next day but one, Ben was out by the
wood-pile, trying to break up some kindlings for

Polly, who was washing up the dishes, and otherwise preparing for the delights of baking day.

" Hello! " said a voice he thought he knew.

He turned around to see the merry-faced boy and the big black dog, that immediately began to wag his tail, as if willing to recognize him.

" You see I thought you'd *never* look round," said the boy, with a laugh. " How's the little girl? "

" Oh! you have come, really," cried Ben, springing over the wood-pile with a beaming face. " Polly! "

But Polly was already by the door, with dish-cloth in hand.

" This is my sister, Polly," began Ben—and then stopped, not knowing the boy's name.

" I'm Jasper King," said the boy, stepping upon the flat stone by Polly's side; and taking off his cap, he put out his hand. " And this is Prince," he added.

Polly put her hand in his, and received a hearty shake; and then she sprang over the big stone, dish-cloth and all, and just flung her arms around the dog's neck.

" Oh, you splendid fellow, you! " said she.

"Don't you know we all think you're as good as gold?"

The dog submitted to this astonishing proceeding as if he liked it, while Jasper, delighted with Polly's appreciation, beamed down on them, and struck up a friendship with her on the instant.

"Now, I must call Phronsie," said Polly, getting up, her face as red as a rose.

"Is her name Phronsie?" asked the boy, with interest.

"No, it's Sophronia," said Polly, "but we call her Phronsie."

"What a very funny name," said Jasper, "Sophronia is, for such a little thing—and yours is Polly, is it not?" he asked, turning around suddenly on her.

"Yes," said Polly; "no, not truly Polly; it's Mary, my real name is—but I've always been Polly."

"I like Polly best, too," declared Jasper, "it sounds so nice."

"And his name is Ben," said Polly.

"Ebenezer, you mean," said Ben, correcting her.

"Well, we call him Ben." said Polly; "it

doesn't ever seem as if there was any Ebenezer about it."

"I should think not," laughed Jasper.

"Well, I must get Phronsie," Polly reiterated, running back into the bedroom, where that small damsel was busily engaged in washing "Baby" in the basin of water that she had with extreme difficulty succeeded in getting down on the floor. She had then, by means of a handful of soft soap, taken from Polly's soap-bowl during the dish-washing, and a bit of old cotton, plastered both herself and "Baby" to a comfortable degree of stickiness.

"Phronsie," said Polly—"goodness me! what are you doing? the big dog's out there, you know, that scared the naughty organ-man; and the boy" —but before the words were half out, Phronsie had slipped from under her hands, and, to Polly's extreme dismay, clattered out into the kitchen.

"Here she is!" cried Jasper, meeting her at the door. The little soapy hands were grasped, and kissing her—"Ugh!" he said, as the soft soap plentifully spread on her face met his mouth.

"Oh, Phronsie! you shouldn't," cried Polly, and then they all burst out into a peal of laughter at Jasper's funny grimaces.

"She's been washing 'Baby,'" explained Polly, wiping her eyes, and looking at Phronsie, who was hanging over Prince in extreme affection. Evidently Prince still regarded her as his especial property.

"Have you got a baby?" asked Jasper. "I thought *she* was the baby," pointing to Phronsie.

"Oh, I mean her littlest dolly; she always calls her 'Baby,'" said Polly. "Come, Phronsie, and have your face washed, and a clean apron on."

When Phronsie could be fairly persuaded that Prince would not run away during her absence, she allowed herself to be taken off; and soon reappeared, her own dainty little self. Ben, in the meantime, had been initiating Jasper into the mysteries of cutting the wood, the tool-house, and all the surroundings of the Little Brown House. They had received a reinforcement in the advent of Joel and David, who stared delightedly at Phronsie's protector, made friends with the dog, and altogether had such a thoroughly good time, that Phronsie, coming back, clapped her hands in glee to hear them.

"I wish mamsie was home," said Polly, polishing up the last cup carefully.

"Let me put it up," said Jasper, taking it from

her; "it goes up here, doesn't it, with the rest?" reaching up to the upper shelf of the old cupboard.

"Yes," said Polly.

"Oh, I should think you'd have real good times!" said the boy, enviously. "I haven't a single sister or brother."

"Haven't you?" said Polly, looking at him in extreme pity. "Yes, we do have real fun," she added, answering his questioning look; "the house is just brimful sometimes, even if we are poor."

"We ain't poor," said Joel, who never could bear to be pitied. Then, with a very proud air, he said, in a grand way, "At any rate, we ain't going to be, long, for something's a-coming!"

"What *do* you mean, Jocy?" asked Ben, while the rest looked equally amazed.

"Our ships," said Joel, confidently, as if they were right before their eyes; at which they all screamed!

"See Polly's stove!" cried Phronsie, wishing to entertain in her turn. "Here 'tis," running up to it, and pointing with her fat little finger.

"Yes, I see," cried Jasper, pretending to be greatly surprised; "it's new, isn't it?"

"Yes," said the child; "it's very all new; four yesterdays ago!"

And then Polly stopped in sweeping up and related, with many additions and explanations from the others, the history of the stove, and good Doctor Fisher (upon whom they all dilated at great length), and the dreadful measles, and everything. And Jasper sympathized, and rejoiced with them to their hearts' content, and altogether got so very homelike, that they all felt as if they had known him for a year. Ben neglected his work a little, but then visitors didn't come every day to the Peppers; so while Polly worked away at her bread, which she was "going to make like biscuits," she said, the audience gathered in the little old kitchen was in the merriest mood, and enjoyed everything to the fullest extent.

"Do put in another stick, Bensie dear," said Polly; "this bread won't be fit for anything!"

"Isn't this fun, though?" cried Jasper, running up to try the oven; "I wish I could ever bake," and he looked longingly at the little brown biscuits waiting their turn out on the table.

"You come out some day," said Polly, sociably, "and we'll all try baking—mammy'd like to have you, I know," feeling sure that nothing would be too much for Mrs. Pepper to do for the protector of little Phronsie.

" I will! " cried Jasper, perfectly delighted. " You can't think how awfully dull it is out in Hingham! "

" Don't you *live* there? " asked Polly, with a gasp, almost dropping a tin full of little brown lumps of dough she was carrying to the oven.

" *Live there!* " cried Jasper; and then he burst out into a merry laugh. " No, *indeed!* I hope not! Why, we're only spending the summer there, father and I, in the hotel."

" Where's your mother? " asked Joel, squeezing in between Jasper and his audience. And then they all felt instinctively that a very wrong question had been asked.

" I haven't any mother," said the boy, in a low voice.

They all stood quite still for a moment; then Polly said, " I wish you'd come out sometime; and you may bake—or anything else," she added; and there was a kinder ring to her voice than ever.

No mother! Polly for her life couldn't imagine how anybody *could* feel without a mother, but the

very words alone smote her heart; and there was
nothing she wouldn't have done to give pleasure
to one who had done so much for them.

"I wish you could see *our* mother," she said,
gently. "Why, here she comes now! oh! mamsie,
dear," she cried. "Do, Joe, run and take her
bundle."

Mrs. Pepper stopped a minute to kiss Phronsie—her baby was dearer than ever to her now.
Then her eye fell on Jasper, who stood respectfully waiting and watching her with great interest.

"Is this," she asked, taking it all in at the first
glance—the boy with the honest eyes as Ben had
described him—and the big black dog—"is this
the boy who saved my little girl?"

"Oh, ma'am," cried Jasper, " *I* didn't do much;
'twas Prince."

"I guess you never'll know how much you *did*
do," said Mrs. Pepper. Then looking with a long,
keen gaze into the boy's eyes that met her own
so frankly and kindly: "I'll trust him," she said
to herself; "a boy with those eyes can't help but
be good."

"Her eyes are just the same as Polly's,"
thought Jasper, "just such laughing ones, only
Polly's are brown," and he liked her on the spot.

And then, somehow, the hubbub ceased. Polly went on with her work, and the others separated, and Mrs. Pepper and Jasper had a long talk. When the mother's eyes fell on Phronsie playing around on the floor, she gave the boy a grateful smile that he thought was beautiful.

"Well, I declare," said Jasper, at last, looking up at the old clock in the corner by the side of the cupboard, "I'm afraid I'll miss the stage, and then father never'll let me come again. Come, Prince."

"Oh, don't go," cried Phronsie, wailing. "Let doggie stay! Oh, *make* him stay, mammy!"

"I can't, Phronsie," said Mrs. Pepper, smiling, "if he thinks he ought to go."

"I'll come again," said Jasper, eagerly, "if I may, ma'am." He looked up at Mrs. Pepper as he stood cap in hand, waiting for the answer.

"I'm sure we should be glad, if your father'll be willing," she added; thinking, proudly, "My children are an honor to anybody," as she glanced around on the bright little group she could call her own. "But be sure, Jasper," and she laid her hand on his arm as she looked down into his eyes, "that your father *is* willing, that's all."

" Oh, yes, ma'am," said the boy; " but he will be, I guess, if he feels well."

" Then come on Thursday," said Polly; " and can't we bake something then, mammy? "

" I'm sure I don't care," laughed Mrs. Pepper; " but you won't find much but brown flour and meal to bake with."

" Well, we can pretend," said Polly; " and we can cut the cakes with the heart-shape, and they'll do for anything."

" Oh, I'll come," laughed Jasper, ready for such lovely fun in the old kitchen; " look out for me on Thursday, Ben! "

So Jasper and Prince took their leave, all the children accompanying them to the gate; and then after seeing him fairly started on a smart run to catch the stage, Prince scampering at his heels, they all began to sing his praises and to wish for Thursday to come.

But Jasper didn't come! Thursday came and went; a beautiful, bright, sunny day, but with no signs of the merry boy whom all had begun to love, nor of the big black dog. The children had made all the needful preparations with much ostentation and bustle, and were in a state of excited happiness, ready for any gale. But the last hope had to be given up, as the old clock ticked away hour after hour. And at last Polly had to put Phronsie to bed, who wouldn't stop crying enough to eat her supper at the dreadful disappointment.

"He *couldn't* come, I know," said both Ben and Polly, standing staunchly up for their new friend; but Joel and David felt that he had broken his word.

"He promised," said Joel, vindictively.

"I don't believe his father'd let him," said Polly, wiping away a sly tear; "I know Jasper would have come, if he could."

Mrs. Pepper wisely kept her own counsel, simply giving them a kindly caution:

"Don't you go to judging him, children, till you know."

"Well, he *promised*," said Joel, as a settler.

"Aren't you ashamed, Joe," said his mother, "to talk about any one whose back is turned? Wait till he tells you the reason himself."

Joel hung his head, and then began to tease David in the corner, to make up for his disappointment.

The next morning Ben had to go to the store

after some more meal. As he was going out rather
dismally, the storekeeper, who was also postmaster, called out, " Oh, hello, there! "

" What is it? " asked Ben, turning back, thinking perhaps Mr. Atkins hadn't given him the right
change.

" Here," said Mr. Atkins, stepping up to the
post-office department, quite smart with its array
of boxes and official notices, where Ben had always
lingered, wishing there might be *sometime* a letter
for him—or for some of them. " You've got a sister Polly, haven't you? "

" Yes," said Ben, wondering what was coming
next.

" Well, she's got a letter," said the postmaster,
holding up a nice big envelope, looking just like
those that Ben had so many times wished for.
That magic piece of white paper danced before
the boy's eyes for a minute; then he said:

" It can't be for her, Mr. Atkins; why, she's
never had one."

" Well, she's got one now, sure enough," said
Mr. Atkins; " here 'tis, plain enough," and he read
what he had no need to study much, as it had
already passed examination by his own and his
wife's faithful eyes: " ' Miss Polly Pepper, near

the Turnpike, Badgertown '—that's her, isn't it? "
he added, laying it down before Ben's eyes.
" Must be a first time for everything, you know,
my boy! " and he laughed long over his own joke;
" so take it and run along home." For Ben still
stood looking at it, and not offering to stir.

" If you say so," said the boy, as if Mr. Atkins
had given him something out of his own pocket;
" but I'm afraid 'tisn't for Polly." Then button-
ing up the precious letter in his jacket, he spun
along home as never before.

"Polly! Polly! " he screamed. " Where is she,
mother?"

" I don't know," said Mrs. Pepper, coming out
of the bedroom. " Dear me! is anybody hurt,
Ben? "

" I don't know," said Ben, in a state to believe
anything, " but Polly's got a letter."

" Polly got a letter! " cried Mrs. Pepper; "what
do you mean, Ben? "

" I don't know," repeated the boy, still holding
out the precious letter; " but Mr. Atkins gave it
to me; where is Polly? "

" I know where she is," said Joel; " she's up-
stairs." And he flew out in a twinkling, and soon

reappeared with Polly scampering after him in the wildest excitement.

And then the kitchen was in an uproar as the precious missive was put into Polly's hands; and they all gathered around her, wondering and examining, till Ben thought he would go wild with the delay.

"I wonder where it did come from," said Polly, in the greatest anxiety, examining again the address.

"Where does the postmark say?" asked Mrs. Pepper, looking over her shoulder.

"It's all rubbed out," said Polly, peering at it, "you can't see anything."

"Do *open* it," said Ben, "and then you'll find out."

"But p'r'aps 'tisn't for me," said Polly, timidly.

"Well, Mr. Atkins says 'tis," said Ben, impatiently; "here, I'll open it for you, Polly."

"No, let her open it for herself, Ben," protested his mother.

"But she *won't*," said Ben; "do *tear* it open, Polly."

"No, I'm going to get a knife," she said.

"I'll get one," cried Joel, running up to the table drawer; "here's one, Polly."

" O dear," groaned Ben; " you never'll get it open at this rate! "

But at last it was cut; and they all, holding their breath, gazed awestruck, while Polly drew out the mysterious missive.

" What *does* it say? " gasped Mrs. Pepper.

" Dear Miss Polly," began both Ben and Polly in a breath.

" Let Polly read," said Joel, who couldn't hear in the confusion.

" Well, go on, Polly," said Ben; " *hurry!* "

" ' Dear Miss Polly, I was *so* sorry I couldn't come on Thursday ——' "

" Oh, it's Jasper! it's Jasper! " cried all the children in a breath.

" I told you so! " cried Ben and Polly, perfectly delighted to find their friend vindicated fully— " *there,* Jocy Pepper! "

" Well, I don't care," cried Joe, nothing daunted, " he *didn't* come, anyway—do go on, Polly."

" ' I was *so* sorry I couldn't come ——' " began Polly.

" You read that," said Joel.

" I know it," said Polly, " but it's just lovely; ' on Thursday; but my father was sick, and I couldn't leave him. If you don't mind I'll come again—I mean I'll come some other day, if it's just as convenient for you, for I do *so want* the baking, and the nice time. I forgot to say that I had a cold, to'" (here Jasper had evidently had a struggle in his mind whether there should be two o's or one, and he had at last decided it, by crossing out one), "'but my father is willing I should come when I get well. Give my love to all, and especially remember me respectfully to your mother.   Your friend,

"'Jasper Elyot King.'"

"Oh, *lovely! lovely!*" cried Polly, flying around with the letter in her hand; "so he is coming really and truly!"

Ben was just as wild as she was, for no one knew but Polly just how the new friend had stepped into his heart. Phronsie went to sleep happy, hugging "Baby."

"And don't you think, Baby, dear," she whispered, sleepily, and Polly heard her say as she was tucking her in, "that Jasper is *really* coming; really—and the big, be-you-ti-ful doggie, too!"

XIII

PHRONSIE PAYS A DEBT OF GRATITUDE

" AND now I tell you," said Polly, the next day,
" let's make Jasper something; can't we, ma? "

" Oh, *do! do!* " cried all the other children,
" *let's;* but what'll it be, Polly? "

" I don't know about this," interrupted Mrs.
Pepper; " I don't see how you could get anything
to him if you could make it."

" Oh, we could, mamsie," said Polly, eagerly,
running up to her; " for Ben knows; and he says
we can do it."

" Oh, well, if Ben and you have had your heads
together, I suppose it's all right," laughed Mrs.
Pepper, " but I don't see how you can do it."

" Well, we can, mother, truly," put in Ben.
" I'll tell you how, and you'll say it'll be splendid.
You see Deacon Blodgett's going over to Hingham, to-morrow; I heard him tell Mrs. Blodgett
so; and he goes right past the hotel; and we can
do it up real nice—and it'll please Jasper so—do,
mammy! "

"And it's real dull there, Jasper says," put in Polly, persuasively; "and just think, mammy, no brothers and sisters!" And Polly looked around on the others.

After that there was no need to say anything more; her mother would have consented to almost any plan then.

"Well, go on, children," she said; "you may do it; I don't see but that you can get 'em there well enough; but I'm sure I don't know what you can make."

"Can't we," said Polly—and she knelt down by her mother's side and put her face in between the sewing in Mrs. Pepper's lap, and the eyes bent kindly down on her—"make some little cakes, real cakes, I mean? Now don't say no, mamsie!" she said, alarmed, for she saw a "no" slowly coming in the eyes above her, as Mrs. Pepper began to shake her head.

"But we haven't any white flour, Polly," began her mother.

"I know," said Polly; "but we'll make 'em of brown; it'll do, if you'll give us some raisins—you know there's *some* in the bowl, mammy."

"I was saving them for a nest-egg," said Mrs. Pepper; meaning at some future time to indulge in another plum-pudding that the children so loved.

"Well, do give 'em to us," cried Polly; "do, ma!"

"I want 'em for a plum-pudding sometime," said Mrs. Pepper.

"*Ow!* "—and Joel with a howl sprang up from the floor where he had been trying to make a cart for "Baby" out of an old box, and joined Mrs. Pepper and Polly. "No, don't give 'em away, ma!" he screamed; "let's have our plum-pudding —now, Polly Pepper, you're a-going to bake up all our raisins in nasty little cakes—and——"

"*Joey!* " commanded Mrs. Pepper, "*hush!* what word did you say?"

"Well," blubbered Joel, wiping his tears away with his grimy little hand, "Polly's—a-going—to give——"

"I should rather you'd *never* have a plum-pudding than to say such words," said Mrs. Pepper, sternly, taking up her work again. "And besides, do you think what Jasper has done for you?" and her face grew very white around the lips.

"Well. he can have plum-puddings," said Joel,

whimpering, " for ever an' ever, if he wants 'em—
and—and ——"

"Well, Joey," said Polly, "there, don't feel
bad," and she put her arms around him, and tried
to wipe away the tears that still rolled down his
cheeks. "We won't give 'em if you don't want us
to; but Jasper's sick, and there isn't anything for
him to do, and "—here she whispered slyly up
into his ear—" don't you remember how you
liked folks to send *you* things when you had the
measles?"

"Yes, I know," said Joel, beginning to smile
through his tears; "wasn't it fun, Polly?"

"I guess *'twas*," laughed Polly back again,
pleased at the return of sunshine. "Well, Jasper'll be just as pleased as you were, 'cause we
love him and want to do something for him, he
was so good to Phronsie."

"I will, Polly, I will," cried Joel, completely
won over; "do let's make 'em for him; and put
'em in thick; oh! thick as you can; " and determined to do nothing by halves, Joel ran generously for the precious bowl of raisins, and after
setting it on the table, began to help Polly in all
needful preparations.

Mrs. Pepper smiled away to herself to see happiness restored to the little group. And soon a pleasant hum and bustle went on around the baking-table, the centre of attraction.

"Now," said Phronsie, coming up to the table and standing on tiptoe to see Polly measure out the flour, "I'm a-going to bake something for my sick man, I *am*."

"Oh, no, Phronsie, you can't," began Polly.

"Hey?" asked Joel, with a daub of flour on the tip of his chubby nose, gained by too much peering into Polly's flour-bag. "What did she say, Polly?" watching her shake the clouds of flour in the sieve.

"She said she was going to bake something for Jasper," said Polly. "There," as she whisked in the flour, "now that's done."

"No, I didn't say Japser," said Phronsie; "I didn't *say* Japser," she repeated, emphatically.

"Why, what did you say, Pet?" asked Polly, astonished, while little Davie repeated, "What did you say, Phronsie?"

"I said my sick *man*," said Phronsie, shaking her yellow head; "poor sick man!"

"Who *does* she mean?" said Polly, in despair, stopping a moment her violent stirring that threatened to overrun the whole cake-bowl.

"I guess she means Prince," said Joel. "Can't I stir, Polly?"

"Oh, no," said Polly; "only one person must stir cake."

"Why?" asked Joel; "why, Polly?"

"Oh, I don't know," said Polly, "'cause 'tis so; never mind now, Joel. *Do* you mean Prince, Phronsie?"

"*No,* I don't mean Princey," said the child, decisively; "I mean my sick *man.*"

"It's Jasper's father, I guess she means," said Mrs. Pepper, over in the corner; "but what in the world!"

"Yes, yes," cried Phronsie, perfectly delighted at being at last understood, and hopping on one toe; "my sick man."

"I *shall* give up!" said Polly, tumbling over in a chair, with the cake spoon in her hand, from which a small sticky lump fell on her apron, which Joel immediately pounced upon and devoured. "*What do* you want to bake, Phronsie?" she gasped, holding the spoon sticking up straight, and staring at the child.

"A gingerbread boy," said Phronsie, promptly; "he'd like that best; poor sick man!" and she commenced to climb up to active preparations.

XIV

A LETTER TO JASPER

"Mamsie, what *shall* we do?" implored Polly of her mother.

"I don't know," said her mother; "how ever did that get into her head, do you suppose?"

"I am sure I can't tell," said Polly, jumping up and beginning to stir briskly to make up for lost time. "P'r'aps she heard us talking about Jasper's having to take care of his sick father, and how hard it must be to be sick away from home."

"Yes," said Phronsie, "but he'll be glad to see my gingerbread boy, I guess; poor, sick man."

"Oh, Phronsie," cried Polly, in great distress, "you aren't ever going to make a 'gingerbread boy' to-day! see, we'll put in a cunning little cake for Mr. King—full of raisins, Phronsie; won't that be lovely!" and Polly began to fill a little scalloped tin with some of the cake mixture.

"N-no," said the child, eyeing it suspiciously; "that isn't like a 'gingerbread boy,' Polly; he'll like that best."

"Mamsie," said Polly, "we *can't* let her make a dreadful, horrid 'gingerbread boy' to send Mr. King! he never'll let Jasper come here again."

"Oh, let her," cried Joel; "she can bake it, and Dave an' I'll eat it," and he picked up a raisin that had fallen under the table and began crunching it with great gusto.

"That wouldn't be fair," said Polly, gloomily. "Do get her off from it, mammy."

"Phronsie," said Mrs. Pepper, going up back of the child, who sat patiently in her high chair waiting for Polly to let her begin, "hadn't you rather wait and give your 'gingerbread boy' to Jasper for his father when he comes?"

"Oh, no, no!" cried Phronsie, twisting in her chair in great apprehension, "I want to send it now, I *do*."

"Well, Polly," said her mother, laughing, "after all it's best, I think, to let her; it can't do any harm, anyway—and instead of Mr. King's not letting Jasper come, if he's a sensible man that won't make any difference; and if he isn't, why, then there'd be sure to something come up sometime to make trouble."

"Well," said Polly, "I suppose she's got to; and p'r'aps," as a consoling idea struck her,

" p'r'aps she'll want to eat it up herself when it's done. Here, Phronsie," giving her a handful of the cake mixture, which she stiffened with flour to the right thickness, " there, you can call that a ' gingerbread boy; ' see, won't it make a beautiful one! "

" You needn't think," said Mrs. Pepper, seeing Phronsie's delighted face, and laughing as she went back to her work, " but that that gingerbread boy'll go."

When the little cakes were done, eight of them, and set upon the table for exhibition, they one and all protested that they never saw so fine a lot. Polly was delighted with the praise they received, and her mother's commendation that she was " growing a better cook every day." " How glad Jasper'll be, won't he, mamsie? " said she.

The children walked around and around the table, admiring and pointing out the chief points of attraction, as they appeared before their discriminating eyes.

" I should choose that one," said Joel, pointing at one which was particularly plummy, with a raisin standing up on one end with a festive air, as if to say, " There's lots of us inside, you better believe! "

"I wouldn't," said Davie; "*I'd* have that— that's cracked so pretty."

"So 'tis," said Mrs. Pepper; "they're all as light as a feather, Polly."

"But my 'gingerbread boy,'" cried Phronsie, running eagerly along with a particularly ugly looking specimen of a cake figure in her hand, "is the be-you-ti-fullest, isn't it, Polly?"

"O dear!" groaned Polly, "it looks just awful, doesn't it, Ben?"

"Hoh, hoh!" laughed Joel, in derision; "his leg is crooked, see, Phronsie—you better let Davie an' me have it."

"No, *no*," screamed the child in terror; "that's my sick man's 'gingerbread boy,' it *is!*"

"Joe, put it down," said Ben. "Yes, Phronsie, you shall have it; there, it's all safe;" and he put it carefully into Phronsie's apron, when she breathed easier.

"And he hasn't but one eye," still laughed Joel, while little Davie giggled, too.

"He did have two," said Polly, "but she punched the other in with her thumb; don't, boys," she said, aside, "you'll make her feel bad; do stop laughing. Now, how'll we send the things?"

"Put 'em in a basket," said Ben; "that's nicest."

"But we haven't got any basket," said Polly, "except the potato basket, and they'd be lost in that."

"Can't we take your work-basket, mamsie?" asked Ben; "they'd look so nice in that."

"Oh," said Mrs. Pepper, "that wouldn't do; I couldn't spare it, and besides, it's all broken at the side, Ben; that doesn't look nice."

"O dear," sighed Polly, sitting down on one of the hard wooden chairs to think, "I *do* wish we had things nice to send to sick people." And her forehead puckered up in a little hard knot.

"We'll have to do 'em up in a paper, Polly," said Ben; "there isn't any other way; they'll look nice in anything, 'cause they *are* nice," he added, comfortingly.

"If we only had some flowers," said Polly, "that would set 'em off perfectly lovely."

"You're always thinking of flowers, Polly," said Ben. "I guess the cakes'll have to go without 'em."

"I suppose they will," said Polly, stifling a little sigh. "Where's the paper?"

"I've got a nice piece up-stairs," said Ben, "just right; I'll get it."

"Put my gingerbread boy on top," cried Phronsie, handing him up.

So Polly packed the little cakes neatly in two rows, and laid the "gingerbread boy" in a fascinating attitude across the top.

"He looks as if he'd been struck by lightning!" said Ben, viewing him critically as he came in the door with the paper.

"Be still," said Polly, trying not to laugh; "that's because he baked so funny; it made his feet stick out."

"Children," said Mrs. Pepper, "how'll Jasper know where the cakes come from?"

"Why, he'll know it's us," said Polly, "of course; 'cause it'll make him think of the baking we're going to have when he gets well."

"Well, but you don't say so," said Mrs. Pepper, smiling; "'tisn't polite to send it this way."

"Whatever'll we do, mamsie?" said all four children, in dismay, while Phronsie simply stared. "Can't we send 'em at all?"

"Why, yes," said their mother; "I hope so, I'm sure, after you've got 'em baked; but you might answer Jasper's letter, I should think, and tell him about 'em, and the ' gingerbread boy.' "

" O dear! " said Polly, ready to fly, " I *couldn't,* mamsie; I *never* wrote a letter."

" Well, you never had one before, did you? " said her mother, composedly biting her thread. " Never say you can't, Polly, 'cause you don't know what you can do till you've tried."

" You write, Ben," said Polly, imploringly.

" No," said Ben, " I think the nicest way is for all to say something, then 'twon't be hard for any of us."

" Where's the paper," queried Polly, " coming from, I wonder! "

" Joel," said Mrs. Pepper, " run to the bureau in the bedroom, and open the top drawer, and get a green box there."

So Joel, quite important at the errand, departed, and presently put the designated box into his mother's hand.

" There, now I'm going to give you this," and she took out a small sheet of paper slightly yellowed by age; but being gilt-edged, it looked very magnificent to the five pairs of eyes directed to it.

" Now, Ben, you get the ink-bottle and the pen, and then go to work."

So Ben reached down from the upper shelf in the cupboard the ink-bottle, and a pen in a black wooden penholder.

"Oh, mamsie," cried Polly, "that's where Phronsie bit it off when she was a baby, isn't it?" holding up the stubby end where the little ball had disappeared.

"Yes," said Mrs. Pepper, "and now you're going to write about her 'gingerbread boy' with it —well, time goes, to be sure." And she bent over her work again, harder than ever. Poor woman! if she could only scrape together enough money to get her children into school—that was the earnest wish of her heart. She *must* do it soon, for Ben was twelve years old; but with all her strivings and scrimpings she could only manage to put bread into their mouths, and live from day to day. "I s'pose I'd ought to be thankful for that," she said to herself, not taking time even to cry over her troubles. "But, oh, the learning! they *must* have that!"

"Now," said Polly, "how'll we do it, Ben?" as they ranged themselves around the table, on which reposed the cakes; "you begin."

"How *do* folks begin a letter?" asked Ben, in despair, of his mother.

"How did Jasper begin his?" asked Mrs. Pepper back again.

"Oh!" cried Polly, running into the bedroom to get the precious missive. "'Dear Miss Polly' —that's what it says."

"Well," said Mrs. Pepper, "then you'd better say, 'Dear Mister Jasper,'—or you might say, 'Dear Mr. King.'"

"O misery!" cried Polly, "that would be the father, then—s'pose he should think we wrote to *him!*" and Polly looked horror-stricken to the last degree.

"There, there 'tis," said Ben: "'Dear Mister Jasper'—now what'll we say?"

"Why say about the cakes," replied Polly.

"And the gingerbread boy," cried Phronsie. "Oh, tell about him, Polly, *do.*"

"Yes, yes, Phronsie," said Polly, "we will— why, tell him how we wish he could have come, and that we baked him some cakes, and that we do so want him to come again just as soon as he can."

"All right!" said Ben; so he went to work laboriously; only his hard breathing showing what a difficult task it was, as the stiff old pen scratched up and down the paper.

" There, that's done," he cried at length, in great satisfaction, holding it up for inspection.

" Oh, I do wish," cried Polly, in intense admiration, " I could write so nice and so fast as you can, Ben."

" Read it, Polly," said Mrs. Pepper, in pride.

So Polly began: " ' Dear Mister Jasper, we were all dreadfully sorry that you didn't come, and so we baked you some cakes.'—You didn't say anything about his being sick, Ben."

" I forgot it," said Ben, " but I put it in farther down—you'll see if you read on."

" ' Baked you some cakes—that is, Polly did, for this is Ben that's writing.' "

" You needn't have said that, Ben," said Polly, dissatisfied; " we all baked 'em, I'm sure. ' And just as soon as you get well we do want you to come over and have the baking. We're real sorry you're sick—boneset's good for colds.' "

" Oh, Ben! " said Mrs. Pepper, " I guess his father knows what to give him."

" And oh! the bitter stuff! " cried Polly, with a wry face.

" Well, it's hard work to write," said Ben, yawning. " I'd rather chop wood."

"I wish I knew how," exclaimed Joel, long-ingly.

"Just you try every day; Ben'll teach you, Joe," said his mother, eagerly, "and then I'll let you write."

"I will!" cried Joe; "then, Dave, you'll see how I'll write—I tell you!"

"And I'm going to—ma, can't I?" asked Davie, unwilling to be outdone.

"Yes, you may, to be sure," said Mrs. Pepper, delighted; "that'll make a man of you fast."

"Oh, boys," said Polly, lifting a very red face, "you joggle the table so I can't do anything."

"I wasn't joggling," said Joel; "the old thing tipped. Whickets!" he whispered to Davie, "see Polly, she's writing crooked."

So while the others hung around her and looked over her shoulder as they made their various comments, Polly finished her part, and also held it up for inspection.

"Let us see," said Ben, taking it up.

"It's after 'boneset's good for colds,'" said Polly, puckering up her face again at the thought.

"'We most of us knew you were sick—I'm Polly now—because you didn't come; and we liked your letter telling us so'"——

"Oh, Polly! we weren't glad to hear he was sick!" cried Ben, in horror.

"I didn't say so!" cried Polly, starting up. "Why, Ben Pepper, I *never* said so!" and she looked ready to cry.

"It sounds something like it, doesn't it, mammy?" said Ben, unwilling to give her pain, but appealing to Mrs. Pepper.

"Polly didn't mean it," said her mother, consolingly; "but if I were you, I'd say something to explain it."

"I can't put anything in now," said poor Polly; "there isn't any room and no more paper either— what *shall* I do! I told you, Ben, I couldn't write." And Polly looked helplessly from one to the other for comfort.

"Yes, you can," said Ben; "there, now I'll show you: write it fine, Polly—you write so big— little bits of letters, like these."

So Polly took the pen again with a sigh. "Now he won't think so, I guess," she said, much relieved, as Ben began to read again.

"I'll begin yours again," Ben said:

"'We most of us knew you were sick because you didn't come, and we liked your letter telling us so because we'd all felt so badly, and Phronsie

cried herself to sleep'—(that's good, I'm sure).
'The "gingerbread boy" is for your father—
please excuse it, but Phronsie would make it for
him because he is sick. There isn't any more to
write, and besides I can't write good, and Ben's
tired. From all of us.'"

"Why, how's he to know?" cried Ben. "That
won't do to sign it."

"Well, let's say from Ben and Polly, then," said
Polly; "only all the others want to be in the letter."

"Well, they can't write," said Ben.

"We might sign their names for 'em," suggested Polly.

"Here's mine," said Ben, putting under the
"From all of us" a big, bold "Ben."

"And here's mine," echoed Polly, setting a
slightly crooked "Polly" by its side.

"Now, Joe, you better let Ben hold your hand,"
said Polly, warningly. But Joel declaring he
could write, had already begun, so there was no
hope for it; and a big drop of ink falling from
the pen, he spattered the "J" so that no one
could tell what it was. The children looked at
each other in despair.

"Can we ever get it out, mamsie?" asked
Polly, running to Mrs. Pepper with it.

"I don't know," said her mother. "I
you do it, Joe?"

"I didn't mean to," said Joel, loo
downcast and ashamed. "The ugly ol
it!"

"Well," said Polly, "it's got to go ;
help it." But she looked so sorrowful o
half the pleasure was gone for Ben ;
wanted everything just right, and was
ticular about things.

"Now, Dave." Ben held his h
"David" went down next to Joel.

But when it was Phronsie's turn, she
that Polly, and no one else, must hold he

"It's a dreadful hard name to write
is," said Polly, as she guided Phronsie's
hand that clung faithfully to the stubby
"There, it's over now," she cried ;
thankful! I wouldn't write another
thing!"

"Read it all over now, Ben," cried N
per, "and don't speak, children, till
through."

"Doesn't it sound elegant!" said Pol
ing her hands, when he had finished.
think we ever could do it so nice, did you

cried herself to sleep '—(that's good, I'm sure).
'The "gingerbread boy" is for your father—
please excuse it, but Phronsie would make it for
him because he is sick. There isn't any more to
write, and besides I can't write good, and Ben's
tired. From all of us.' "

"Why, how's he to know?" cried Ben. "That
won't do to sign it."

"Well, let's say from Ben and Polly, then," said
Polly; "only all the others want to be in the letter."

"Well, they can't write," said Ben.

"We might sign their names for 'em," suggested Polly.

"Here's mine," said Ben, putting under the
"From all of us" a big, bold "Ben."

"And here's mine," echoed Polly, setting a
slightly crooked "Polly" by its side.

"Now, Joe, you better let Ben hold your hand,"
said Polly, warningly. But Joel declaring he
could write, had already begun, so there was no
hope for it; and a big drop of ink falling from
the pen, he spattered the "J" so that no one
could tell what it was. The children looked at
each other in despair.

"Can we ever get it out, mamsie?" asked
Polly, running to Mrs. Pepper with it.

"I don't know," said her mother. "How could you do it, Joe?"

"I didn't mean to," said Joel, looking very downcast and ashamed. "The ugly old pen did it!"

"Well," said Polly, "it's got to go; we can't help it." But she looked so sorrowful over it that half the pleasure was gone for Ben; for Polly wanted everything just right, and was very particular about things.

"Now, Dave." Ben held his hand, and "David" went down next to Joel.

But when it was Phronsie's turn, she protested that Polly, and no one else, must hold her hand.

"It's a dreadful hard name to write—Phronsie is," said Polly, as she guided Phronsie's fat little hand that clung faithfully to the stubby old pen. "There, it's over now," she cried; "and I'm thankful! I wouldn't write another for anything!"

"Read it all over now, Ben," cried Mrs. Pepper, "and don't speak, children, till he gets through."

"Doesn't it sound elegant!" said Polly, clasping her hands, when he had finished. "I didn't think we ever could do it so nice, did you, Ben?"

" No, indeed, I didn't," replied Ben, in a highly ecstatic frame of mind. "Now—oh! what'll we do for an envelope? " he asked, in dismay.

" You'll have to do without that," said Mrs. Pepper, " for there isn't any in the house—but see here, children," she added, looking into the sorry faces before her—" you just fold up the letter and put it inside the parcel; that'll be just as good."

" O dear! " said Polly; " but it would have been splendid the other way, mammy—just like other folks! "

" You must make believe this is like other folks," said Mrs. Pepper, cheerily, " when you can't do any other way."

" Yes," said Ben, " we've got to, Polly; tie 'em up quick's you can, and I'll take 'em over to Deacon Blodgett's, for he's going to start early in the morning."

So after another last look all around, Polly put the cakes in the paper, and tied it with four or five strong knots, to avoid all danger of its undoing.

" He never'll untie it, Polly," said Ben; " that's just like a girl's knots! "

" Why didn't you tie it, then? " said Polly; " I'm sure it's as good as a boy's knots, and they always muss up a parcel so." And she gave a loving, approving little pat to the top of the package, which, despite its multitude of knots, was certainly very neat indeed.

"Now," said Ben, grasping the pen again, "here goes for the direction."

"O my, yes!" said Polly. "I forgot all about that; I thought 'twas done."

"How'd you s'pose he'd get it?" asked Ben, coolly beginning the "M."

"I don't know," replied Polly, looking over his shoulder; "s'pose anybody else *had* eaten 'em up, Ben!" And she turned pale at the very thought of such a thing.

"There," said Ben, at last, after a good many flourishes, "now *'tis* done! you can't think of another thing to do to it, Polly!"

"Mamsie, see!" cried Polly, running with it to Mrs. Pepper, "isn't that fine! 'Mr. Jasper E. King, at the Hotel Hingham.'"

"Yes," said Mrs. Pepper, admiringly, to the content of all the children, "I should think it was!"

"Let me take it in my hand," screamed Joel, reaching eagerly up for the tempting brown parcel.

" Be careful then, Joe," said Polly, with an important air.

So Joel took a comfortable feel, and then Davie must have the same privilege. At last it was off, and with intense satisfaction the children watched Ben disappear with it down the long hill to Deacon Blodgett's.

The next day Ben came running in from his work at the deacon's.

"Oh, Polly, you had 'em! " he screamed, all out of breath. "You had 'em! "

"Had what? " asked Polly, in astonishment. "Oh, Bensie, what *do* you mean? "

"Your flowers," he panted. "You sent some flowers to Jasper."

"*Flowers to Jasper!* " repeated Polly, afraid Ben had gone out of his wits.

"Yes," said Ben; "I'll begin at the beginning. You see, Polly, when I went down this morning, Betsy was to set me to work. Deacon Blodgett and Mrs. Blodgett had started early, you know; and while I was cleaning up the wood-shed as she told me, all of a sudden she said, as she stood in the door looking on, ' Oh, Ben, Mis' Blodgett took some posies along with your parcel.' ' *What?* ' said I; I didn't know as I'd heard straight.

'*Posies*, I said,' says Betsy; 'beautiful ones they were, too, the best in the garding. I heard her tell Mr. Blodgett it would be a pity if that sick boy couldn't have some flowers, and she knew the Pepper children were crazy about 'em, so she twisted 'em in the string around the parcel, and there they stood up and looked *fine*, I tell you, as they drove away.' So, Polly! "

"Bensie Pepper!" cried Polly, taking hold of his jacket, and spinning him round, "I told you so! Now those cakes look perfectly lovely!"

"I know you did," said Ben, as she gave him a parting whirl, "but whoever could s'pose we'd get flowers, Polly?"

XV

JOLLY DAYS

"Oh, Ben," cried Jasper, overtaking him by a smart run as he was turning in at the little brown gate one morning three days after, "do wait."

"Hello!" cried Ben, turning around, and setting down his load—a bag of salt and a basket of potatoes—and viewing Jasper and Prince with great satisfaction.

"Yes, here I am," said Jasper. "And how I've run; that fellow on the stage was dreadfully slow in getting here—oh, you're so good," he said, and his eyes, brimful of gladness, beamed on Ben. "The cakes were awfully good, and 'twas great fun to get your letter."

"Did you like it?" asked Ben, the color up all over his brown face.

"*Like* it!" cried Jasper. "Why, 'twas just splendid; and the cakes were royal! Isn't Polly smart though, to bake like that?" he added, admiringly.

"I guess she *is*," said Ben, drawing himself up

191

to his very tallest dimensions. " She knows how to do everything, Jasper King! "

" I should think she did," responded the boy, quickly. " I wish she was my sister," he finished, longingly.

" Well, I don't," quickly replied Ben, " for then she wouldn't be mine; and I couldn't think of being without Polly! Was your father angry about —about—' the gingerbread boy ' ? " he asked, timidly, trembling for an answer.

" O dear! " cried Jasper, tumbling over on the grass, " don't, *don't!* I sha'n't be good for anything if you make me laugh! Oh, wasn't it funny! " and he rolled over and over, shaking with glee.

" Yes," said Ben, immensely relieved to find that no offence had been taken. " But she would send it; Polly tried not to have her, and she 'most cried when Phronsie was so determined, 'cause she said your father never'd let you come again ——"

" 'Twas just lovely in Phronsie," said the boy, sitting up and wiping his eyes, " but, oh, it was *so* funny! you *ought* to have seen my father, Ben Pepper."

" Oh, then he *was* angry," cried Ben.

" No, indeed he wasn't! " said Jasper; " don't

you think it! Do you know, it did him lots of good, for he'd been feeling real badly that morning, he hadn't eaten any breakfast, and when he saw that gingerbread boy "—here Jasper rolled over again with a peal of laughter—" and heard the message, he just put back his head, and he laughed—why, I never heard him laugh as he did then! and he ate a big dinner, and all that afternoon he felt as good as could be. And he says he's coming to see the little girl that baked it for him before we go home."

Ben nearly tumbled over by the side of Jasper at these words—" *Coming to see us!* " he gasped.

"Yes," said Jasper, who had scarcely gotten over his own astonishment about it, for nothing could have amazed him more than to hear his father say cheerily: " Well, Jasper, my boy, I guess I shall have to drive over and see your little girl, since she's been polite enough to bake me this," pointing to the wild-looking " gingerbread boy."

" Come in and tell 'em about it! " cried Ben, radiantly, picking up his potatoes and salt. " It's all right, Polly! " he said, in a jubilant voice, " for here's Jasper, and he'll tell you so himself."

" *Hush!* " said Jasper, warningly, " don't let

Phronsie hear; well, here's my pet now," and after bobbing lovingly to the others, with eyes beaming over with fun, he caught up the little girl who was screaming—" Oh, here's Jasper! and my be-you-ti-ful doggie! "

"Now, Phronsie," he cried, " give me a kiss; you haven't any soft soap to-day, have you? No; that's a good, nice one, now; your ' gingerbread boy' was just splendid! "

"Did he *eat* it?" asked the child, in grave delight.

"Well—no—he hasn't eaten it yet," said Jasper, smiling on the others; "he's keeping it to look at, Phronsie."

"I should think so!" groaned Polly.

"Never mind, Polly," Ben whispered; " Jasper's been telling me about it; his father liked it—he did truly."

"*Oh!*" said Polly, " I'm *so* glad! "

"He had eyes," said Phronsie, going back to the charms of the " gingerbread boy."

"I know it," said Jasper, admiringly; "so he did."

"Rather deep sunk, one of 'em was," muttered Ben.

"And I'll bake you one, Jasper," said the child.

as he put her down; " I will very truly—some day."

" Will you? " smiled Jasper; " well, then," and there was a whispered conference with Phronsie that somehow sent that damsel into a blissful state of delight. And then while Phronsie monopolized Prince, Jasper told them all about the reception of the parcel—how very dull and forlorn he was feeling that morning, Prince and he shut up indoors—and how his father had had a miserable night, and had eaten scarcely any breakfast, and just at this juncture there came a knock at the door, " and," said Jasper, " your parcel walked in, all dressed up in flowers! "

" They weren't our flowers," said Polly, honestly. " Mrs. Blodgett put 'em on."

" Well, she couldn't have, if you hadn't sent the parcel," said Jasper, in a tone of conviction.

Then he launched out into a description of how they opened the package—Prince looking on, and begging for one of the cakes.

" Oh, didn't you give him one? " cried Polly, at this. " Good old Prince! "

" Yes, I did," said Jasper, " the biggest one of all."

" The one, I guess," interrupted Joel, " with the big raisin on top."

Polly spoke up quickly to save any more remarks on Joel's part. " Now tell us about your father—and the ' gingerbread boy.' "

So Jasper broke out with a merry laugh, into this part of the story, and soon had them all in such a gale of merriment that Phronsie stopped playing out on the door-step with Prince, and came in to see what the matter was.

" Never mind," said Polly, trying to get her breath, just as Jasper was relating how Mr. King set up the " gingerbread boy " on his writing-table before him, while he leaned back in his chair for a hearty laugh.

" And to make it funnier still," said Jasper, " don't you think, a little pen-wiper he has, made like a cap, hanging on the pen-rack above him, tumbled off just at this very identical minute right on the head of the ' gingerbread boy,' and there it stuck! "

" Oh! " they all screamed, " if we could only have seen it."

" What was it? " asked Phronsie, pulling Polly's sleeve to make her hear.

So Jasper took her in his lap, and told how

funny the " gingerbread boy " looked with a cap on, and Phronsie clapped her hands, and laughed with the rest, till the little old kitchen rang and rang again.

And then they had the baking! and Polly tied one of her mother's ample aprons on Jasper, as Mrs. Pepper had left directions if he should come while she was away; and he developed such a taste for cookery, and had so many splendid improvements on the Peppers' simple ideas, that the children thought it the most fortunate thing in the world that he came; and one and all voted him a most charming companion.

" You could cook a Thanksgiving dinner in this stove, just as easy as not," said Jasper, putting into the oven something on a little cracked plate that would have been a pie if there had been any centre; but lacking that necessary accompaniment, probably was a short-cake. " Just as easy as not," he repeated, with emphasis, slamming the door, to give point to his remarks.

" No, you couldn't, either," said Ben, at the table, with equal decision; " not a bit of it, Jasper King! "

" Why, Ben Pepper! " exclaimed Jasper, " that

oven's awful big!   I should like to know why not?"

" 'Cause there isn't anything to cook," said Ben, coolly, cutting out a piece of dough for a jumble; "we don't keep Thanksgiving."

" *Not keep Thanksgiving!* " said Jasper, standing quite still; " *never had a Thanksgiving!* well, I declare," and then he stopped again.

"Yes," answered Ben; "we had one once; 'twas last year—but that wasn't much."

"Well, then," said Jasper, leaning over the table, "I'll tell you what I should think you'd do—try Christmas."

"Oh, that's always worse," said Polly, setting down her rolling-pin to think—which immediately rolled away by itself off from the table.

"We never had a Christmas," said little Davie, reflectively; "what are they like, Jasper?"

Jasper sat quite still, and didn't reply to this question for a moment or two.

To be among children who didn't like Thanksgiving, and who never had seen a Christmas, and didn't know what it was like, was a revelation to him.

"They hang up stockings," said Polly, softly.

How many, many times she had begged her

mother to try it for the younger ones; but there was never anything to put in them, and the winters were cold and hard, and only the strictest economy carried them through.

"Oh!" said little Phronsie in horror, "are their feet in 'em, Polly?"

"No, dear," said Polly; while Jasper, instead of laughing, only stared. Something requiring a deal of thought was passing through the boy's mind just then. "They *shall* have a Christmas!" he muttered. "I know father'll let me." But he kept his thoughts to himself; and becoming his own gay, kindly self, he explained, and told to Phronsie and the others so many stories of past Christmases he had enjoyed, that the interest over the baking soon dwindled away, until a horrible smell of something burning brought them all to their senses.

"Oh! the house is a-burning!" cried Polly. "Oh, get a pail of water!"

"'Tisn't either," said Jasper, snuffing wisely; "oh! I know—I forgot all about it—I do beg your pardon." And running to the stove, he knelt down and drew out of the oven a black, odorous mass, which with a crestfallen air he brought to Polly.

" I'm no end sorry I made such a mess of it," he said, " I meant it for you."

" 'Tisn't any matter," said Polly, kindly.

" And now do you go on," cried Joel and David, both in the same breath, " all about the Tree, you know."

" Yes, yes," said the others; " if you're not tired, Jasper."

" Oh, no," cried their accommodating friend, " I love to tell about it; only wait—let's help Polly clear up first."

So after all traces of the frolic had been tidied up, and made nice for the mother's return, they took seats in a circle, and Jasper regaled them with story and reminiscence, till they felt as if fairyland were nothing to it!

" How did you ever live through it, Jasper King? " said Polly, drawing the first long breath she had dared to indulge in. " Such an *elegant* time! "

Jasper laughed. " I hope I'll live through plenty more of 'em," he said, merrily. " We're going to sister Marian's again, father and I; we always spend our Christmas there, you know, and she's to have all the cousins, and I don't know how many more; and a tree—but the best of all, there's going to be a German carol sung by choir-boys—I shall like that best of all."

"What are choir-boys?" asked Polly, who was intensely fond of music.

"In some of the churches," explained Jasper, "the choir is all boys; and they do chant, and sing anthems perfectly beautifully, Polly!"

"Do you play on the piano and sing?" asked Polly, looking at him in awe.

"Yes," said the boy, simply; "I've played ever since I was a little fellow, no bigger'n Phronsie."

"Oh, Jasper!" cried Polly, clasping her hands, her cheeks all aflame—"do you mean to say you do *really and truly play on the piano?*"

"Why, yes," said the boy, looking into her flashing eyes.

"Polly's always crazy about music," explained Ben; "she'll drum on the table, and anywhere, to make believe it's a piano."

"There's Doctor Fisher going by," said Joel, who, now that they had gotten on the subject of music, began to find prickles running up and down his legs from sitting so still. "I wish he'd stop."

"Is he the one who cured your measles—and

Polly's eyes?" asked Jasper, running to the window. "I want to see him."

"Well, there he is," cried Ben, as the doctor put his head out of the gig and bowed and smiled to the little group in the window.

"He's just lovely!" cried Polly. "Oh! I wish you knew him."

"If father's sick again," said Jasper, "we'll have him—he looks nice, anyway—for father doesn't like the doctor over in Hingham—do you know perhaps we'll come again next summer; wouldn't that be nice!"

"Oh!" cried the children, rapturously; "do come, Jasper, *do!*"

"Well, maybe," said Jasper, "if father likes it and sister Marian and her family will come with us; they do some summers. You'd like little Dick, I know," turning to Phronsie. "And I guess all of you'd like all of them," he added, looking at the group of interested listeners. "They wanted to come this year awfully; they said, 'Oh, grandpapa, do let us go with you and Jappy, and——'"

"*What!*" said the children.

"Oh," said Jasper, with a laugh, "they call me Jappy—it's easier to say than Jasper; ever so many people do for short. You may if you want to," he said, looking around on them all.

"How funny!" laughed Polly, "but I don't know as it's any worse than Polly or Ben."

"Or Phronsie," said Jappy. "Don't *you* like Jappy?" he said, bringing his head down to her level, as she sat on the little stool at his feet, content in listening to the merry chat.

"Is that the same as Japser?" she asked, gravely.

"Yes, the very same," he said.

When they parted, Jappy and the little Peppers were sworn friends; and the boy, happy in his good times in the cheery little home, felt the hours long between the visits that his father, when he saw the change that they wrought in his son, willingly allowed him to make.

"Goodness me!" exclaimed Mrs. Pepper, one day in the last of September, as a carriage, drawn by a pair of handsome horses, stopped at their door, "here comes Mr. King I do believe; we never looked worse'n we do to-day!"

"I don't care," said Polly, flying out of the bedroom. "Jappy's with him, mamma, and it'll be nice, I guess. At any rate, Phronsie's clean as a pink," she thought to herself, looking at the little maiden, busy with " Baby," to whom she was teaching deportment, in the corner. But there was no time to " fix up; " for a tall, portly gentleman, leaning on his heavy gold-headed cane, was walking up from the little brown gate to the big flat stone that served as a step. Jasper and Prince followed decorously.

" Is this little Miss Pepper? " he asked, pompously, of Polly, who answered his rap on the door. Now whether she was little " Miss Pepper " she never had stopped to consider.

" I don't know, sir; I'm Polly." And then she blushed bright as a rose, and the laughing brown eyes looked beyond to Jasper, who stood on the walk, and smiled encouragingly.

" Is your mother in? " asked the old gentleman, who was so tall he could scarcely enter the low door. And then Mrs. Pepper came forward, and Jasper introduced her, and the old gentleman bowed, and sat down in the seat Polly placed for him. And Mrs. Pepper thanked him with a heart overflowing with gratitude, through lips that *would* tremble even then, for all that Jasper had done for them. And the old gentleman said, " Humph! " but he looked at his son, and something shone in his eye just for a moment.

Phronsie had retreated with "Baby" in her arms behind the door on the new arrival. But seeing everything progressing finely, and overcome by her extreme desire to see Jappy and Prince, she began by peeping out with big eyes to observe how things were going on. Just then the old gentleman happened to say, "Well, where is my little girl that baked me a cake so kindly?"

Then Phronsie, forgetting all else but her "poor sick man," who also was "Jasper's father," rushed out from behind the door, and coming up to the stately old gentleman in the chair, she looked up pityingly, and said, shaking her yellow head, "Poor sick man, was my boy good?"

After that there was no more gravity and ceremony. In a moment, Phronsie was perched upon old Mr. King's knee, and playing with his watch; while the others, freed from all restraint, were chatting and laughing happily, till some of the cheeriness overflowed and warmed the heart of the old gentleman.

"We go to-morrow," he said, rising, and looking at his watch. "Why, is it possible that we have been here an hour! there, my little girl, will you give me a kiss?" and he bent his handsome old head down to the childish face upturned to his confidingly.

"Don't go," said the child, as she put up her little lips in grave confidence. "I do like you—I *do!*"

"Oh, Phronsie," began Mrs. Pepper.

"Don't reprove her, madam," said the old gentleman, who liked it immensely. "Yes, we go to-morrow," he said, looking around on the group to whom this was a blow they little expected. They had surely thought Jasper was to stay a week longer.

"I received a telegram this morning, that I must be in the city on Thursday. And besides, madam," he said, addressing Mrs. Pepper, "I think the climate is bad for me now, as it induces rheumatism. The hotel is also getting unpleasant; there are many annoyances that I cannot put up with; so that altogether, I do not regret it."

Mrs. Pepper, not knowing exactly what to say to this, wisely said nothing. Meantime, Jappy and the little Peppers were having a sorry time over in the corner by themselves.

"Well, I'll write," cried Jasper, not liking to look at Polly just then, as he was sure he shouldn't want any one to look at him, if he felt like crying. "And you must answer 'em all."

"Oh, we will! we will!" they cried. "And, Jappy, do come next summer," said Joel.

"If father'll only say yes, we will, I tell you!" he responded, eagerly.

"Come, my boy," said his father the third time; and Jasper knew by the tone that there must be no delay.

Mr. King had been nervously putting his hand in his pocket during the last few moments that the children were together; but when he glanced at Mrs. Pepper's eyes, something made him draw it out again hastily, as empty as he put it in. "No, 'twouldn't do," he said to himself; "she isn't the kind of woman to whom one could offer money."

The children crowded back their tears, and hastily said their last good-by, some of them hanging on to Prince till the last moment.

And then the carriage door shut with a bang, Jasper giving them a bright parting smile, and they were gone.

And the Peppers went into their Little Brown House, and shut the door.

XVI

AND so October came and went. The little Peppers were very lonely after Jasper had gone; even Mrs. Pepper caught herself looking up one day when the wind blew the door open suddenly, half-expecting to see the merry, whole-souled boy and the faithful dog come scampering in.

But the letters came—and that was a comfort; and it was fun to answer them. The first one spoke of Jasper's being under a private tutor, with his cousins; then they were less frequent, and they knew he was studying hard. Full of anticipations of Christmas himself, he urged the little Peppers to try for one. And the life and spirit of the letter was so catching that Polly and Ben found their souls fired within them to try at least to get for the little ones a taste of Christmastide.

" Now, mamsie," they said at last, one day in the latter part of October, when the crisp, fresh air filled their little healthy bodies with springing

208

vitality that must bubble over and rush into something, "we don't want a Thanksgiving—truly we don't. But may we try for a Christmas—just a *little* one," they added, timidly, "for the children?" Ben and Polly always called the three younger ones of the flock "the children."

To their utter surprise, Mrs. Pepper looked mildly assenting, and presently she said:

"Well, I don't see why you can't try; 'twon't do any harm, I'm sure."

You see, Mrs. Pepper had received a letter from Jasper, which at present she didn't feel called upon to say anything about.

"Now," said Polly, drawing a long breath, as she and Ben stole away into a corner to "talk over" and lay plans, "what does it mean?"

"Never mind," said Ben; "as long as she's given us leave I don't care what it is."

"I don't, either," said Polly, with a delicious feeling as if the whole world were before them in which to choose; "it'll be just *gorgeous*, Ben!"

"What's that?" asked Ben, who was not as much given to long words as Polly, who dearly loved to be fine in language as well as other things.

"Oh, it's something Jappy said one day; and I

asked him, and he says it's fine, and lovely, and all that," answered Polly, delighted that she knew something she could really tell Ben.

"Then why not *say* fine?" commented Ben, practically, with a little upward sniff of his nose.

"Oh, I d'know, I'm sure," laughed Polly. "Let's think what'll we do for Christmas—how many weeks are there, anyway, Ben?" And she began to count on her fingers.

"That's no way," said Ben, "I'm going to get the Almanac."

So he went to the old clock, where hanging up by its side was a "Farmer's Almanac."

"Now we'll know," he said, coming back to their corner. So with heads together they consulted and counted up till they found that eight weeks and three days remained in which to get ready.

"O my!" said Polly, "it's 'most a year, isn't it, Ben?"

"'Twon't be much time for us," said Ben, who thought of the many hours to be devoted to hard work that would run away with the time. "We'd better begin right away, Polly."

"Well, all right," said Polly, who could scarcely keep her fingers still, as she thought of the many

things she should so love to do if she could.
"But first, Ben, what let's do?"

"Would you rather hang up their stockings?"
asked Ben, as if he had unlimited means at his
disposal; "or have a tree?"

"Why," said Polly, with wide-open eyes at the
two magnificent ideas, "we haven't got anything
to put *in* the stockings when we hang 'em, Ben."

"That's just it," said Ben. "Now, wouldn't
it be better to have a tree, Polly? I can get that
easy in the woods, you know."

"Well," interrupted Polly, eagerly, "we haven't
got anything to hang on that, either, Ben. You
know Jappy said folks hang all sorts of presents
on the branches. So I don't see," she continued,
impatiently, "as that's any good. We can't do
anything, Ben Pepper, so there!" and with a
flounce Polly sat down on the old wooden stool,
and folding her hands looked at Ben in a most
despairing way.

"I know," said Ben, "we haven't got much."

"We haven't *anything*," said Polly, still looking at him.

"Why, we've got a tree," replied Ben, hopefully.

"Well, what's a tree!" retorted Polly, scornfully.   " Anybody can go out and look at a tree outdoors."

" Well, now, I tell you, Polly," said Ben, sitting down on the floor beside her, and speaking very slowly and decisively, " we've got to do something 'cause we've begun; and we might make a tree real pretty."

" How? " asked Polly, ashamed of her ill-humor, but not in the least seeing how anything could be made of a tree.   " How, Ben Pepper? "

" Well," said Ben, pleasantly, " we'd set it up in the corner ——"

" Oh, no, not in the corner," cried Polly, whose spirits began to rise a little as she saw Ben so hopeful.   " Put it in the middle of the room, *do!* "

" I don't care where you put it," said Ben, smiling, happy that Polly's usual cheerful energy had returned, " but I thought—'twill be a little one, you know, and I thought 'twould look better in the corner."

" What else? " asked Polly, eager to see how Ben would dress the tree.

" Well," said Ben, " you know the Henderson boys gave me a lot of corn last week."

" I don't see how that helps much," said Polly, still incredulous.   " Do you mean hang the cobs on the branches, Ben? That would be just awful! "

" I should think likely," laughed Ben. " No, indeed, Polly Pepper! but if we should pop a lot, oh! a bushel, and then we should string 'em, we could wind it all in and out among the branches, and——"

" Why, wouldn't that be pretty? " cried Polly, " real pretty—and we can do that, I'm sure."

" Yes," continued Ben; " and then, don't you know, there's some little candle-ends in that box in the Provision Room, maybe mammy'd give us them."

" I don't believe but she would," cried Polly; " 'twould be just like Jappy's if she would! Let's ask her now—this very minute! "

And they scampered hurriedly to Mrs. Pepper, who to their extreme astonishment, after all, said, " Yes," and smiled encouragingly on the plan.

" Isn't mamsie good? " said Polly, with loving gratitude, as they seated themselves again.

" Now, we're all right," exclaimed Ben, " and I tell you we can make the tree look perfectly *splendid*, Polly Pepper! "

" And I'll tell you another thing, Ben," Polly said, " oh! something elegant! You must get ever so many hickory nuts; and you know those bits of bright paper I've got in the bureau drawer? Well, we can paste them on to the nuts and hang 'em on for the balls Jappy tells of."

"Polly," cried Ben, "it'll be such a tree as never was, won't it?"

"Yes; but dear me," cried Polly, springing up, "the children are coming! Wasn't it good, grandma wanted 'em to come over this afternoon, so's we could talk! Now *hush!*" as the door opened to admit the noisy little troop.

"If you think of any new plan," whispered Ben, behind his hand, while Mrs. Pepper engaged their attention, "you'll have to come out into the woodshed to talk after this."

"I know it," whispered Polly back again; "oh! we've got just heaps of things to think of, Bensie!"

Such a contriving and racking of brains as Polly and Ben set up after this! They would bob over at each other, and smile with significant gestures as a new idea would strike one of them, in the most mysterious way that, if observed, would drive the others almost wild. And then, frightened lest in some hilarious moment the secret should pop out, the two conspirators would be-

take themselves to the wood-shed as before agreed
on. But Joel, finding this out, followed them one
day—or, as Polly said, tagged—so that was no
good.

"Let's go behind the wood-pile," she said to
Ben, in desperation; "he can't hear there, if we
whisper real soft."

"Yes, he will," said Ben, who knew Joel's hearing faculties much better. "We'll have to wait
till they're abed."

So after that, when nightfall first began to
make its appearance, Polly would hint mildly
about bedtime.

"You hustle us so!" said Joel, after he had
been sent off to bed for two or three nights unusually early.

"Oh, Joey, it's good for you to get to bed," said
Polly, coaxingly; "it'll make you grow, you know,
real fast."

"Well, I don't grow abed," grumbled Joel, who
thought something was in the wind. "You and
Ben are going to talk, I know, and wink your
eyes, as soon as we're gone."

"Well, go along, Joe, that's a good boy," said
Polly, laughing, "and you'll know some day."

"What'll you give me?" asked Joel, seeing a

bargain, his foot on the lowest stair leading to the loft, "say, Polly?"

"Oh, I haven't much to give," she said, cheerily; "but I'll tell you what, Joey—I'll tell you a story every day that you go to bed."

"Will you?" cried Joe, hopping back into the room. "Begin now, Polly, begin now!"

"Why, you haven't been to bed yet," said Polly, "so I can't till to-morrow."

"Yes, I have—you've made us go for three— no, I guess, fourteen nights," said Joel, indignantly.

"Well, you were *made* to go," laughed Polly. "I said if you'd go good, you know; so run along, Joe, and I'll tell you a nice one to-morrow."

"It's got to be long," shouted Joel, when he saw he could get no more, making good time up to the loft.

To say that Polly, in the following days, was Master Joel's slave, was stating the case lightly. However, she thought by her story-telling she got off easily, as each evening saw the boys drag their unwilling feet bedward, and leave Ben and herself in peace to plan and work undisturbed. There they would sit by the little old table, around the one tallow candle, while Mrs. Pepper sewed away busily, looking up to smile or to give some bits of advice; keeping her own secret meanwhile, which made her blood leap fast, as the happy thoughts nestled in her heart, of her little ones and their coming glee. And Polly made the loveliest of paper dolls for Phronsie out of the rest of the bits of bright paper; and Ben made windmills and whistles for the boys; and a funny little carved basket with a handle, for Phronsie, out of a hickory-nut shell; and a new pink calico dress for Seraphina peered out from the top drawer of the old bureau in the bedroom, whenever any one opened it, for Mrs. Pepper kindly let the children lock up their treasures there as fast as completed.

" I'll make Seraphina a bonnet," said Mrs. Pepper, " for there's that old bonnet-string in the bag, you know, Polly, that'll make a beautiful one."

" Oh, do, mother," cried Polly, " she's been wanting a new one awfully."

" And I'm going to knit some mittens for Joel and David," continued Mrs. Pepper; " because I can get the yarn cheap now. I saw some down at the store yesterday I could have at half-price."

" I don't believe anybody'll have as good a Christmas as we shall," cried Polly, pasting on a bit of trimming to the gayest doll's dress; "no, not even Jappy."

An odd little smile played around Mrs. Pepper's mouth, but she said not a word, and so the fun and the work went on.

The tree was to be set up in the Provision Room; that was finally decided, as Mrs. Pepper showed the children how utterly useless it would be to try to have it in the kitchen.

" I'll find the key, children," she said, " I think I know where 'tis, and then we can keep them out."

" Well, but it looks so," said Polly, demurring at the prospect.

" Oh, no, Polly," said her mother; " at any rate, it's clean."

" Polly," said Ben, " we can put evergreen around, you know."

" So we can," said Polly, brightly; " oh, Ben, you do think of the best things; we couldn't have had them in the kitchen."

" And don't let's hang the presents on the tree," continued Ben; " let's have the children hang up their stockings; they want to, awfully—for I heard David tell Joel this morning before we got up—they thought I was asleep, but I wasn't—

that he did so wish they could, but, says he, ' Don't tell mammy, 'cause that'll make her feel bad.' "

" The little dears! " said Mrs. Pepper, impulsively, " they shall have their stockings, too."

" And we'll make the tree pretty enough," said Polly, enthusiastically; " we sha'n't want the presents to hang on; we've got so many things. And then we'll have hickory nuts to eat; and p'r'aps mamsie'll let us make some molasses candy the day before," she said, with a sly look at her mother.

" You may," said Mrs. Pepper, smiling.

" O goody! " they both cried, hugging each other ecstatically.

" And we'll have a frolic in the Provision Room afterwards," finished Polly; " oh! ooh! "

And so the weeks flew by—one, two, three, four, five, six, seven, eight! till only the three days remained, and to think of the fun that Polly and Ben had had already!

" It's better'n a Christmas," they told their mother, " to get ready for it! "

" It's too bad you can't hang up *your* stockings," said Mrs. Pepper, looking keenly at their flushed faces and bright eyes; "you've never hung them up."

"That isn't any matter, mamsie," they both said, cheerily; "it's a great deal better to have the children have a nice time—oh, won't it be elegant! p'r'aps we'll have ours next year!"

For two days before, the house was turned upside down for Joel to find the biggest stocking he could; but on Polly telling him it must be his own, he stopped his search, and bringing down his well-worn one, hung it by the corner of the chimney to be ready.

"You put yours up the other side, Dave," he advised.

"There isn't any nail," cried David, investigating.

"I'll drive one," said Joel, so he ran out to the tool-house, as one corner of the wood-shed was called, and brought in the hammer and one or two nails.

"Phronsie's is going in the middle," he said, with a nail in his mouth.

"Yes, I'm going to hang up my stocking," cried the child, hopping from one toe to the other.

"Run get it, Phronsie," said Joel, "and I'll hang it up for you."

"Why, it's two days before Christmas yet," said Polly, laughing; "how they'll look hanging there so long."

"I don't care," said Joel, giving a last thump to the nail; "we're going to be ready. O dear! I wish 'twas to-night!"

"Can't Seraphina hang up her stocking?" asked Phronsie, coming up to Polly's side; "and Baby, too?"

"Oh, let her have part of yours," said Polly, "that'll be best—Seraphina and Baby and you have one stocking together."

"Oh, yes," cried Phronsie, easily pleased; "that'll be best."

So for the next two days, they were almost distracted; the youngest ones asking countless questions about Santa Claus, and how he possibly could get down the chimney, Joel running his head up as far as he dared, to see if it was big enough.

"I guess he can," he said, coming back in a sooty state, looking very much excited and delighted.

"Will he be black like Joey?" asked Phronsie, pointing to his grimy face.

"No," said Polly; "he doesn't ever get black."

"Why?" they all asked; and then, over and over they wanted the delightful mystery explained.

"We never'll get through this day," said Polly, in despair, as the last one arrived. "I wish 'twas to-night, for we're all ready."

"Santy's coming! Santy's coming!" sang Phronsie, as the bright afternoon sunlight went down over the fresh, crisp snow, "for it's night now."

"Yes, Santa is coming!" sang Polly; and "Santa Claus is coming!" rang back and forth through the kitchen, till it seemed as if the three little old stockings would hop down and join in the dance going on so merrily.

"I'm glad mine is red," said Phronsie, at last, stopping in the wild jig, and going up to see if it was all safe, "'cause then Santy'll know it's mine, won't he, Polly?"

"Yes, dear," cried Polly, catching her up. "Oh, Phronsie! you *are* going to have a Christmas!"

"Well, I wish," said Joel, "I had my name on mine! I know Dave'll get some of my things."

"Oh, no, Joe," said Mrs. Pepper, "Santa Claus is smart; he'll know yours is in the left-hand corner."

"Will he?" asked Joel, still a little fearful.

"Oh, yes, indeed," said Mrs. Pepper, confidently. "I never knew him to make a mistake."

"Now," said Ben, when they had all made a pretence of eating supper, for there was such an excitement prevailing that no one sat still long enough to eat much, "you must every one fly off to bed as quick as ever can be."

"Will Santa Claus come faster then?" asked Joel.

"Yes," said Ben, "just twice as fast."

"I'm going then," said Joel; "but I ain't going to sleep, 'cause I mean to hear him come over the roof; then I'm going to get up, for I do so want a squint at the reindeer!"

"I am, too," cried Davie, excitedly. "Oh, do come, Joe!" and he began to mount the stairs.

"Good night," said Phronsie, going up to the centre of the chimney-piece, where the little red stocking dangled limpsily, "lift me up, Polly, do."

"What do you want to do?" asked Polly, running to give her a jump. "What are you going to do, Phronsie?"

"I want to kiss it good night," said the child, with eyes big with anticipation and happiness,

hugging the well-worn toe of the little old stocking affectionately. "I wish I had something to
give Santa, Polly, I *do*," she cried as she held her
fast in her arms.

"Never mind, Pet," said Polly, nearly smoth-
ering her with kisses; "if you're a good girl,
Phronsie, that pleases Santa the most of anything."

"Does it?" cried Phronsie, delighted beyond
measure, as Polly carried her into the bedroom,
"then I'll be good always, I *will!*"

XVII

In the middle of the night Polly woke up with a start.

"What in the world!" she said, and she bobbed up her head and looked over at her mother, who was still peacefully sleeping, and was just going to lie down again, when a second noise out in the kitchen made her pause and lean on her elbow to listen. At this moment she thought she heard a faint whisper, and springing out of bed she ran to Phronsie's crib—it was empty! As quick as a flash she sped out into the kitchen. There, in front of the chimney, were two figures. One was Joel, and the other, unmistakably, was Phronsie!

"What *are* you doing?" gasped Polly, holding on to a chair.

The two little nightgowns turned round at this.

"Why, I thought it was morning," said Joel, "and I wanted my stocking. Oh!" as he felt the toe, which was generously stuffed, "give it to me, Polly Pepper, and I'll run right back to bed again!"

225

"Goodness!" cried Polly; "and you, too, Phronsie! Why, it's the middle of the night! Did I ever!" and she had to pinch her mouth together tight to keep from bursting out into a loud laugh. "O dear, I *shall* laugh! don't look so scared, Phronsie, there won't anything hurt you." For Phronsie, who, on hearing Joel fumbling around the precious stockings, had been quite willing to hop out of bed and join him, had now, on Polly's saying the dire words, "in the middle of the night," scuttled over to her protecting side like a frightened rabbit.

"It never'll be morning," said Joel, taking up first one cold toe and then the other; "you might let us have 'em now, Polly, *do!*"

"No," said Polly, sobering down; "you can't have yours till Davie wakes up, too. Scamper off to bed, Joey, dear, and forget all about 'em— and it'll be morning before you know it."

"Oh, I'd rather go to bed," said Phronsie, trying to tuck up her feet in the little flannel nightgown, which was rather short, "but I don't know the way back, Polly. Take me, Polly, do," and she put up her arms to be carried.

"Oh, *I* ain't going back alone, either," whimpered Joel, coming up to Polly, too.

"Why, you came down alone, didn't you?" whispered Polly, with a little giggle.

"Yes, but I thought 'twas morning," said Joel, his teeth chattering with something beside the cold.

"Well, you must think of the morning that's coming," said Polly, cheerily. "I'll tell you— you wait till I put Phronsie into the crib, and then I'll come back and go half-way up the stairs with you."

"I won't ever come down till it's morning again," said Joel, bouncing along the stairs, when Polly was ready to go with him, at a great rate.

"Better not," laughed Polly, softly. "Be careful and not wake Davie nor Ben."

"I'm *in*," announced Joel, in a loud whisper; and Polly could hear him snuggle down among the warm bedclothes. "Call us when 'tis morning, Polly."

"Yes," said Polly, "I will; go to sleep."

Phronsie had forgotten stockings and everything else on Polly's return, and was fast asleep in the old crib. The result of it was that the children slept over, when morning did really come; and Polly had to keep her promise, and go to the foot of the stairs and call:

" MERRY CHRISTMAS!   Oh, Ben! and Joel! and Davie! "

" Oh!—oh!—oo-h! " and then the sounds that answered her, as with smothered whoops of expectation they one and all flew into their clothes!

Quick as a flash Joel and Davie were down and dancing around the chimney.

" Mammy!   mammy! " screamed Phronsie, hugging her stocking, which Ben lifted her up to unhook from the big nail, " Santy did *come,* he *did!* " and then she spun around in the middle of the floor, not stopping to look in it.

" Well, open it, Phronsie," called Davie, deep in the exploring of his own; " oh, ain't that a splendid windmill, Joe! "

" Yes," said that individual, who, having found a big piece of molasses candy, was so engaged in enjoying a huge bite, that, regardless alike of his other gifts or of the smearing his face was getting, he gave himself wholly up to its delights.

" Oh, Joey," cried Polly, laughingly, " molasses candy for breakfast! "

" That's *prime!* " cried Joel, swallowing the last morsel.   " Now I'm going to see what's this—oh, Dave, see here! see here! " he cried in intense excitement, pulling out a nice little parcel which, unrolled, proved to be a bright pair of stout mittens. "See if you've got some—look quick! "

"Yes, I have," said Davie, picking up a parcel about as big. "No, that's molasses candy."

"Just the same as I had," said Joel; "do look for the mittens. P'r'aps Santa Claus thought you had some—O dear! "

"Here they are! " screamed Davie. "I *have* got some, Joe, just exactly like yours! See here, Joe! "

"Goody! " said Joel, immensely relieved; for now he could quite enjoy his to see a pair on Davie's hands, also. "Look at Phron," he cried, " she hasn't got only half of her things out! "

To tell the truth, Phronsie was so bewildered by her riches that she sat on the floor with the little red stocking in her lap, laughing and cooing to herself amid the few things she had drawn out. When she came to Seraphina's bonnet she was quite overcome. She turned it over and over, and smoothed out the little white feather that had once adorned one of Grandma Bascom's chickens, until the two boys with their stockings, and the others sitting around in a group on the floor watching them, laughed in glee to see her enjoyment.

"O dear," said Joel at last, shaking his stocking; "I've got all there is. I wish there were forty Christmases coming! "

" I haven't! " screamed Davie; " there's something in the toe."

" It's an apple, I guess," said Joel; " turn it up, Dave."

" 'Tisn't an apple," exclaimed Davie; " 'tisn't round—it's long and thin; here 'tis." And he pulled out a splendid long whistle on which he blew a blast long and terrible, and Joel immediately following, all quiet was broken up, and the wildest hilarity reigned.

" I don't know as you'll want any breakfast," at last said Mrs. Pepper, when she had got Phronsie a little sobered down.

" I do, I do! " cried Joel.

" Goodness! after your candy? " said Polly

" That's all gone," said Joel, tooting around the table on his whistle. " What are we going to have for breakfast? "

" Same as ever," said his mother; " it can't be Christmas all the time."

" I wish 'twas," said little Davie; " forever and ever! "

" Forever an' ever," echoed little Phronsie, flying up, her cheeks like two pinks, and Seraphina in her arms with her bonnet on upside down.

"Dear, dear!" said Polly, pinching Ben to keep still as they tumbled down the little rickety steps to the Provision Room, after breakfast. The children, content in their treasures, were holding high carnival in the kitchen. "Suppose they *should* find it out now—I declare I should feel most awfully. Isn't it *elegant?*" she asked, in a subdued whisper, going all around and around the tree, magnificent in its dress of bright red and yellow balls, white festoons, and little candle-ends all ready for lighting. "Oh, Ben, did you lock the door?"

"Yes," he said. "That's a mouse," he added, as a little rustling noise made Polly stop where she stood back of the tree and prick up her ears in great distress of mind. "'Tis elegant," he said, turning around in admiration, and taking in the tree which, as Polly said, was quite "gorgeous," and the evergreen branches twisted up on the beams and rafters, and all the other festive arrangements. "I don't believe Jappy's is any better."

"I wish Jappy was here," said Polly, with a small sigh.

"Well, he isn't," said Ben. "Come, we must go back into the kitchen, or all the children will be out here. Look your last, Polly; 'twon't do to come again till it's time to light up."

"Mammy says she'd rather do the lighting up," said Polly.

"Had she?" said Ben, in surprise. "Oh, I suppose she's afraid we'll set something afire. Well, then, we sha'n't come in till we *have* it."

"I can't bear to go," said Polly, turning reluctantly away; "it's most beautiful—oh, Ben, is your Santa Claus dress all safe?"

"Yes," said Ben, "I'll warrant they won't find that in one hurry! Such a time as we've had to make it!"

"I know it," laughed Polly; "doesn't that cotton wool look just like bits of fur, Ben?"

"Yes," said Ben, "and when the flour's shaken over me, it'll be Santa himself."

"We've got to put back the hair into mamsie's cushion the first thing to-morrow," whispered Polly, anxiously, "and we mustn't forget it, Bensie."

"I want to keep the wig awfully," said Ben. "You did make that just magnificent, Polly!"

"If you could see yourself," giggled Polly;

"did you put it *in* the straw bed? and are you sure you pulled the ticking over it smoothly?"

"Yes, *sir*," replied Ben, "sure's my name's Ben Pepper! if you'll only keep them from seeing me when I'm in it till we're ready—that's all I ask."

"Well," said Polly, a little relieved, "but I hope Joe won't look."

"Come on! they're coming!" whispered Ben; "quick!"

"Polly!" rang a voice dangerously near; so near that Polly, speeding over the stairs to intercept it, nearly fell on her nose.

"Where have you been?" asked one.

"Let's have a concert," put in Ben; Polly was so out of breath that she *couldn't* speak. "Come, now, each take a whistle, and we'll march round and round and see which can make the biggest noise."

In the rattle and laughter which this procession made, all mystery was forgotten, and the two conspirators began to breathe freer.

Five o'clock! The small ones of the Pepper flock, being pretty well tired out with noise and excitement, all gathered around Polly and Ben, and clamored for a story.

" Do, Polly, do," begged Joel. " It's Christmas, and 'twon't come again for a year."

" I can't," said Polly, in such a twitter that she could hardly stand still, and for the first time in her life refusing, " I can't think of a thing."

" I will, then," said Ben; " we must do something," he whispered to Polly.

" Tell it good," said Joel, settling himself.

So for an hour the small tyrants kept their entertainers well employed.

" Ain't it growing awful dark? " said Davie, rousing himself at last, as Ben paused to take breath.

Polly pinched Ben.

" Mammy's going to let us know," he whispered in reply. " We must keep on a little longer."

" Don't stop," said Joel, lifting his head where he sat on the floor. " What are you whispering for, Polly? "

" I'm not," said Polly, glad to think she hadn't spoken.

" Well, do go on, Ben," said Joel, lying down again.

" Polly'll have to finish it," said Ben; " I've got to go up-stairs now."

So Polly launched out into such an extravagant story that they all, perforce, had to listen.

All this time Mrs. Pepper had been pretty busy in *her* way. And now she came into the kitchen and set down her candle on the table. "Children," she said. Everybody turned and looked at her—her tone was so strange; and when they saw her dark eyes shining with such a new light, little Davie skipped right out into the middle of the room. "What's the matter, mammy?"

"You may all come into the Provision Room," said she.

"What for?" shouted Joel, in amazement; while the others jumped to their feet, and stood staring.

Polly flew around like a general, arranging her forces. "Let's march there," said she; "Phronsie, you take hold of Davie's hand, and go first."

"I'm going first," announced Joel, squeezing up past Polly.

"No, you mustn't, Joe," said Polly, decidedly: "Phronsie and David are the youngest."

"They're *always* the youngest," said Joel, falling back with Polly to the rear.

"*Forward!* MARCH!" sang Polly. "Follow mamsie!"

Down the stairs they went with military step, and into the Provision Room. And then, with one wild look, the little battalion broke ranks, and tumbling one over the other, in decidedly unmilitary style, presented a very queer appearance!

And Captain Polly was the queerest of all; for she just gave one gaze at the tree, and then sat right down on the floor, and said, " O MY! "

Mrs. Pepper was flying around delightedly, and saying, " Please to come right in," and " How do you do? "

And before anybody knew it, there were the laughing faces of Mrs. Henderson and the parson himself, Doctor Fisher, and old Grandma Bascom; while the two Henderson boys, unwilling to be defrauded of any of the fun, were squeezing themselves in between everybody else, and coming up to Polly every third minute, and saying, " There—aren't you surprised? "

" It's Fairyland! " cried little Davie, out of his wits with joy; " oh! aren't we in Fairyland, ma? "

The whole room was in one buzz of chatter and fun; and everybody beamed on everybody else; and nobody knew what they said, till Mrs. Pepper called, " *Hush!* Santa Claus is coming! "

A rattle at the little old window made everybody look there, just as a great snow-white head popped up over the sill.

" *Oh!* " screamed Joel, " *'tis Santy!* "

" He's coming in! " cried Davie, in chorus, which sent Phronsie flying to Polly. In jumped a little old man, quite spry for his years; with a jolly, red face and a pack on his back, and flew into their midst, prepared to do his duty; but what should he do, instead of making his speech, " this jolly old Saint "—but first fly up to Mrs. Pepper, and say—" *Oh, mamsie, how did you do it?* "

" It's Ben! " screamed Phronsie; but the little old Saint didn't hear, for he and Polly took hold of hands, and pranced around that tree while everybody laughed till they cried to see them go!

And then it all came out!

" *Order!* " said Parson Henderson, in his deepest tones; and then he put into Santa Claus's hands a letter, which he requested him to read. And the jolly old Saint, although he was very old, didn't need any spectacles, but piped out in Ben's loudest tones:

"'DEAR FRIENDS:—A Merry Christmas to you all! And that you'll have a good time, and enjoy it as much as I've enjoyed my good times at your house, is the wish of your friend,

"'JASPER ELYOT KING.'"

"Hurrah for Jappy!" cried Santa Claus, pulling his beard; and "Hurrah for Jasper!" went all around the room; and this ended in three good cheers—Phronsie coming in too late with her little crow—which was just as well, however!

"Do your duty, now, Santa Claus!" commanded Doctor Fisher, as master of ceremonies; and everything was as still as a mouse!

And the first thing she knew, a lovely brass cage, with a dear little bird with two astonished black eyes in it, was put into Polly's hands. The card on it said: "*For Miss Polly Pepper, to give her music every day in the year.*"

"Mamsie," said Polly; and then she did the queerest thing of the whole performance! She just burst into tears! "I never thought I should have a bird for *my very own!*"

"Hello!" said Santa Claus, "I've got something myself!"

"Santa Claus's clothes are too old," laughed

Doctor Fisher, holding up a stout, warm suit that a boy about as big as Ben would delight in.

And then that wonderful tree just rained down all manner of lovely fruit. Gifts came flying thick and fast, till the air seemed full, and each one was greeted with a shout of glee, as it was put into the hands of its owner. A shawl flew down on Mrs. Pepper's shoulders; and a work-basket tumbled on Polly's head; and tops and balls and fishing-poles sent Joel and David into a corner with howls of delight!

But the climax was reached when a large wax doll in a very gay pink silk dress was put into Phronsie's hands, and Doctor Fisher, stooping down, read in loud tones: " FOR PHRONSIE, FROM ONE WHO ENJOYED HER GINGERBREAD BOY."

After that, nobody had anything to say! Books jumped down unnoticed, and gay boxes of candy. Only Polly peeped into one of her books, and saw in Jappy's plain hand, "*I hope we'll both read this next summer.*" And turning over to the title-page, she saw " A Complete Manual of Cookery."

" The best is to come," said Mrs. Henderson, in her gentle way. When there was a lull in the gale, she took Polly's hand, and led her to a little

stand of flowers in the corner concealed by a
sheet—pinks and geraniums, heliotropes and
roses, blooming away, and nodding their pretty
heads at the happy sight—Polly had her flowers.

"Why didn't we know?" cried the children at
last, when everybody was tying on their hoods,
and getting their hats to leave the festive scene,
"how *could* you keep it secret, mammy?"

"They all went to Mrs. Henderson's," said Mrs.
Pepper; "Jasper wrote me, and asked where to
send them, and Mrs. Henderson was so kind as to
say that they might come there. And we brought
them over last evening, when you were all abed.
I couldn't have done it," she said, bowing to the
parson and his wife, "if it hadn't been for their
kindness—never in the world!"

"And I'm sure," said the minister, looking
around on the bright group, "if we can help along
a bit of happiness like this, it is a blessed thing!"

And here Joel had the last word. "You said
'twasn't going to be Christmas always, mammy.
I say," looking around on the overflow of treasures and the happy faces—"it'll be just *forever!*"

XVIII

EDUCATION AHEAD

AFTER that they couldn't thank Jasper enough!
They tried to, lovingly, and an elaborate letter of
thanks, headed by Mrs. Pepper, was drawn up and
sent with a box of the results of Polly's diligent
study of Jasper's book. Polly stripped off recklessly her choicest buds and blossoms from the
gay little stand of flowers in the corner, that had
already begun to blossom, and tucked them into
every little nook in the box that could possibly
hold a posy. But as for thanking him enough!

"We can't do it, mamsie," said Polly, looking
around on all the happy faces, and then up at
Cherry, who was singing in the window, and who
immediately swelled up his little throat and
poured out such a merry burst of song that she
had to wait for him to finish. "No, not if we
tried a thousand years!"

"I'm going," said Joel, who was busy as a bee
with his new tools that the tree had shaken down
for him, "to make Jappy the splendidest box *you*
ever saw, Polly! I guess that'll thank him!"

"Do," cried Polly; "he'd be so pleased, Joey."

"And I," said Phronsie, over in the corner with her children, "I'm going to see my poor sick man sometime, Polly, I *am!*"

"O horrors!" cried Polly, whirling around, and looking at her mother in dismay. "She'll be going to-morrow! Oh, no, Phronsie, you can't; he lives miles and miles away—oh, ever so far!"

"Does he live as far as the moon?" asked little Phronsie, carefully laying Seraphina down, and looking up at Polly, anxiously.

"Oh, I don't know," said Polly, giving Cherry a piece of bread, and laughing to see how cunning he looked. "Oh, no, of course not, but it's an *awfully* long ways, Phronsie."

"I don't care," said Phronsie, determinedly, giving the new doll a loving little pat, "I'm going sometime, Polly, to thank my poor sick man, yes, I am!"

"You'll see him next summer, Phronsie," sang Polly, skipping around the kitchen, "and Jappy's sister Marian, the lovely lady, and all the boys. Won't that be nice?" and Polly stopped to pat the yellow head bending in motherly attentions over her array of dolls.

"Ye-es," said Phronsie, slowly; "the whole of 'em, Polly?"

"Yes, indeed!" said Polly, gaily; "the whole of 'em, Phronsie!"

"Hooray!" shouted the two boys, while Phronsie only gave a long sigh, and clasped her hands.

"Better not be looking for summer," said Mrs. Pepper, "until you do your duty by the winter; then you can enjoy it," and she took a fresh needleful of thread.

"Mamsie's right," said Ben, smiling over at her. And he threw down his book and jumped for his cap. "Now for a good chop!" he cried, and snatching a kiss from Phronsie, he rushed out of the door to his work, whistling as he went.

"Isn't Mr. Henderson good, ma," asked Polly, watching his retreating figure, "to teach Ben?"

"Yes, he is," replied Mrs. Pepper, enthusiastically. "We've got a parson, if anybody has in this world!"

"And Ben's learning," said Polly, swelling with pride, as she sat down by her mother, and began to sew rapidly, "so that he'll be a big man right off! O dear!" as a thought made her needle pause a minute in its quick flying in and out.

"What is it, Polly?" Mrs. Pepper looked keenly at the troubled face and downcast eyes.

"Why ——" began Polly, and then she finished very slowly, "I sha'n't know anything, and Ben'll be ashamed of me."

"Yes, you will!" cried Mrs. Pepper, energetically, "you keep on trying, and the Lord'll send some way; don't you go to bothering your head about it now, Polly—it'll come when it's time."

"Will it?" asked Polly, doubtfully, taking up her needle again.

"Yes, indeed!" cried Mrs. Pepper, briskly; "come, fly at your sewing; that's *your* learning now."

"So 'tis," said Polly, with a little laugh. "Now let's see which'll get their seam done first, mamsie!"

And now letters flew thick and fast from the city to the little brown house, and back again, warming Jasper's heart, and filling the tedious months of that winter with more of jollity and fun than the lad ever had enjoyed before; and never were fun and jollity more needed than now; for Mr. King, having nothing to do, and each year finding himself less inclined to exercise and thoughtful energy for others, began to look at life something in the light of a serious bore, and accordingly made it decidedly disagreeable for all around him, and particularly for Jasper, who was his constant companion. But the boy was looking forward to summer, and so held on bravely.

"I do verily believe, Polly," he wrote, "that Badgertown'll see the gayest times it ever knew! Sister Marian wants to go, so *that's* all right. Now, hurrah for a good time—it's surely coming!"

But alas! for Jasper! as spring advanced, his father took a decided aversion to Hingham, Badgertown, and all other places that could be mentioned in that vicinity.

"It's a wretched climate," he asserted, over and over; "and the foundation of all my ill feelings this winter was laid, I'm convinced, in Hingham last summer."

No use to urge the contrary; and all Jasper's pleadings were equally vain. At last, Sister Marian, who was kind-hearted to a fault, sorry to see her brother's dismay and disappointment, said, one day, "Why not have one of the children come here? I should like it very much—do invite Ben."

"I don't want Ben," said Jasper, gloomily, "I want Polly." He added this in much the same tone as Phronsie's when she had rushed up to him the day she was lost, declaring, "I want Polly!"

"Very well, then," said sister Marian, laughing, "I'm sure I didn't mean to dictate which one; let it *be* Polly, then; yes, I should prefer Polly myself, I think, as we've enough boys now," smiling to think of her own brood of wide-awake youngsters.

"If you only will, father, I'll try to be *ever* so good!" said Jasper, turning suddenly to his father.

"Jasper needs some change," said sister Marian, kindly, "he really has grown very pale and thin."

"*Hey!*" said Mr. King, sharply, looking at him over his eye-glasses. "The boy's well enough; well enough!" But he twisted uneasily in his chair, all the same. At last he flung down his paper, twitched his fingers through his hair two or three times, and then burst out:

"Well, why don't you send for her? I'm sure I don't care—I'll write myself, and I had better do it now. Tell Thomas to be ready to take it right down; it must get into this mail."

When Mr. King had made up his mind to do anything everybody else must immediately give up their individual plans, and stand out of the way for him to execute his at just that particular moment! Accordingly Thomas was dragged from his work to post the letter, while the old gentle-man occupied the time in pulling out his watch every third minute until the slightly-out-of-breath Thomas reported on his return that the letter did get in. Then Mr. King settled down satisfied, and everything went on smoothly as before.

But Polly didn't come! A grateful, apprecia-tive letter, expressed in Mrs. Pepper's own stiff way, plainly showed the determination of that good woman not to accept what was such a favor to her child.

In vain Mr. King stormed, and fretted, and begged, offering every advantage possible—Polly should have the best foundation for a musical education that the city could afford; also lessons in the schoolroom under the boys' private tutor—it was all of no avail. In vain sister Marian sent a gentle appeal, fully showing her heart was in it; nothing broke down Mrs. Pepper's resolve, until, at last, the old gentleman wrote one day that Jasper. being in such failing health, really depended on Polly to cheer him up. That removed the last straw that made it " putting one's self under an obligation," which, to Mrs. Pepper's independent soul, had seemed insurmountable.

And now, it was decided that Polly was *really* to go! and pretty soon all Badgertown knew that Polly Pepper was going to the big city. And there wasn't a man, woman, or child but what greatly rejoiced that a sunny time was coming to one of the chicks in the Little Brown House. With many warm words, and some substantial gifts, kind friends helped forward the " outing." Only one person doubted that this delightful chance should be grasped at once—and that one was Polly herself!

" I *can't*," she said, and stood quite pale and still, when the Hendersons advised her mother's approval, and even Grandma Bascom said, " Go." " I can't go and leave mamsie to do all the work."

" But don't you see, Polly," said Mrs. Henderson, drawing her to her side, " that you will help your mother twice as much as you possibly could here, by getting a good education? Think what your music will be; only think, Polly! "

Polly drew a long breath at this, and turned away.

"Oh, Polly!" cried Ben, though his voice choked, "if you give this up, there never'll be another chance," and the boy put his arm around her, and whispered something in her ear.

"I know," said Polly, quietly—and then she burst out, "oh, but I can't! 'Tisn't right."

"Polly," said Mrs. Pepper—and never in all their lives had the children seen such a look in mamsie's eyes as met them then; "it does seem as if my heart would be broken if you didn't go!" And then she burst out crying, right before them all!

"Oh, mamsie," cried Polly, breaking away from everybody, and flinging herself into her arms "I'll go—if you think I ought to. But it's too good! don't cry—*don't*, mammy, dear," and Polly stroked the careworn face lovingly, and patted the smooth hair that was still so black.

"And, Polly," said Mrs. Pepper, smiling through her tears, "just think what a comfort you'll be to me, and us all," she added, taking in the children who were crowding around Polly as the centre of attraction. "Why, you'll be the making of us," she added, hopefully.

"I'll do *something*," said Polly, her brown eyes kindling, "or I sha'n't be worthy of you, mammy."

"Oh, you'll do it," said Mrs. Pepper, confidently, "now that you're going I can trust you, Polly."

But when Polly stepped into the stage, with her little hair trunk strapped on behind, containing her one brown merino that Mrs. Henderson had made over for her out of one of her own, and her two new ginghams, her courage failed again, and she astonished everybody, and nearly upset a mild-faced old lady who was in the corner placidly eating doughnuts, by springing out and rushing up through the little brown gateway, past all the family, drawn up to see her off. She flew over the old flat door-stone, and into the bedroom, where she flung herself down between the old bed and Phronsie's crib, in a perfect torrent of tears. "I *can't* go!" she sobbed—"oh, I *can't!*"

"Why, Polly!" cried Mrs. Pepper, hurrying in, followed by Joel and the rest of the troop at his heels. "What are you thinking of!"

"Think of by and by, Polly," put in Ben, patting her on the back with an unsteady hand, while Joel varied the proceedings by running back and forth, screaming at the top of his lungs, "The stage is going—with your trunk on top!"

"O dear!" cried Mrs. Pepper, "do stop it,

somebody! there, Polly; come, be mother's good girl."

"I'll try again," said poor Polly, choking back her sobs, and getting on her feet.

Then Polly's tears were wiped away, her hat straightened, after which she was kissed all round again by the whole family, Phronsie waiting for the last two, and then was helped again into the stage, the bags and parcels, and a box for Jappy, which, as it wouldn't go into the trunk, Joel had insisted Polly should carry in her hand, were again piled around her, and Mr. Tisbett mounted to his seat, and, with a crack of the whip, bore her safely off this time.

The doughnut lady, viewing poor Polly with extreme sympathy, immediately forced upon her acceptance three of the largest and sugariest.

"'Twill do you good," she said, falling to, herself, on another with good zeal. "I always eat 'em, and then there ain't no room for homesickness!"

And away, and away, and away they rumbled and jumbled to the cars.

Here Mr. Tisbett put Polly and her numerous bundles under the care of the conductor, with manifold charges and explicit directions, to see

her safely into Mr. King's own hands. He left
her sitting straight up among her parcels, her
sturdy little figure drawn up to its full height, and
the clear brown eyes regaining a little of their
dancing light; for although an *awful* feeling
tugged at her heart, as she thought of the Little
Brown House she was fast flying away from, there
was something else; our Polly had begun to realize that now she was going to "help mother."

And now they neared the big city and everybody began to bustle around, and get ready to
jump out, and the minute the train stopped the
crowd poured out from the cars, making way for
the crowd pouring in, for this was a through train.

"All *aboard!*" sang the conductor. "O *gracious!*" springing to Polly; "I forgot you—*here!*"

But as quick as a flash he was pushed aside,
and a bright, boyish figure dashed up.

"Oh, Polly!" he said, in such a ringing voice!
and in another second, Polly and her bag, and the
bundle of cakes and apples that Grandma Bascom
had put up for her, and Joel's box, were one and
all bundled out upon the platform, and the train
whizzed on, and there Mr. King was fuming up
and down, berating the departing conductor, and
speaking his mind in regard to all the railroad of-

ficials he could think of. He pulled himself up long enough to give Polly a hearty welcome; and then away again he flew in righteous indignation, while Jasper rushed off into the baggage-room with Polly's check.

However, every now and then, turning to look down into the little rosy face beside him, the old gentleman would burst forth, " Bless me, child! I'm glad you're here, Polly!—how could the fellow forget when——"

" Oh, well, you know," said Polly, with a happy little wriggle under her brown coat, " I'm here now."

" So you are! so you are! " laughed the old gentleman, suddenly; " where can Jasper be so long? "

" They're all in the carriage," answered the boy, skipping back. " Now, father! now, Polly! "

He was fairly bubbling over with joy, and Mr. King forgot his dudgeon and joined in the general glee, which soon became so great that travellers gave many a glance at the merry trio who bundled away to Thomas and the waiting grays.

" You're sure everything is all right? " asked Mr. King, nervously, getting into a handsome coach lined with dark green satin, and settling down among its ample cushions with a sigh of relief.

"Oh, yes," laughed Jasper; "Polly didn't have any one else's check, I guess!"

Over through the heart of the city, down narrow, noisy, busy streets, out into wide avenues, with handsome stately mansions on either side—they flew along.

"Oh!" said Polly; and then she stopped, and blushed very hard.

"What is it, my dear?" asked Mr. King, kindly.

Polly couldn't speak at first, but when Jasper stopped his merry chat and begged to know what it was, she turned on him, and burst out, "You *live* here?"

"Why, yes," laughed the boy; "why not?"

"*Oh!*" cried Polly, again, her cheeks as red as two roses, "it's *so lovely!*"

And then the carriage turned in at a brown stone gateway, and winding up among some fine old trees, stopped before a large, stately residence that in Polly's eye seemed like one of the castles of Ben's famous stories. And then Mr. King got out, and gallantly escorted Polly out, and up the steps, while Jasper followed with Polly's bag,

which he couldn't be persuaded to resign to
Thomas. A stiff butler held the door open—and
then, the rest was only a pleasant, confused
jumble of kind welcoming words, smiling faces,
with a background of high spacious walls, bright
pictures, and soft, elegant hangings, everything
and all inextricably mixed—till Polly herself
seemed floating—away—away, fast to the Fairyland of her dreams; now, Mr. King was handing
her around, like a precious parcel, from one to the
other—now Jasper was bobbing in and out everywhere, introducing her on all sides, and then
Prince was jumping up and trying to lick her face
every minute—but it was best of all when a
lovely face looked down into hers, and Jasper's
sister bent to kiss her.

" I am *very* glad to have you here, little Polly."
The words were simple, but Polly, lifting up her
clear brown eyes, looked straight into the heart of
the speaker, and from that moment never ceased
to love her.

"It was a good inspiration," thought Mrs.
Whitney to herself; " this little girl is going to be
a comfort, I know." And then she set herself to
conduct successfully her three boys into friendli-
ness and good fellowship with Polly, for each of

them was following his own sweet will in the capacity of host, and besides staring at her with all his might, was determined to do the whole of the entertaining, a state of things which might become unpleasant. However, Polly stood it like a veteran.

"This little girl must be very tired," said Mrs. Whitney at last, with a bright smile. "Besides, I am going to have her to myself now."

"Oh, no, no," cried little Dick, in alarm; "why, she's just come; we want to see her."

"For shame, Dick!" said Percy, the eldest, a boy of ten years, who took every opportunity to reprove Dick in public; "she's come a great way, so she ought to rest, you know."

"You wanted her to come out to the greenhouse yourself, you know you did," put in Van, the next to Percy, who never would be reproved or patronized, "only she wouldn't go."

"You'll come down to dinner," said Percy, politely, ignoring Van. "Then you won't be tired, perhaps."

"Oh, I'm not very tired now," said Polly, brightly, with a merry little laugh, "only I've never been in the cars before, and——"

"Never been in the cars before!" exclaimed

Van, crowding up, while Percy made a big round O with his mouth, and little Dick's eyes stretched to their widest extent.

"No," said Polly, simply, "never in all my life."

"Come, dear," said sister Marian, rising quickly, and taking Polly's hand; while Jasper, showing unmistakable symptoms of pitching into all the three boys, followed with the bag.

Up the broad oak staircase they went, Polly holding Mrs. Whitney's soft hand as if for dear life, and Jasper tripping up two steps at a time, in front of them. They turned after reaching the top, down a hall soft to the foot and brightly lighted.

"Now, Polly," said sister Marian, "I'm going to have you here, right next to my dressing-room; this is your nest, little bird, and I hope you'll be very happy in it."

And here Mrs. Whitney turned up the gas, and then, just because she couldn't help it, gathered Polly up in her arms without another word. Jasper set down the bag on a chair, and came and stood by his sister's side, looking down at her as she stroked the brown wavy hair on her bosom.

"It's *so* nice to have Polly here, sister," he said

and he put his hand on Mrs. Whitney's neck; and then with the other hand took hold of both of Polly's chubby ones, who looked up and smiled; and in that smile the Little Brown House seemed to hop right out, and bring back in a flash all the nice times those eight happy weeks had brought him.

"Oh, 'twas so perfectly splendid, sister Marian," he cried, flinging himself down on the floor by her chair. "You don't know *what* good times we had —does she, Polly?" and then he launched out into a perfect shower of "Don't you remember this?" or, "Oh, Polly! you surely haven't forgotten that!" Mrs. Whitney good-naturedly entering into it and enjoying it all with them, until, warned by the lateness of the hour, she laughingly reminded Jasper of dinner, and dismissed him to prepare for it.

When the three boys saw Polly coming in again, they welcomed her with a cordial shout, for one and all, after careful measurement of her, had succumbed entirely to Polly; and each was unwilling that the others should get ahead of him in her regard.

"This is your seat, Polly," said sister Marian, touching the chair next to her own.

Thereupon a small fight ensued between the little Whitneys, while Jasper looked decidedly discomfited.

"Let Polly sit next to me," said Van, as if a seat next to him was of all things most to be desired.

"Oh, no, I want her," said little Dick.

"Pshaw, Dick! you're too young," put in Percy. "You'd spill the bread and butter all over her."

"I wouldn't, either," said little Dick, indignantly, and beginning to crawl into his seat; "I don't spill bread and butter, now, Percy, you know."

"See here," said Jasper, decidedly, "she's coming up here by father and me; that is, sister Marian," he finished more politely, "if you're willing."

All this while Polly had stood quietly watching the group, the big, handsome table, the bright lights, and the well-trained servants with a curious feeling at her heart—what were the Little-Brown-House people doing?"

"Polly shall decide it," said sister Marian, laughing. "Now, where will you sit, dear?" she added, looking down on the little quiet figure beside her.

"Oh, by Jappy, please," said Polly, quickly, as if there could be no doubt; "and kind Mr. King," she added, smiling at him.

"That's right; that's right, my dear," cried the old gentleman, pleased beyond measure at her honest choice. And he pulled out her chair, and waited upon her into it so handsomely that Polly was happy at once; while Jasper, with a proud toss of his dark, wavy hair, marched up delightedly, and took the chair on her other side.

And now, in two or three minutes it seemed as if Polly had always been there; it was the most natural thing in the world that sister Marian should smile down the table at the bright-faced narrator, who answered all their numerous questions, and entertained them all with accounts of Ben's skill, of Phronsie's cunning ways, of the boys who made fun for all, and above everything else of the dear mother whom they all longed to help, and of all the sayings and doings in the Little Brown House. No wonder that the little boys forgot to eat; and for once never thought of the attractions of the table. And when, as they left the table at last, little Dick rushed impulsively up to Polly, and flinging himself into her arms, declared:

"I love you!—and you're my sister!" Nothing more was needed to make Polly feel at home.

"Yes," said Mrs. Whitney, and nodded to herself in the saying, "it *was* a good thing; and a comfort, I believe, has come to this house this day!"

XIX

BRAVE WORK AND THE REWARD

AND on the morrow came Polly's music teacher!

The big drawing-room, with its shaded light and draped furniture, with its thick soft carpet, on which no footfall could be heard, with all its beauty and loveliness on every side, was nothing to Polly's eyes, only the room that contained the piano!

That was all she saw! And when the teacher came he was simply the Fairy (an ugly little one, it is true, but still a most powerful being) who was to unlock its mysteries, and conduct her into Fairyland itself. He was a homely little Frenchman, with a long curved nose, and an enormous black moustache, magnificently waxed, who bowed elaborately, and called her " Mademoiselle Pep-paire; " but he had music in his soul, and Polly couldn't reverence him too much.

And now the big piano gave out new sounds; sounds that told of a deep purpose and strong patience. Every note was struck for mother and the home brood. Monsieur Tourtelotte, after watching her keenly out of his little black eyes, would nod to himself like a mandarin, and the nod would be followed by showers of extra politeness, expressing his appreciation of her patient energy and attention.

Every chance she could get, Polly would steal away into the drawing-room from Jappy and the three boys and all the attractions they could offer, and laboriously work away over and over at the tedious scales and exercises that were to be stepping-stones to so much that was glorious beyond. Never had she sat still for so long a time in her active little life; and now, with her arms at just such an angle, with the stiff, chubby fingers kept under training and restraint—well, Polly realized, years after, that only her love of the Little Brown House could *ever* have kept her from flying up and spinning around in perfect despair.

"She likes it!" said Percy, in absolute astonishment, one day, when Polly had refused to go out driving with all the other children in the park, and had gone resolutely, instead, into the drawing-room and shut the door. "She likes those hateful old exercises and she doesn't like anything else."

"Much you know about it," said Jappy; "she's perfectly aching to go, now Percy Whitney!"

"Well, why doesn't she then?" said Percy, opening his eyes to their widest extent.

"'Cause," said Jasper, stopping on his way to the door to look him full in the face, "she's commenced to learn to play, and there won't *anything* stop her."

"I'm going to try," said Percy, gleefully. "I know lots of ways I can do to try, anyway."

"See here, now," said Jasper, turning back, "you let her alone! Do you hear?" he added, and there must have been something in his eye to command attention, for Percy instantly signified his intention not to tease this young music student in the least.

"Come on then, old fellow," and Jasper swung his cap on his head, "Thomas will be like forty bears if we keep him waiting much longer."

And Polly kept at it steadily day after day; getting through with the lessons in the schoolroom as quickly as possible to rush to her music, until presently the little Frenchman waxed enthusiastic to that degree that, as day after day progressed and swelled into weeks, and each lesson came to an end, he would skip away on the tips of his toes, his nose in the air, and the waxed ends of his moustache fairly trembling with delight:

"Ah, such patience as Mademoiselle Pep-paire has! I know no other such little Americaine!"

"I think," said Jasper, one evening after dinner, when all the children were assembled as usual in their favorite place on the big rug in front of the fire in the library, Prince in the middle of the group, his head on his paws, watching everything in infinite satisfaction—"I think that Polly's getting on in music as I never saw any one do; and that's a fact!"

"*I* mean to begin," said Van, ambitiously, sitting up straight and staring at the glowing coals. "I guess I will to-morrow," which announcement was received with a perfect shout—Van's taste being anything rather than of a musical nature.

"If you do," said Jappy, when the merriment had a little subsided, "I shall go out of the house at every lesson; there won't any one stay in it, Van."

"I can bang all I want to, then," said Van, in no way disturbed by the reflection, and pulling one of Prince's long ears, "you think you're so big, Jappy, just because you're thirteen."

"He's only three ahead of me, Van," bristled Percy, who never could forgive Jappy for being his uncle, much less the still greater sin of having been born three years earlier than himself.

"Three's just as bad as four," said Van.

"Let's tell stories," began Polly, who never could remember such goings on in the Little Brown House; "we must each tell one," she added, with the great enthusiasm, "and see which will be the biggest and the best."

"Oh, no," said Van, who perfectly revelled in Polly's stories, and who now forgot his trials in the prospect of one, "you tell, Polly—you tell alone."

"Yes, do, Polly," said Jasper; "we'd rather hear you."

So Polly launched out into one of her gayest and finest; and soon they were in such a peal of laughter, and had reached such heights of enjoyment, that Mr. King popped his head in at the door, and then came in, and took a seat in a big rocking-chair in the corner to hear the fun go on.

"O dear!" said Van, leaning back with a long sigh, and wiping his flushed face as Polly wound up with a triumphant flourish, "how ever do you think of such things, Polly Pepper?"

"That isn't anything," said Jappy, bringing his handsome face out into the strong light; "why, it's just nothing to what she has told time and again in the Little Brown House in Badgertown; " and then he caught sight of Polly's face, which turned a little pale in the firelight as he spoke; and the brown eyes had such a pathetic droop in them that it went to the boy's very heart.

Was Polly homesick? and so soon!

XX

POLLY IS COMFORTED

Yes, it must be confessed. Polly was homesick. All her imagination of her mother's hard work, increased by her absence, loomed up before her, till she was almost ready to fly home without a minute's warning. At night, when no one knew it, the tears would come racing over the poor, forlorn little face, and would not be squeezed back. It got to be noticed finally; and one and all redoubled their exertions to make everything twice as pleasant as ever.

The only place, except in front of the grand piano, where Polly approached a state of comparative happiness, was in the greenhouse.

Here she would stay, comforted and soothed among the lovely plants and rich exotics, rejoicing the heart of old Turner the gardener, who, since Polly's first rapturous entrance, had taken her into his good graces for all time.

Every chance she could steal after practice hours were over, and after the clamorous demands of the boys upon her time were fully satisfied, was seized to fly on the wings of the wind to the flowers.

But even with the music and flowers the dancing light in the eyes went down a little; and Polly, growing more silent and pale, moved around with a little droop in the small figure that had only been wont to fly through the wide halls and spacious rooms with gay and springing step.

"Polly doesn't like us," at last said Van, one day, in despair.

"Then, dear," said Mrs. Whitney, "you must be kinder to her than ever; think what it would be for one of you to be away from home even among friends."

"I'd like it first-rate to be away from Percy," said Van, reflectively; "I wouldn't come back in three, no, six weeks."

"My son," said his mamma, "just stop and think how badly you would feel, if you really couldn't see Percy."

"Well," said Van, and he showed signs of relenting a little at that; "but Percy is perfectly awful, mamma, you don't know; and he feels so smart, too," he added, vindictively.

"Well," said Mrs. Whitney, softly, "let's think

what we can do for Polly; it makes me feel very badly to see her sad little face."

"I don't know," said Van, running over in his mind all the possible ways he could think of for entertaining anybody, " unless she'd like my new book of travels—or my velocipede," he added.

" I'm afraid those wouldn't quite answer the purpose," said his mamma, smiling—" especially the last; yet we must think of something."

But just here Mr. King thought it about time to take matters into *his* hands. So, with a great many chucklings and shruggings when no one was by, he had departed after breakfast one day, simply saying he shouldn't be back to luncheon.

Polly sat in the drawing-room, near the edge of the twilight, practising away bravely. Somehow, of all the days when the home feeling was the strongest, this day it seemed as if she could bear it no longer. If she could only see Phronsie for just one moment! " I shall *have* to give up! " she moaned. " I *can't* stand it! " and over went her head on the music-rack.

" Where is she? " asked a voice over in front of the piano, in the gathering dusk—unmistakably Mr. King's.

" Oh, she's always at the piano," said Van.

"She must be there now, somewhere," and then somebody giggled. Then came in the loudest of whispers from little Dick, "Oh, Jappy, what'll she say?"

"*Hush!*" said one of the other boys; "do be still, Dick!"

Polly bounced up straight and whisked off the tears quickly. Up came Mr. King with an enormous bundle in his arms; and he marched up to the piano, puffing with his exertions.

"Here, Polly, hold your lap," he had only strength to gasp. And then he broke out into a loud burst of merriment, in which all the troop joined, until the big room echoed with the sound.

At this, the bundle opened suddenly, and—out popped Phronsie!

"Here I am! I'm here, Polly!"

But Polly couldn't speak; and if Jasper hadn't caught her just in time, she would have tumbled over backward from the stool, Phronsie and all!

"Aren't you glad I've come, Polly?" asked Phronsie, with her little face close to Polly's own.

That brought Polly to. "Oh, *Phronsie!*" she cried, and strained her to her heart; while the boys crowded around, and plied her with sudden questions.

"Now you'll stay," cried Van; "say, Polly, won't you?"

"Weren't you awfully surprised?" cried Percy; "say, Polly, *awfully?*"

"Is her name Phronsie?" put in Dick, unwilling to be left out, and not thinking of anything else to ask.

"Boys," whispered their mother, warningly, "she *can't* answer you; just look at her face."

And, to be sure, our Polly's face was a study to behold. All its old sunniness was as nothing to the joy that now transfigured it.

"*Oh!*" she cried, coming out of her rapture a little, and springing over to Mr. King with Phronsie still in her arms. "Oh, you are the dearest and best Mr. King I ever saw! but how *did you make mammy let her come?*"

"Isn't he splendid!" cried Jasper, in intense pride, swelling up. "Father knew how to do it."

But Polly's arms were around the old gentleman's neck, so she didn't hear. "There, there," he said, soothingly, patting her brown, fuzzy head. Something was going down the old gentleman's neck, that wet his collar, and made him whisper very tenderly in her ear, "Don't give way now, Polly: Phronsie'll see you."

"I know," gasped Polly, keeping down her sobs; "I won't—only—I *can't* thank you!"

"Phronsie," said Jasper, quickly, "what do you suppose Prince said the other day?"

"What?" asked Phronsie, in intense interest, slipping down out of Polly's arms, and crowding up close to Jasper's side. "What did he, Japser?"

"Oh-ho, how funny!" laughed Van, while little Dick burst right out, "*Japser!*"

"Be still," said Jappy, warningly, while Phronsie stood surveying them all with grave eyes.

"Well, I asked him, 'Don't you want to see Phronsie Pepper, Prince?' And do you know, he just stood right upon his hind legs, Phronsie, and said: '*Bark!* yes, *Bark! Bark!*'"

"Did he *really*, Japser?" cried Phronsie, delighted beyond measure; and clasping her hands in rapture, "all alone by himself?"

"Yes, all alone by himself," asserted Jasper, vehemently, and winking furiously to the others to stop their laughing; "he did now, truly, Phronsie."

"Then mustn't I go and see him *now*, Japser? yes, pretty soon *now?*"

"So you must," cried Jasper, enchanted at his success in amusing; "and I'll go with you."

"Oh, no," cried Phronsie, shaking her yellow head. "Oh, no, Japser; I must go by my very own self."

"There, Jap, you've caught it," laughed Percy; while the others screamed at the sight of Jasper's face.

"Oh, Phronsie!" cried Polly, turning around at the last words; "how *could* you!"

"Don't mind it, Polly," whispered Jasper; "'twasn't her fault."

"Phronsie," said Mrs. Whitney, smilingly, stooping over the child, "would you like to see a little pussy I have for you?"

But the chubby face didn't look up brightly as usual: and the next moment, without a bit of warning, Phronsie sprang past them all, even Polly, and flung herself into Mr. King's arms, in a perfect torrent of sobs. "Oh! let's *go back!*" was all they heard.

"Dear me!" ejaculated the old gentleman, in the utmost amazement; "and such a time as I've had to get her here, too!" he added, staring around on the astonished group, none of whom had a word to say.

But Polly stood like a statue! All Jasper's frantic efforts at comfort utterly failed. To think that Phronsie had left her for any one!—even good Mr. King! The room seemed to buzz, and everything to turn upside down—and just then, she heard another cry—" Oh, I *want* Polly, I *do!* "

With one jump, Polly was at Mr. King's side, with her face on his coat, close to the little tear-stained one. The fat, little arms unclasped their hold, and transferred themselves willingly to Polly's neck; and Phronsie hugged up comfortingly to Polly's heart, who poured into her ear all the loving words she had so longed to say.

Just then there was a great rush and a scuffling noise; and something bounced up to Phronsie. "*Oh!*" And then the next minute, she had her arms around Prince's neck, and he was jumping all over her and trying as hard as he could to express his overwhelming delight.

" She's the cunningest little thing I ever saw," said Mrs. Whitney, enthusiastically, afterward, aside to Mr. King. " Such lovely yellow hair, and such exquisite brown eyes—the combination is very striking. How did her mother ever let her go? " she asked, impulsively, " I didn't believe you could persuade her, father."

" I didn't have any fears, if I worked it rightly," said the old gentleman, complacently. " I wasn't

coming without her, Marian, if it could possibly
be managed. The truth is, that Phronsie had
been pining for Polly to such an extent, that there
was no other way but for her to *have* Polly; and
her mother was just on the point, although it
almost killed her, of sending for Polly—as if we
should have let her go! " he cried in high dudgeon; just as if he owned the whole of the Peppers, and could dispose of them all to suit his
fancy! "So you see, I was just in time; in the
very nick of time, in fact! "

" So her mother was willing? " asked his daughter, curiously.

" Oh, she couldn't help it," cried Mr. King, beginning to walk up and down the floor, and beaming as he recalled his successful strategy; " there
wasn't the smallest use in thinking of anything
else. I told her 'twould just stop Polly from ever
being a musician if she broke off now—and so
'twould, you know, yourself, Marian, for we
should never get the child here again, if we let
her go now; and I talked—well, I had to talk
some; but, well—the upshot is I *did* get her, and
I *did* bring her—and here she is! " And the old
gentleman was so delighted with his success, that
he had to burst out into a series of short, happy

bits of laughter, that occupied quite a space of time. At last he came out of them, and wiped his face vigorously.

"And to think how fond the little girl is of you, father!" said Mrs. Whitney, who hadn't yet gotten over her extreme surprise at the old gentleman's complete subjection to the little Peppers: he, whom all children had by instinct always approached so carefully, and whom every one found it necessary to conciliate!

"Well, she's a nice child," he said, "a *very* nice child; and," straightening himself up to his fullest height, and looking so very handsome, that his daughter could not conceal her admiration, "I shall always take care of Phronsie Pepper, Marian!"

"So I hope," said Mrs. Whitney; "and, father, I believe they'll repay you; for I do think there's good blood there; these children have a look about them that shows them worthy to be trusted."

"So they have: so they have," assented Mr. King, and then the conversation dropped.

XXI

PHRONSIE

PHRONSIE was toiling up and down the long oak staircase the next morning; slowly going from one step to the other, drawing each little fat foot into place laboriously, but with a pleased expression on her face that only gave some small idea of the rapture within. Up and down she had been going for a long time, perfectly fascinated; seeming to care for nothing else in the world but to work her way up to the top of the long flight, only to turn and come down again. She had been going on so for some time, till at last, Polly, who was afraid she would tire herself all out, sat down at the foot and begged and implored the little girl, who had nearly reached the top, to stop and rest.

" You'll be tired to death, Phronsie! " she said, looking up at the small figure on its toilsome journey. " Why, you must have gone up a million times! Do sit down, pet; we're all going out riding, Phronsie, this afternoon; and you can't go if you're all tired out."

" I won't be tired, Polly," said Phronsie, turning around and looking at her, " do let me go just once more! "

" Well," said Polly, who never could refuse her anything, " just once, Phronsie, and then you must stop."

So Phronsie kept on her way rejoicing, while Polly still sat on the lowest stair, and drummed impatiently on the step above her, waiting for her to get through.

Jappy came through the hall and found them thus.

" Hello, Polly! " he said, stopping suddenly; " what's the matter? "

" Oh, Phronsie's been going so," said Polly, looking up at the little figure above them, which had nearly reached the top in delight, " that I can't stop her. She has really, Jappy, almost all the morning; you can't think how crazy she is over it."

" Is that so? " said Jasper, with a little laugh. " Hello, Phronsie, is it nice? " and he tossed a kiss to the little girl, and then sat down by Polly.

" Oh," said Phronsie, turning to come down,

" it's the be-you-tiflest place I ever saw, Japser! the very be-you-tiflest! "

" I wish she could have her picture painted," whispered Jasper, enthusiastically. " Look at her now, Polly, quick! "

" Yes," said Polly, " isn't she sweet! "

" Sweet! " said Jasper. " Indeed she is! why, she's Phronsie! "

The sunlight through an oriel window fell on the childish face and figure, glinting the yellow hair, and lighting up the radiant face, that had a tender, loving glance for the two who waited for her below. One little foot was poised, just in the act of stepping down to the next lower stair, and the fat hand grasped the polished railing, expressive of just enough caution to make it truly childish. In after years Jasper never thought of Phronsie without bringing up this picture on that April morning, when Polly and he sat at the foot of the stairs, and looked up and saw it.

" Where's Jap? " called one of the boys; and then there was a clatter out in the hall.

" What are you doing? " and Van came to a full stop of amazement and stared at them.

" Resting," said Jappy, concisely, " what do you want, Van? "

" I want you," said Van, " we can't do anything without you, Jappy; you know that."

" Very well," said Jasper, getting up. " Come on, Polly, we must go."

" And Phronsie," said Van, anxiously, looking up to Phronsie, who had nearly reached them by this time, " we want her, too."

" Of course," said Polly, running up and meeting her to give her a hug; " *I* don't go unless she does."

" Where are we going, Polly? " asked Phronsie, looking back longingly to her beloved stairs as she was borne off.

" To the greenhouse, chick! " said Jasper, " to help Turner; and it'll be good fun, won't it, Polly? "

" What is a greenhouse? " asked the child, wonderingly. " All green, Japser? "

" O dear me! " said Van, doubling up, " *do* you suppose she thinks it's painted green? "

" It's green inside, Phronsie, dear," said Jasper, kindly, " and that's the best of all."

When Phronsie was really let loose in the greenhouse she thought it decidedly best of all! and she went into nearly as much of a rapture as Polly did on her first visit to it.

In a few moments she was cooing and jumping among the plants, while old Turner, staid and particular as he was, laughed to see her go.

"She's your sister, Miss Mary, ain't she?" at last he asked, as Phronsie bent lovingly over a pot of heath, and just touched one little leaf carefully with her finger.

"Yes," said Polly, "but she doesn't look like me."

"She *is* like you," said Turner, respectfully, "if she don't look like you; and the flowers know it, too," he added, "and they'll love to see her coming, just as they do you."

For Polly had won the old gardener's heart completely by her passionate love for flowers, and nearly every morning a little nosegay, fresh and beautiful, came up to the house for "Miss Mary."

And now nobody liked to think of the time, or to look back to it, when Phronsie hadn't been in the house. When the little feet went pattering through halls and over stairs, it seemed to bring sunshine and happiness into every one's heart just to hear the sounds. Polly and the boys in the schoolroom would look up from their books and nod away brightly to each other, and then fall to faster than ever on their lessons, to get through the quicker to be with her again.

One thing Phronsie always insisted on, and kept to it pertinaciously—and that was to go into the drawing-room with Polly when she went to practise, and there, with one of her numerous family of dolls, to sit down quietly in some corner and wait till she got through.

Day after day she did it, until Polly, who was worried to think how tedious it must be for her, would look around and say:

" Oh, childie, do run out and play."

" I want to stay," Phronsie would beg in an injured tone; " please let me, Polly."

So Polly would jump and give her a kiss, and then, delighted to know that she was there, would go at her practising with twice the vigor and enthusiasm.

But Phronsie's chief occupation, at least when she wasn't with Polly, was the entertainment and amusement of Mr. King. And never was she very long absent from his side, which so pleased the old gentleman that he could scarcely contain himself, as, with a gravity befitting the importance of her office, she would follow him around in a happy contented way, that took with

him immensely. And nowadays, no one ever saw
the old gentleman going out of a morning, when
Jasper was busy with his lessons, without Phronsie by his side, and many people turned to see the
portly figure with the handsome head bent to
catch the prattle of a little sunny-haired child,
who trotted along, clasping his hand confidingly.
And nearly all of them stopped to gaze the second
time before they could convince themselves that
it was really that stately old Mr. King of whom
they had heard so much.

And now the accumulation of dolls in the house
became something alarming, for Mr. King, observing Phronsie's devotion to her family, thought
there couldn't possibly be too many of them; so
he scarcely ever went out without bringing home
one at least to add to them, until Phronsie had
such a remarkable collection as would have driven
almost any other child nearly crazy with delight.
She, however, regarded them something in the
light of a grave responsibility, to be taken care of
tenderly, to be watched over carefully as to the
right kind of bringing up; and to have small
morals and manners taught in just the correct
way.

Phronsie was playing in the corner of Mrs. Whitney's little boudoir, engaged in sending out invitations for an elaborate tea-party to be given by one of the dolls, when Polly rushed in with consternation in her tones, and dismay written all over her face.

" What is it, dear? " asked Mrs. Whitney, looking up from her embroidery.

" Why," said Polly, " how *could* I! I don't see —but I've forgotten to write to mamsie to-day; it's Wednesday, you know, and there's Monsieur coming." And poor Polly looked out in despair to see the lively little music-teacher advancing towards the house at an alarming rate of speed.

" That is because you were helping Van so long last evening over his lessons," said Mrs. Whitney; " I am so sorry."

" Oh, no," cried Polly, honestly, " I had plenty of time—but I forgot 'twas mamsie's day. What *will* she do! "

" You will have to let it go now till the afternoon, dear; there's no other way; it can go in the early morning mail."

" O dear! " sighed Polly, " I suppose I must." And she went down to meet Monsieur with a very distressed little heart.

Phronsie laid down the note of invitation she was scribbling, and stopped to think; and a moment or two after, at a summons from a caller, Mrs. Whitney left the room.

"I know I ought to," said Phronsie to herself and the dolls, "yes, I know I had; mamsie will feel, oh! so bad, when she doesn't get Polly's letter; and I know the way, I do, truly."

She got up and went to the window, where she thought a minute; and then, coming back, she took up her little stubby pencil, and bending over a small bit of paper, she commenced to trace, with laborious efforts and much hard breathing, some very queer hieroglyphics that to her seemed to be admirable, as at last she held them up with great satisfaction.

"Good-by," she said, then, getting up and bowing to the dolls, who sat among the interrupted invitations, "I won't be gone but a little bit of one minute," and she went out determinedly and shut the door.

Nobody saw the little figure going down the carriage drive, so of course nobody could stop her. When Phronsie got to the gateway she looked up and down the street carefully, each way.

"Yes," she said, at last, "it was down here, I'm

very sure, I went with grandpapa," and immediately turned down the wrong way, and went on
and on, grasping carefully her small, and by this
time rather soiled, bit of paper.

At last she reached the business street; and although she didn't come to the post-office, she
comforted herself by the thought: " It must bo
coming soon. I guess it's round this corner."

She kept turning corner after corner, until, at
last, a little anxious feeling began to tug at her
heart; and she began to think—" I wish I *could*
see Polly——"

And now, she had all she could do to get out
of the way of the crowds of people who were pouring up and down the thoroughfare. Everybody
jostled against her, and gave her a push. " O
dear! " thought Phronsie, " there's *such* a many
big people! " and then there was no time for
anything else but to stumble in and out, to keep
from being crushed completely beneath their feet.
At last, an old huckster woman, in passing along,
knocked off her bonnet with the end of her big
basket, which flew around and struck Phronsie's
head. Not stopping to look into the piteous
brown eyes, she strode on without a word. Phronsie turned in perfect despair to go down a street

that looked as if there might be room enough for her in it. Thoroughly frightened, she plunged over the crossing to reach it!

"*Look out!*" cried a ringing voice. "*Stop!*"

"The little girl'll be killed!" said others, with bated breath, as a powerful pair of horses, whose driver could not pull them up in time, dashed along just in front of her! With one cry, Phronsie sprang between their feet, and reached the opposite curbstone in safety!

The plunge brought her up against a knot of gentlemen who were standing talking on the corner.

"What's this!" asked one, whose back being next to the street, hadn't seen the commotion, as the small object dashed into their midst, and fell up against him.

"Didn't you see that narrow escape?" asked a second, whose face had paled in witnessing it. "This little girl was nearly killed a moment ago— careless driving enough!" And he put out his hand to catch the child.

"Bless me!" cried a third, whirling around suddenly, "bless me! you don't say so! why ——"

With a small cry, but gladsome and distinct in

its utterance, Phronsie gave one look—" Oh, *grandpapa!* " was all she could say.

" Oh! *where* "—Mr. King couldn't possibly have uttered another word, for then his breath gave out entirely, as he caught the small figure.

" I went to the post-office," said the child, clinging to him in delight, her tangled hair waving over the little white face, into which a faint pink color was quickly coming back. " Only it wouldn't come; and I walked and walked—where is it, grandpapa? " And Phronsie gazed up anxiously into the old gentleman's face.

" *She went to the post-office!* " turning around on the others fiercely, as if they had contradicted him—" Why, my child, what were you going to do? "

" Mamsie's letter," said Phronsie, holding up for inspection the precious bit, which by this time, was decidedly forlorn—" Polly couldn't write; and mamsie'd feel *so* bad not to get one—she would really," said the child, shaking her head very soberly, " for Polly said so."

" And you've been—oh! I can't *think* of it," said Mr. King, tenderly taking her up on his shoulder, " well, we must get home now, or I don't know *what* Polly will do! " And without stopping to say a word to his friends, he hailed a passing carriage, and putting Phronsie in, he commanded the driver to get them as quickly as possible to their destination.

In a few moments they were home. Mr. King pushed into the house with his burden. " Doesn't anybody know," he burst out, puffing up the stairs, and scolding furiously at every step, " enough to take better care of this child, than to have such goings on! "

" What is the matter, father? " asked Mrs. Whitney, coming up the stairs, after him. " What has happened out of the way? "

"Out of the way! " roared the old gentleman, irascibly, " well, if you want Phronsie racing off to the post-office by herself, and nearly getting killed, poor child! yes, Marian, I say nearly killed! " he continued.

" What *do* you mean? " gasped Mrs. Whitney.

" Why, where have you been? " asked the old gentleman, who wouldn't let Phronsie get down out of his arms, under any circumstances; so there she lay, poking up her head like a little bird, and trying to say she wasn't in the least hurt. " Where's everybody been not to know she'd

gone?" he exclaimed, "where's Polly—and Jasper—and all of them?"

"Polly's taking her music lesson," said Mrs. Whitney. "Oh, Phronsie, darling!" and she bent over the child in her father's arms, and nearly smothered her with kisses.

"'Twas a naughty horse," said Phronsie, sitting up straight and looking at her, "or I should have found the post-office; and I lost off my bonnet, too," she added, for the first time realizing it, putting her hand to her head; "a bad old woman knocked it off with a basket—and now mamsie won't get her letter!" and she waved the bit, which she still grasped firmly between her thumb and finger, sadly towards Mrs. Whitney.

"O dear!" groaned that lady, "how could we talk before her! But who would have thought it! Darling," and she took the little girl from her father's arms, who at last let her go, "don't think of your mamma's letter; we'll tell her how it was," and she sat down in the first chair that she could reach; while Phronsie put her tumbled little head down on the kind shoulder and gave a weary little sigh.

"It was *so* long," she said, "and my shoes hurt," and she stuck out the dusty little boots, that spoke pathetically of the long and unaccustomed tramp.

"Poor little lamb!" said Mr. King, getting down to unbutton them. "What a shame!" he mumbled, pulling off half of the buttons in his frantic endeavors to get the shoes off quickly.

But Phronsie never heard the last of his objurgations, for in a minute she was fast asleep! The tangled hair fell off from the tired little face; the breathing came peaceful and regular, and with her little hand fast clasped in Mrs. Whitney's she slept on and on.

Polly came flying up-stairs, two or three at a time, and humming a scrap of her last piece that she had just conquered.

"Phronsie," she called, with a merry little laugh, "where ——"

"Hush!" said Mr. King, warningly, and then just because he couldn't explain there without waking Phronsie up, he took hold of Polly's two shoulders and marched her into the next room, where he carefully closed the door, and told her the whole thing, using his own discretion about the very narrow escape she had passed through. He told enough, however, for Polly to see what had been so near them: and she stood there so quietly, alternately paling and flushing as he proceeded, till at last, when he finished, Mr. King was frightened almost to death at the sight of her face.

"O goodness me, Polly!" he said, striding up to her, and then fumbling around on the table to find a glass of water, "you are not going to faint, are you? Phronsie's all well now, she isn't hurt in the least, I assure you; I assure you—where *is* a glass of water! Marian ought to see that there's some here—that stupid Jane!" and in utter bewilderment he was fussing here and there, knocking down so many things in general, that the noise soon brought Polly to, with a little gasp.

"Oh, don't mind me, dear Mr. King—I'm—all well."

"So you are," said the old gentleman, setting up a toilet-bottle that he had knocked over, "so you are; I didn't think you'd go and tumble over, Polly, I really didn't," and he beamed admiringly down on her.

And then Polly crept away to Mrs. Whitney's side, where she flung herself down on the floor, to watch the little sleeping figure. Her hand was gathered up, into the kind one that held Phronsie's: and there they watched and waited.

"O dear!" said Phronsie, suddenly, turning over with a little sigh, and bobbing up her head to look at Polly; "I'm so hungry! I haven't had anything to eat in ever an' ever so long, Polly!" and she gazed at her with a very injured countenance.

"So you must be," said Mrs. Whitney, kissing the flushed little face. "Polly must ring the bell for Jane to bring this little bird some crumbs."

"Can I have a great many?" asked Phronsie, lifting her eyes, with the dewy look of sleep still lingering in them, "as many as *two* birdies?"

"Yes, dear," said Mrs. Whitney, laughing; "I think as many as *three* little birdies could eat, Phronsie."

"Oh," said Phronsie, and leaned back satisfied, while Polly gave the order, which was presently executed by Jane with a well-filled tray.

"Now," said Jappy, when he heard the account of the adventure, "*I* say that letter ought to go to your mother, Polly."

"Oh," said Polly, "it would scare mamsie 'most to death, Jappy!"

"Don't tell her the whole," said Jasper, quickly. "I didn't mean that—about the horses and all

that—but only enough to let her see how Phronsie tried to get it to her."

" And I'm going to write to your brother Joel,"
said Van, drawing up to the library table; " I'll
scare *him*, Polly, I guess; he won't tell your
mother."

" Your crow-tracks'll scare him enough without
anything else," pleasantly remarked Percy, who
really could write very nicely, while Polly broke
out in an agony:

" Oh, no, Van, you mustn't! you mustn't! "

" If Van does," said Jasper, decidedly, " it'll be
the last time he'll write to the ' Brown House,' I
can tell him; and besides, he'll go to Coventry."
This had the desired effect.

" Let's all write," said Polly.

So a space on the table was cleared, and the
children gathered around it, when there was great
scratching of pens and clearing of ideas; which
presently resulted in a respectable budget of letters, into which Phronsie's was lovingly tucked in
the centre; and then they all filed out to put it
into the letter-box in the hall, for Thomas to mail
with the rest in the morning.

XXII

"AND I'll tell you, Marian, what I am going to do."

Mr. King's voice was pitched on a higher key than usual; and extreme determination was expressed in every line of his face. He had met Mrs. Whitney at the foot of the staircase, dressed for paying visits. "Oh, are you going out?" he said, glancing impatiently at her attire. "And I'd just started to speak to you on a matter of great importance. Of the greatest importance *indeed!*" he repeated, irritably, as he stood with one gloved hand resting on the balustrade.

"Oh, it's no matter, father," she replied, pleasantly; "if it's really important, I can postpone going for another day, and ——"

"*Really important!*" repeated the old gentleman, irascibly. "Haven't I just told you it's of the greatest importance? There's no time to be lost; and with my state of health, too, it's of the

296

utmost consequence that I shouldn't be troubled. It's very bad for me; I should think you would realize that, Marian."

" I'll tell Thomas to take the carriage directly back," said Mrs. Whitney, stepping to the door. " Or stay, father; I'll just run up and send the children out for a little drive. The horses ought to be used, you know," she said, lightly, preparing to run up to carry out the changed plan.

"Never mind that now," said Mr. King, abruptly. " I want you to give me your attention directly." And walking towards the library door, getting a fresh accession of impatience with every step, he beckoned her to follow.

But his progress was somewhat impeded by little Dick—or, rather, little Dick and Prince, who were standing at the top of the stairs to see Mrs. Whitney off. When he saw his mother retrace her steps, supposing her yielding to the urgent entreaties that he was sending after her to stay at home, the child suddenly changed his " Goodbys " to vociferous howls of delight, and speedily began to plunge down the stairs to welcome her.

But the staircase was long, and little Dick was in a hurry, and besides, Prince was in the way. The consequence was, nobody knew just how,

that a bumping noise struck into the conversation
that made the two below in the hall look up
quickly, to see the child and dog come rolling
over the stairs at a rapid rate.

"Goodness!" cried the old gentleman. "Here,
Thomas, *Thomas!*" But as that individual was
waiting patiently outside the door on the car-
riage-box, there was small hope of his being in
time to catch the boy, who was already in his
mother's arms, not quite clear by the suddenness
of the whole thing, as to how he came there.

"Oh! oh! Dicky's hurt!" cried somebody up
above—followed by every one within hearing distance, and all came rushing to the spot to ask a
thousand questions all in the same minute.

There sat Mrs. Whitney in one of the big covered chairs, with little Dick in her lap, and Prince
walking gravely around and around him with the
greatest expression of concern on his noble face.
Mr. King was storming up and down, and calling
on everybody to bring a "bowl of water, and
some brown paper; and *be quick!*" interpolated
with showers of blame on Prince for sitting on
the stairs, and tripping people up; while Dick
meanwhile was laughing and chatting, and enjoying the distinction of making so many people

run, and of otherwise being the object of so much attention.

"I don't think he was sitting on the stairs, father," said Jasper, who, when he saw that Dicky was really unhurt, began to vindicate his dog. "He never does that; do you, sir?" he said, patting the head that was lifted up to him, as if to be defended.

"And I expect we shall all be killed some day, Jasper," said Mr. King, warming with his subject, and forgetting all about the brown paper and water which he had ordered, and which was now waiting for him at his elbow, "just by that creature."

"He's the noblest ——" began Jasper, throwing his arms around his neck; an example which was immediately followed by the Whitney boys, and the two little Peppers. When Dick saw this, he began to struggle to get down to add himself to the number.

"Where's the brown paper?" began Mr. King, seeing this and whirling around suddenly. "Hasn't anybody brought it yet?"

"Here 'tis, sir," said Jane, handing him a generous supply.

"Oh, I don't want to," cried little Dick, in dis-

may, seeing his grandfather advance with an
enormous piece of paper, which, previously wet in
the bowl of water, was now unpleasantly clammy
and wet—" oh, no, I don't want to be all stuck
up with old horrid wet paper! "

" Hush, dear! " said his mamma, soothingly, as
Mr. King dropped it scientifically on his head,
" grandpapa wants to put it on—there "—and
then proceeded to paste another one over his left
eye.

" And I hope they'll all drop off," cried Dick,
savagely, shaking his head to facilitate matters.
" Yes, I do, every single one of 'em! " he added,
with an expression that seen under the brown bits
was anything but benign.

" Was Prince on the stairs, Dick? " asked Jasper, coming up and peering under his several
adornments. " Tell us how you fell."

" No," said little Dick, crossly, and giving his
head another shake. " He was up in the hall—O
dear, I want to get down," and he began to stretch
his legs and to struggle with so much energy that
two or three pieces fell off, and landed on the
floor, to his intense delight.

" And how did you fall, then? " asked Jasper,

perseveringly. "Can't you remember, Dicky, boy?"

"I pushed Princey," said Dick, feeling, with freedom from some of his encumbrances, more disposed for conversation, "and made him go ahead—and then I fell on top of him—that's all."

"I guess Prince has saved him, father," cried Jasper, turning around with eyes full of pride and love on the dog, who was trying as hard as he could to tell all the children how much he enjoyed their caresses.

And so it all came about that the consultation so summarily interrupted was never held. For, as Mrs. Whitney was about to retire that evening, Mr. King rapped at her door on his way to bed.

"Oh," he said, popping in his head, in response to her invitation to come in, "it's nothing—only I thought I'd just tell you a word or two about what I've decided to do."

"Do you mean what you wanted to see me about this afternoon?" asked Mrs. Whitney, who hadn't thought of it since. "Do come in, father."

"It's of no consequence," said the old gentleman; "no consequence at all," he repeated, waving his hand emphatically, "because I've made up my mind and arranged all my plans—it's only about the Peppers ——"

"The Peppers?" repeated Mrs. Whitney.

"Yes. Well, the fact of it is, I'm going to have them here for a visit—the whole of them, you understand; that's all there is to it. And I shall go down to see about all the arrangements—Jasper and I—day after to-morrow," said the old gentleman, as if he owned the whole Pepper family, and was the only responsible person to be consulted about their movements.

"Will they come?" asked Mrs. Whitney, doubtfully.

"Come? of course," said Mr. King, sharply, "there isn't any other way; or else Mrs. Pepper will be sending for her children—and of course you know, Marian, we couldn't allow *that*—well, that's all; so good night," and the door closed on his retreating footsteps.

And so Polly and Phronsie soon knew that mamsie and the boys were to be invited! And then the grand house, big as it was, didn't seem large enough to contain them.

"I declare," said Jasper, next day, when they had been laughing and planning till they were all as merry as grigs, "if this old dungeon doesn't begin to seem a little like 'the Little Brown House,' Polly."

" 'Twon't," answered Polly, hopping around on one toe, followed by Phronsie, "till mamsie and the boys get here, Jasper King! "

"Well, they'll be here soon," said Jappy, pleased at Polly's exultation over it, "for we're going to-morrow to do the inviting."

"And Polly's to write a note to slip into Marian's," said Mr. King, putting his head in at the door. "And if you want your mother to come, child, why, you'd better mention it as strong as you can."

"I'm going to write," said Phronsie, pulling up after a prolonged skip, all out of breath. "I'm going to write, and beg mamsie dear. *Then* she'll come, I guess."

"I guess she will," said Mr. King, looking at her. "You go on, Phronsie, and write; and that letter shall go straight in my coat pocket alone by itself."

"Will it? " asked Phronsie, coming up to him, " and nobody will take it out till you give it to mamsie? "

"No, nobody shall touch it," said the old gentleman, stooping to kiss the upturned face, " till I put it into her own hand."

" Then," said Phronsie, in the greatest satisfaction, " I'm going to write this very one minute! " and she marched away to carry her resolve into immediate execution.

Before they got through they had quite a bundle of invitations and pleadings; for each of the three boys insisted on doing his part, so that when they were finally done up in an enormous envelope and put into Mr. King's hands, he told them with a laugh that there was no use for Jappy and himself to go, as those were strong enough to win almost anybody's consent.

However, the next morning they set off, happy in their hopes, and bearing the countless messages, which the children would come up every now and then to entrust to them, declaring that they had forgotten to put them in the letters.

" You'd have needed an express-wagon to carry the letters if you had put them all in," at last cried Jasper. " You've given us a bushel of things to remember."

" And oh! don't forget to ask Ben to bring Cherry," cried Polly the last minute, as they were driving off, although she had put it in her letter at least a dozen times; "and O dear! of course the flowers can't come."

"We have plenty here," said Jasper. "You wouldn't know what to do with them, Polly."

"Well, I do wish mamsie would give some to kind Mrs. Henderson, then," said Polly, on the steps, clasping her hands anxiously, while Jasper told Thomas to wait till he heard the rest of the message, "and to grandma—you know Grandma Bascom; she was so good to us," she said, impulsively. "And oh! don't let her forget to carry some to dear, *dear* Doctor Fisher; and don't forget to give him our love, Jappy; *don't* forget that!" and Polly ran down the steps to the carriage door, where she gazed up imploringly to the boy's face.

"I guess I won't," cried Jasper, impulsively, "when I think how he saved your eyes, Polly!"

"And don't let mamsie forget to carry some in to good old Mr. and Mrs. Beebe in town—where Phronsie got her shoes, you know; that is, if mamsie can," she added, remembering how very busy her mother would be.

"I'll carry them myself," said Jasper; "we're going to stay over till the next day, you know."

"Oh!" cried Polly, radiant as a rose, "will you, really, Jappy? you're *so* good!"

"Yes, I will," said Jasper, "everything you want done, Polly; anything else?" he asked, quickly, as Mr. King, impatient to be off, showed unmistakable symptoms of hurrying up Thomas.

"Oh, no," said Polly, "only do look at the Little Brown House, Jasper, as much as you can," and Polly left the rest unfinished. Jasper seemed to understand, however, for he smiled brightly as he said, looking into the brown eyes, "I'll do it all, Polly; every single thing." And then they were off.

Mamsie and the boys! could Polly ever wait till the next afternoon that would bring the decision?

Long before it was possibly time for the carriage to come back from the depot, Polly, with Phronsie and the three boys, who, improving Jasper's absence, had waited upon her with the grace and persistence of cavaliers of the olden time, were drawn up at the old stone gateway.

"O dear!" said Van, with an impatient fling; "they *never* will come!"

"Won't they, Polly?" asked Phronsie, anxiously, and standing quite still.

"Deary me, yes," said Polly, with a little laugh. "Van only means they'll be a good while, Phronsie. They're *sure* to come some time."

"Oh!" said Phronsie, quite relieved; and she commenced her capering again in extreme enjoyment.

"I'm going," said little Dick, "to run down and meet them."

Accordingly off he went, and was immediately followed by Percy, who started with the laudable desire of bringing him back; but finding it so very enjoyable, he stayed himself and frolicked with Dick, till the others, hearing the fun, all took hold of hands and flew off to join them.

"Now," said Polly, when they had recovered their breath a little, "let's all turn our backs to the road; and the minute we hear the carriage we must whirl round; and the one who sees them first can *ask* first, 'Is mamsie coming?'"

"All right," cried the boys.

"Turn round, Dick," said Percy, with a little shove, for Dick was staring with all his might right down the road. And so they all turned around and looked like five statues set up to grace the sidewalk.

"Suppose a big dog should come," suggested Van, pleasantly, " and snap at our backs! "

At this little Dick gave a small howl, and turned around in a fright.

"There isn't any dog coming," said Polly. "What does make you say such awful things, Van?"

"I hear a noise," said Phronsie; and so they all whirled around in expectation. But it proved to be only a market-wagon coming at a furious pace down the road, with somebody's belated dinner. So they all had to whirl back again as before. The consequence was that when the carriage did come nobody heard it.

Jasper, looking out, was considerably astonished to see, drawn up in solemn array with their backs to the road, five children, who stood as if completely petrified.

"What in the world! " he began, and called to Thomas to stop, whose energetic " *Whoa!* " reaching the ears of the frozen line, caused it to break ranks, and spring into life at an alarming rate.

"Oh, *is* she coming, Jappy? *Is* she? *Is* she? " they all screamed together, swarming up to the carriage door, and over the wheels.

"Yes," said Jasper, looking at Polly.

At that, Phronsie made a little cheese and sat right down on the pavement in an ecstasy.

"Get in here, all of you," said Jasper, merrily; "help Polly in first. For shame, Dick! don't scramble so."

"Dick always shoves," said Percy, escorting Polly up with quite an air.

"I don't, either," said Dick; "you pushed me awful, just a little while ago," he added, indignantly.

"Do say 'awfully,'" corrected Van, crowding up to get in. "You leave off your ly's so," he finished, critically.

"I don't know anything about any lees," said little Dick, who, usually so good-natured, was now thoroughly out of temper; "I want to get in and go home," and he showed evident symptoms of breaking into a perfect roar.

"There," said Polly, lifting him up, "there he goes! now—one, two, three!" and little Dick was spun in so merrily that the tears changed into a happy laugh.

"Now then, bundle in, all the rest of you," put in Mr. King, who seemed to be in the best of spirits. "That's it; go on, Thomas!"

"When are they coming?" Polly found time to ask, in the general jumble.

"In three weeks from to-morrow," said Jasper. "And everything's all right, Polly! and the whole of them, Cherry and all, will be here then!"

"*Oh!*" cried Polly.

"Here we are!" screamed Van, jumping out almost before the carriage had stopped. "Mamma, mamma," he shouted to Mrs. Whitney in the doorway, "the Peppers are coming, and the Little Brown House, too!—everything and everybody!"

"They are!" said Percy, as wild as his brother; "and everything's just splendid! Jappy said so."

"Everything's coming," said little Dick, tumbling up the steps—"and the bird—and—and ——"

"And mamsie!" finished Phronsie, impatient to add her part—while Polly didn't say anything —only looked.

Three weeks! "I *can't* wait!" thought Polly at first, in counting over the many hours before the happy day would come. But on Jasper's suggesting that they should all do something to get ready for the visitors, and have a general trimming up with vines and flowers besides, the time passed away much more rapidly than was feared.

Polly chose a new and more difficult piece of music to learn to surprise mamsie. Phronsie had aspired to an elaborate pincushion, that was nearly done, made of bits of worsted and canvas, over whose surface she had wandered according to her own sweet will, in a way charming to behold.

"I don't know what to do," said Van, in despair, "'cause I don't know what she'd like."

"Can't you draw her a little picture?" asked Polly. "She'd like that."

"Does she like pictures?" asked Van, with the greatest interest.

"Yes, indeed!" said Polly, "I guess you'd think so if you could see her!"

"I know what *I* shall do," with a dignified air said Percy, who couldn't draw, and therefore looked down on all Van's attempts with the greatest scorn. "And it won't be any old pictures, either," he added.

"What is it, old fellow?" asked Jasper. "Tell on, now, your grand plan."

"No, I'm not going to tell," said Percy, with the greatest secrecy, "until the very day."

"What will *you* do, sir?" asked Jasper, pulling one of Dick's ears, who stood waiting to speak, as if his mind was made up, and wouldn't be changed for any one!

"I shall give Ben one of my kitties—the littlest and the best!" he said, with heroic self-sacrifice.

A perfect shout greeted this announcement.

"Fancy Ben going round with one of those awful little things," whispered Jappy to Polly, who shook at the very thought.

"Don't laugh! Oh, it's dreadful to laugh at him, Jappy," she said, when she could get voice enough.

"No, I *sha'n't* tell," said Percy, when the fun had subsided; who, finding that no one teased him to divulge his wonderful plan, kept trying to harrow up their feelings by parading it.

"You *needn't*, then," screamed Van, who was nearly dying to know. "I don't believe it's so very dreadful much, anyway."

"What's yours, Jappy?" asked Polly. "I know yours will be just splendid."

"Oh, no, it isn't," said Jasper, smiling brightly, "but as I didn't know what better I could do, I'm going to get a little stand, and then beg some flowers of Turner to fill it, and ——"

"Why, that's *mine!*" screamed Percy, in the

greatest disappointment. "That's just what *I* was going to do!"

"Hoh, hoh!" shouted Van; "I thought you wouldn't tell, Mr. Percy! hoh, hoh!"

"Hoh, hoh!" echoed Dick.

"Hush," said Jappy. "Why, Percy, I didn't know you had thought of that," he said, kindly. "Well, then, you do it, and I'll take something else. I don't care as long as Mrs. Pepper gets them."

"I didn't *exactly* mean that," began Percy; "mine was roots and little flowers growing."

"He means what he gets in the woods," said Polly, explaining; "don't you, Percy?"

"Yes," said the boy. "And then I was going to put stones and things in among them to make them look pretty."

"And they will," cried Jasper. "Go ahead, Percy, they'll look real pretty, and then Turner will give you some flowers for the stand, I know; I'll ask him to-morrow."

"Will you?" cried Percy, "that'll be fine!"

"Mine is the best," said Van, just at this juncture; but it was said a little anxiously, as he saw how things were prospering with Percy; "for my

flowers in the picture will always be there, and
your old roots and things will die."

"What will yours be, then, Jappy?" asked
Polly, very soberly. "The stand of flowers would
have been just lovely! and you do fix them so
nicely," she added, sorrowfully.

"Oh, I'll find something else," said Jappy,
cheerfully, who had quite set his heart on giving
the flowers. "Let me see—I might carve her a
bracket."

"Do," cried Polly, clapping her hands enthusiastically. "And do carve a little bird, like the
one you did on your father's."

"I will," said Jasper, "just exactly like it.
Now, we have something to do, before we welcome
the 'Little Brown House' people—so let's fly at
it, and the time won't seem so long."

And at last the day came when they could all
say—To-morrow they'll be here!

Well, the vines were all up, and pots of lovely
climbing ferns, and all manner of pretty green
things had been arranged and rearranged a dozen
times till everything was pronounced perfect; and
a big green "Welcome" over the library door,
made of laurel leaves, by the patient fingers of all

the children, stared down into their admiring eyes as much as to say, " I'll do *my* part! "

" O dear! " said Phronsie, when evening came, and the children were, as usual, assembled on the rug before the fire, their tongues running wild with anticipation and excitement, " I don't mean to go to bed at all, Polly; I don't, truly."

" Oh, yes, you do," said Polly, laughing; " then you'll be all fresh and rested to see mamsie when she does come."

" Oh, no," said Phronsie, shaking her head soberly, and speaking in an injured tone. " I'm not one bit tired, Polly; not one bit."

" You needn't go yet, Phronsie," said Polly. " You can sit up half an hour longer, if you want to."

" But I don't want to go to bed at all," said the child, anxiously, " for then I may be asleep when mamsie comes, Polly."

" She's afraid she won't wake up," said Percy, laughing. " Oh, there'll be oceans of time before they come, Phronsie."

" What *is* oceans? " asked Phronsie, coming up and looking at him, doubtfully.

" He means mamsie won't get here till afternoon," said Polly, catching her up and kissing her; "then I guess you'll be awake, Phronsie, pet."

So Phronsie allowed herself to be persuaded, at the proper time, to be carried off and inducted into her little nightgown. And when Polly went up to bed, she found the little pincushion, with its hieroglyphics, that she had insisted on taking to bed with her, still tightly grasped in the fat little hand.

"She'll roll over and muss it," thought Polly; "and then she'll feel badly in the morning. I guess I'd better lay it on the bureau."

So she drew it carefully away, without awaking the little sleeper, and placed it where she knew Phronsie's eyes would rest on it the first thing in the morning.

It was going on towards the middle of the night when Phronsie, whose exciting dreams of mamsie and the boys wouldn't let her rest quietly, woke up; and in the very first flash she thought of her cushion.

"Why, where ——" she said, in the softest little tones, only half-awake, "why, Polly, where is it?" and she began to feel all around her pillow to see if it had fallen down there.

But Polly's brown head with its crowd of anticipations and busy plans, was away off in dreamland, and she breathed on and on perfectly motionless.

" I guess I better," said Phronsie to herself, now thoroughly awake and sitting up in bed, "not wake her up. Poor Polly's tired; I can find it myself, I know I can."

So she slipped out of bed, and prowling around on the floor, felt all about for the little cushion.

" 'Tisn't here, oh, no, 'tisn't," she sighed at last, and getting up, she stood still a moment, lost in thought. " Maybe Jane's put it out in the hall," she said, as a bright thought struck her. " I can get it there," and out she pattered over the soft carpet to the table at the end of the long hall, where Jane often placed the children's playthings over night. As she was coming back after her fruitless search, she stopped to peep over the balustrade down the fascinating flight of stairs, now so long and dark. Just then a little faint ray of light shot up from below, and met her eyes.

" Why! " she said, in gentle surprise, " they're all down-stairs! I guess they're making something for mamsie—I'm going to see."

So, carefully picking her way over the stairs

with her little bare feet, and holding on to the balustrade at every step, she went slowly down, guided by the light, which, as she neared the bottom of the flight, she saw came from the library door.

"Oh, isn't it funny!" and she gave a little happy laugh. "They won't know I'm coming!" and now the soft little feet went pattering over the thick carpet, until she stood just within the door. There she stopped perfectly still.

Two dark figures, big and powerful, were bending over something that Phronsie couldn't see, between the two long windows. A lantern on the floor flung its rays over them as they were busily occupied; and the firelight from the dying coals made the whole stand out distinctly to the gaze of the motionless little figure.

"*Why!* what are you doing with my grandpapa's things?"

The soft, clear notes fell like a thunderbolt upon the men. With a start they brought themselves up, and stared—only to see a little white-robed figure, with its astonished eyes uplifted with childlike, earnest gaze, as she waited for her answer.

For an instant they were powerless to move;

and stood as if frozen to the spot, till Phronsie moving one step forward, piped:

"Naughty men, to touch my dear grandpapa's things!"

With a smothered cry one of them started forward with arm uplifted; but the other sprang like a cat and intercepted the blow.

"Stop!" was all he said. A noise above the stairs—a rushing sound through the hall! Something will save Phronsie, for the household is aroused! The two men sprang through the window, having no time to catch the lantern or their tools, as Polly, followed by one and another, rushed in and surrounded the child.

"What!" gasped Polly, and got no farther.

"STOP, THIEF!" roared Mr. King, hurrying over the stairs.

The children, frightened at the strange noises, began to cry and scream, as they came running through the halls to the spot. Jasper rushed for the men-servants.

And there stood Phronsie, surrounded by the pale group.

"'Twas two naughty men," she said, lifting her little face with the grieved, astonished look still in the big brown eyes, " and they were touching my grandpapa's things, Polly! "

" I should think they were," said Jasper, runing over amongst the few scattered tools and the lantern, to the windows, where, on the floor, was a large table-cover hastily caught up by the corners, into which a vast variety of silver, jewelry, and quantities of costly articles were gathered ready for flight. " They've broken open your safe, father! " he cried, in excitement, " see! "

" And they put up their hand—one man did," went on Phronsie. " And the other said ' Stop! ' —oh, Polly, you hurt me! " she cried, as Polly, unable to bear the strain any longer, held her so tightly she could hardly breathe.

" Go on," said Jasper, " how did they look? "

" All black," said the child, pushing back her wavy hair and looking at him, " very all black, Japser."

" And their faces, Phronsie? " said Mr. King, getting down on his old knees on the floor beside her. " Bless me! somebody else ask her, I *can't* talk! "

" How did their faces look, Phronsie dear? " asked Jasper, taking one of the cold hands in his. " Can't you think? "

"Oh!" said Phronsie—and then she gave a funny little laugh, "two big holes, Japser, that's all they had!"

"She means they were masked," whispered Jasper.

"What did you get up for?" Mrs. Whitney asked. "Dear child, what made you get out of bed?"

"Why, my cushion-pin," said Phronsie, looking worried at once. "I couldn't find it, and——"

But just at this, without a bit of warning, Polly tumbled over in a dead faint.

And then it was all confusion again.

And so, on the following afternoon, it turned out that the Peppers, about whose coming there had been so many plans and expectations, just walked in as if they had always lived there. The greater excitement completely swallowed up the less!

XXIII

WHICH TREATS OF A GOOD MANY MATTERS

" PHOOH! " said Joel, a few mornings after the
emptying of the Little Brown House into the big
one, when he and Van were rehearsing for the
fiftieth time all the points of the eventful night,
" phooh! if I'd been here they wouldn't have got
away, I guess! "

" What would *you* have done? " asked Van,
bristling up at this reflection on their courage, and
squaring up to him. " What would you have
done, Joel Pepper? "

" I'd a-pitched right into 'em—like—everything! " said Joel, valiantly; " and a-caught 'em!
Yes, every single one of the bunglers! "

" The *what?* " said Van, bursting into a loud
laugh.

" The bunglers," said Joel, with a red face.
" That's what you said they were, anyway," he
added, positively.

" I said *burglars,*" said Van, doubling up with
amusement, while Joel stood, a little sturdy figure,

regarding him with anything but a sweet countenance.

"Well, anyway, I'd 'a' caught 'em, so there!" he said, as Van at last showed signs of coming out of his fit of laughter, and got up and wiped his eyes.

"How'd you have caught them?" asked Van, scornfully surveying the square little country figure before him. "You can't hit any."

"Can't?" said Joel, the black eyes flashing volumes, and coming up in front of Van. "You'd better believe I can, Van Whitney!"

"Come out in the back yard and try, then," said Van, hospitably, perfectly delighted at the prospect, and flying along towards the door. "Come right out and try."

"All right!" said Joel, following sturdily, equally delighted to show his skill.

"There," said Van, taking off his jacket, and flinging it on the grass, while Joel immediately followed suit with his little homespun one. "Now we can begin perfectly splendid! I won't hit hard," he added, patronizingly, as both boys stood ready.

"Hit as hard as you've a-mind to," said Joel, "I'm a-going to."

"Oh, *you* may," said Van, politely, "because you're company. All right—now!"

So at it they went. Before very many minutes were over, Van relinquished all ideas of treating his company with extra consideration, and was only thinking how he could possibly hold his own with the valiant little country lad. Oh, if he could only be called to his lessons—*anything* that would summon him into the house! Just then a window above their heads was suddenly thrown up, and his mamma's voice in natural surprise and distress called quickly: "Children, what are you doing? Oh, Van, how could you!"

Both contestants turned around suddenly. Joel looked up steadily. "We're a-hitting, ma'am; he said I couldn't, and so we came out and ——"

"Oh, Vanny," said Mrs. Whitney, reproachfully, "to treat a little guest in this way!"

"I wanted to," said Joel, cheerfully; "'twas great fun. Let's begin again, Van!"

"We mustn't," said Van, readily giving up the charming prospect, and beginning to edge quickly towards the house. "Mamma wouldn't like it, you know. He hits splendidly, mamma," he added, generously, looking up. "He does, really."

"And so does Van," cried Joel, his face glowing at the praise. "We'll come out every day," he added, slipping into his jacket, and turning enthusiastically back to Van.

"And perhaps he *could* have pitched into the burglars," finished Van, ignoring the invitation, and tumbling into his jacket with alarming speed.

"I know I could!" cried Joel, scampering after him into the house. "If I'd only been here!"

"Where's Ben?" asked Van, bounding into the hall, and flinging himself down on one of the chairs. "O dear! I'm so hot! Say, Joe, where *do* you s'pose Ben is?"

"I don't know," replied Joel, who didn't even puff.

"I saw him a little while ago with master Percy," said Jane, who was going through the hall.

"There, now! and they've gone off somewhere," cried Van, in extreme irritation, and bouncing up quickly. "I know they have. Which way did they go, Jane? And how long ago?"

"Oh, I don't know," replied Jane, carelessly, "half an hour, maybe; and they didn't go anywhere as I see, at least they were talking at the door, and I was going up-stairs."

"Right here?" cried Van, and stamping with his foot to point out the exact place; "at *this* door, Jane?"

"Yes, yes," said Jane, "at that very door," and then she went into the dining-room to her work.

"O dear me!" cried Van, and flying out on the veranda, he began to peer wildly up and down the drive. "And they've gone to some splendid place, I know, and wouldn't tell us. That's just like Percy!" he added, vindictively, "he's *always* stealing away! don't you see them, Joel? oh, do come out and look!"

"'Tisn't any use," said Joel, coolly, sitting down on the chair Van had just vacated, and swinging his feet comfortably; "they're miles away if they've been gone half an hour. *I'm* going up-stairs," and he sprang up, and energetically pranced to the stairs.

"They aren't up-stairs!" screamed Van, in scorn, bounding into the hall. "Don't go; I know that they've gone down to the museum!"

"The *what?*" exclaimed Joel, nearly at the top, peering over the railing. "What's that you said —what is it?"

"A museum," shouted Van, "and it's a perfectly elegant place, Joel Pepper, and Percy knows

I like to go; and now he's taken Ben off; and he'll show him all the things! and they'll all be old when *I* take him—and—and—oh! I hope the snakes will bite him! " he added, trying to think of something bad enough.

" Do they have snakes there? " asked Joel, staring.

" Yes, they do," snapped out Van. " They have everything! "

" Well, they sha'n't bite *Ben!* " cried Joel, in terror. " Oh! do you suppose they will? " and he whirled around on the stairs, and looked at Van.

" No," said Van, " they won't bite—what's the matter, Joe? "

" Oh, they may! " said Joel, his face working, and screwing both fists into his eyes; at last he burst into a torrent of sobs " Oh, don't let 'em, Van—*don't!* "

" Why, they *can't*," said Van, in an emphatic voice, running up the stairs to Joel's side, frightened to death at his tears. Then he began to shake his jacket-sleeve violently to bring him back to reason. " Wait, Joe! oh, do stop! O dear, what shall I do? I tell you they *can't* bite," he screamed as loud as he could into his ear.

"You said—you—hoped—they—would,"—said Joel's voice, in smothered tones.

"Well, they won't, anyway," said Van, decidedly. "'Cause they're all stuffed—so there, now!"

"Ain't they alive?" asked Joel, bringing one black eye into sight from behind his chubby hands.

"No," said Van, "they're just as dead as anything, Joel Pepper—been dead years! and there's old crabs there, too, old dead crabs—and they're just lovely! Of *such* a lot of eggs as they've got! And there are shells and bugs and stones—and an *awful* old crocodile, and——"

"O dear!" sighed Joel, perfectly overcome at such a vision, and sitting down on the stairs to think. "Well, mamsie'll know where Ben is," he said, springing up. "And then I tell you, Van, we'll just tag 'em!"

"So she will," cried Van. "Why didn't we think of that before?"

"I did," said Joel. "That was where I was going."

Without any more ado they rushed into Mrs. Pepper's big, sunny room, there to see, seated at the square table between the two large windows, the two lost ones bending over what seemed to be an object of the greatest importance, for Polly was hanging over Ben's shoulder with intense pride and delight, which she couldn't possibly conceal, and Davie was crowded as near as he could get to Percy's elbow.

Phronsie and little Dick were perched comfortably on the corner of the table, surveying the whole scene in quiet rapture; and Mrs. Pepper, with her big mending-basket, was ensconced over by the deep window-seat just on the other side of the room, underneath Cherry's cage, and looking up between quick energetic stitches, over at the busy group, with the most placid expression on her face.

" *Oh!*—what are you doing? " cried Joel, flying up to them. " Let us see, do, Ben! "

" What is it? " exclaimed Van, squeezing in between Percy and Ben.

" Don't ——" began Percy. " There, see, you've knocked his elbow and spoilt it! "

" Oh, no, he hasn't," said Ben, putting down his pencil, and taking up a piece of rubber. " There, see, it all comes out—as good as ever."

" Isn't it just *elegant?* " exclaimed Percy, in the

most pleased tone, and wriggling his toes under
the table to express his satisfaction.

"Yes," said Van, craning his neck to get a
better view of the picture, now nearly completed,
"it's perfectly splendid. How'd you do it, Ben?"

"I don't know," replied Ben, with a smile, carefully shading in a few last touches. "It just
drew itself."

"'Tisn't anything to what he *can* do," said
Polly, standing up as tall as she could, and beaming at Ben, "he used to draw most beautifully at
home."

"Better than this?" asked Van, with great respect, and taking up the picture, after some de-
mur on Percy's part, and examining it critically.
"I don't believe it, Polly."

"Phooh; he did!" exclaimed Joel, looking over
his shoulder at a wonderful view of a dog in an
extremely excited state of mind, running down an
interminable hill to bark at a locomotive and train
of cars whizzing along a curve in the foreground.
"Lots better'n that! Ben can do *anything!*" he
added, in an utterly convincing way.

"Now give it back," cried Percy, holding out
his hand in alarm. "I'm going to ask mamma to
have it framed; and then I shall hang it right over

my bed," he finished, as Van reluctantly gave up the treasure.

"Did you draw all the time in the Little Brown House?" asked Van, lost in thought. "How I wish I'd been there!"

"O my, no!" cried Polly, with a little skip, turning away to laugh. "He didn't have hardly any time, and——"

"Why not?" asked Percy.

"'Cause there were things to do," said Polly. "But sometimes when it rained, and he couldn't go out and work, and there wasn't anything to do in the house—then we'd have—oh!" and she drew a long breath at the memory, "such a time, you can't think!"

"Didn't you wish it would always rain?" asked Van, still gazing at the picture.

"Goodness, no!" began Polly.

"I didn't," broke in Joel, in horror. "I wouldn't 'a' had it rain for anything!—only once in a while," he added, as he thought of the good times that Polly had spoken of.

"'Twas nice outdoors," said little Davie, reflectively; "and nice inside, too." And then he glanced over to his mother, who gave him a smile in return. "And 'twas nice *always*."

"Well," said Van, returning to the picture, "I do wish you'd tell me how to draw, Ben. I can't do anything but flowers," he said, in a discouraged way.

"Flowers aren't anything," said Percy, pleasantly. "That's girl's work; but dogs and horses and cars—those are just *good!*"

"Will you, Ben?" asked Van, looking down into the big blue eyes, so kindly turned up to his.

"Yes, indeed, I will," cried Ben, "that is, all I know; 'tisn't much, but everything I can, I'll tell you."

"Then I can learn, can't I?" cried Van, joyfully.

"Oh, tell me, too, Ben," cried Percy, "will you? I want to learn too."

"And me!" cried Dick, bending forward, nearly upsetting Phronsie as he did so. "Yes, say I may, Ben, *do!*"

"You're too little," began Percy. But Ben nodded his head at Dick, which caused him to clap his hands and return to his original position, satisfied.

"Well, I guess we're going to, too," said Joel, "Dave an' me; there isn't anybody going to learn without *us.*"

" Of course not," said Polly, " Ben wouldn't leave you out, Joey."

Phronsie sat quite still all this time, on the corner of the table, her feet tucked up under her, and her hands clasped in her lap, and never said a word. But Ben looking up, saw the most grieved expression settling on her face, as the large eyes were fixed in wonder on the faces before her.

" And there's my pet," he cried, in enthusiasm, and reaching over the table, he caught hold of one of the little fat hands. " Why, we couldn't think of getting along without *her!* She shall learn to draw—she shall! "

" *Really,* Bensie? " said Phronsie, the sunlight breaking all over the gloomy little visage, to set the brown eyes dancing. " Real, true, splendid pictures? "

" Yes, the splendidest," said Ben, " the very splendidest pictures, Phronsie Pepper, you evd saw! "

" *Oh!* " cried Phronsie; and before any one knew what she was about, she tripped right into the middle of the table, over the papers and everything, and gave a happy little whirl!

" My senses, Phronsie! " cried Polly, catching

her up and hugging her; " you mustn't dance **on** the table."

" I'm going to learn," said Phronsie, coming out of Polly's embrace, " to draw whole pictures, all alone by myself—Ben said so! "

" I know it," said Polly, " and then you shall draw one for mamsie—you shall! "

" I will," said Phronsie, dreadfully excited; " I'll draw her a cow and two chickens, Polly, just like Grandma Bascom's! "

" Yes," whispered Polly, " but don't you tell her yet till you get it done, Phronsie."

" I won't," said Phronsie, in the loudest of tones —but putting her mouth close to Polly's ear. " And then she'll be *so* s'prised, Polly! won't she? "

Just then came Jasper's voice at the door. " Can I come in? "

" Oh, do, Jappy," cried Polly, rushing along with Phronsie in her arms to open the door. " We're so glad you're home! "

" So am I," said Jasper, coming in, his face flushed and his eyes sparkling; " I thought father never would be through down-town, Polly! "

" We're going to learn to draw," said Percy, over by the table, who wouldn't on any account leave his seat by Ben, though he was awfully tired of sitting still so long, for fear somebody else would hop into it. " Ben's going to teach us."

" Yes, he is," put in Van, bounding up to Jasper, and pulling at all the buttons on his jacket he could reach, to command attention.

" And us," said Joel, coming up, too. " You forgot *us*, Van."

" The whole of us—every single one in this room," said Van, decidedly, " all except Mrs. Pepper."

" Hello! " said Jasper, " that *is* a class! Well, Professor Ben, you've got to teach me then, for I'm coming, too."

" *You?* " exclaimed Ben, turning around in his chair and looking at him; " I can't teach *you* anything, Jappy. You know everything already —"

" Let him come, anyway," said Polly, hopping up and down.

" Oh, I'm coming, Professor," laughed Jasper. " Never you fear, Polly; I'll be on hand when the rest of the class comes in! "

" And Van," said Mrs. Pepper, pausing a minute in her work, and smiling over at him in a lull in the chatter—" I think flowers are most beautiful! " and she pointed to a little framed picture on the mantel, of the bunch of buttercups and one huge rose that Van had with infinite patience drawn, and then colored to suit his fancy.

" Do you? " cried Van, perfectly delighted; and leaving the group he rushed up to her side. " Do you *really* think they're nice, Mrs. Pepper? "

" Of course I do," said Mrs. Pepper, briskly, and beaming on him; " I think everything of them, and I shall keep them as long as I live, Van! "

" Well, then," said Van, very much pleased, " I shall paint you ever so many more—just as many as you want! "

" Do! " said Mrs. Pepper, taking up her work again. " And I'll hang them every one up."

" Yes, I will," said Van; " and I'll go right to work on one to-morrow. What are you mending our jackets for? " he asked, abruptly, as a familiar hole caught his attention.

" Because they're torn," said Mrs. Pepper, cheerfully, " and they won't mend themselves."

" Why don't you let Jane? " he persisted. " She always does them."

" Jane has enough to do," replied Mrs. Pepper, smiling away as hard as she could, " and I haven't, so I'm going to look around and pick up something to keep my hands out of mischief as much as I can, while I'm here."

"Do you ever get into mischief?" asked little Dick, coming up and looking into Mrs. Pepper's face wonderingly. "Why, you're a big woman!"

"O dear me, yes!" said Mrs. Pepper. "The bigger you are, the more mischief you can get into. You'll find that out, Dicky."

"And then do you have to stand in a corner?" asked Dick, determined to find out just what were the consequences, and reverting to his most dreaded punishment.

"No," said Mrs. Pepper, laughing. "Corners are for little folks; but when people who know better, do wrong, there aren't any corners they can creep into, or they'd get into them pretty quick!"

"I wish," said little Dick, "you'd let me get into your lap. *That* would be a nice corner!"

"Do, mamsie," said Polly, coming up, "that's just the way I used to feel; and I'll finish the mending."

So Mrs. Pepper put down her work, and moved the big basket for little Dick to clamber up, when he laid his head contentedly back in her motherly arms with a sigh of happiness. Phronsie regarded him with a very grave expression. At last she drew near: " I'm tired; do, mamsie, take me! "

" So mamsie will," said Mrs. Pepper, opening her arms, when Phronsie immediately crawled up into their protecting shelter, with a happy little crow.

" Oh, now, tell us a story, Mrs. Pepper," cried Van; " please, *please* do! "

" No, no! " exclaimed Percy, scuttling out of his chair, and coming up, " let's talk of the Little Brown House. Do tell us what you used to do there—that's best."

" So 'tis! " cried Van; " ALL the nice times you used to have in it! Wait just a minute, do." And he ran back for a cricket, which he placed at Mrs. Pepper's feet; and then sitting down on it, he leaned on her comfortable lap, in order to hear better.

" Wait for me, too, till I get a chair," called Percy, starting. " Don't begin till I get there."

" Here, let me, Percy," said Ben; and he drew forward a big easy chair that the boy was tugging at with all his might.

" Now *I'm* ready, too," said Polly, setting small finishing stitches quickly with a merry little flour-

ish, and drawing her chair nearer her mother's as
she spoke.

"Now begin, please," said Van, "all the nice
times you know."

"She couldn't tell *all* the nice times if she had
ten years to tell them in, could she, Polly?" said
Jasper.

"Well, in the first place, then," said Mrs. Pepper, clearing her throat, "the Little Brown House
had *got to be,* you know, so we made up our
minds to make it just the *nicest* brown house that
ever was!"

"And it was!" declared Jasper, with an emphatic ring to his voice. "The very nicest place
in the whole world!"

"O dear!" broke in Van, enviously; "Jappy's
always said so. I wish we'd been there, too!"

"We didn't want anybody but Jappy," said
Joel, not very politely.

"Oh, Joey, for shame!" cried Polly.

"Jappy used to bake," cried little Davie; "and
we all made pies; and then we sat round and ate
them, and then told stories."

"Oh, what fun!" cried Percy. "Do tell us!"

So the five little Peppers and Jasper flew off
into reminiscences and accounts of the funny do-

ings, and Mrs. Pepper joined in heartily till the room got very merry with the glee and enthusiasm called forth; so much so, that nobody heard Mrs. Whitney knock gently at the door, and nobody answering, she was obliged to come in by herself.

"Well, well," she cried, merrily, looking at the swarm of little ones around Mrs. Pepper and the big chair. "You *are* having a nice time! May I come and listen?"

"Oh, if you will, sister," cried Jasper, springing off from his arm of the chair, while Ben flew from the other side, to hurry and get her a chair.

Percy and Van rushed, too, knocking over so many things that they didn't help much; and little Dick poked his head out from Mrs. Pepper's arms when he saw his mamma sitting down to stay, and began to scramble down to get into her lap.

"There now," said Mrs. Whitney, smiling over at Mrs. Pepper, who was smiling at her. "You have your baby, and I have mine! Now, children, what's it all about? What has Mrs. Pepper been telling you?"

"Oh. the Little Brown House!" cried Dicky,

his cheeks all aflame. "The *dearest* little house, mamma! I wish I could live in one!"

" 'Twouldn't be the same without the Peppers in it," said Jasper. "Not a bit of it!"

"And they had such perfectly *elegant* times," cried Percy, enviously, drawing up to her side. "Oh, you can't think, mamma!"

"Well, now," said his mamma, "do go on, and let me hear some of the nice times."

So away they launched again, and Mrs. Whitney was soon enjoying it as hugely as the children, when a heavy step sounded in the middle of the room, and a voice spoke in such a tone that everybody skipped.

"Well, I should like to know what all this means! I've been all over the house, and not a trace of anybody could I find."

"Oh, father!" cried Mrs. Whitney. "Van, dear, get up and get grandpapa a chair."

"No, no!" said the old gentleman, waving him off impatiently. "I'm not going to stay; I must go and lie down. My head is in a bad condition to-day; very bad indeed," he added.

"Oh!" said Phronsie, popping up her head and looking at him. "I must get right down."

"What's the matter, Phronsie?" asked Mrs. Pepper, trying to hold her back.

"Oh, but I *must*," said Phronsie, energetically wriggling. "My poor sick man wants me, he *does*." And flying out of her mother's arms, she ran up to Mr. King, and standing on tiptoe, said, softly, "I'll rub your head, grandpapa, dear, poor sick man; yes, I will."

"And you're the best child," cried the old gentleman, catching her up and marching over to the other side of the room where there was a lounging chair. "There now, you and I, Phronsie, will stay by ourselves. Then my head will feel better."

And he sat down and drew her into his arms.

"Does it ache *very* bad?" asked Phronsie, in a soft little voice. Then reaching up she began to pat and smooth it gently with one little hand, "*Very* bad, dear grandpapa?"

"It won't," said the old gentleman, "if you only keep on taking care of it, little Phronsie."

"Then," said the child, perfectly delighted, "I'm going to take all care of you, grandpapa, *always!*"

"So you shall, so you shall!" cried Mr. King, no less delighted than she was. "Mrs. Pepper!"

"Sir?" said Mrs. Pepper, trying to answer, which she couldn't do very well surrounded as she was by the crowd of little chatterers. "Yes, sir; excuse me, what is it, sir?"

"We've got to come to an understanding about this thing," said the old gentleman, "and I can't talk much to-day, because my headache won't allow it."

Here the worried look came into Phronsie's face again, and she began to try to smooth his head with both little hands.

"And so I must say it all in as few words as possible," he continued.

"What is it, sir?" again asked Mrs. Pepper, wonderingly.

"Well, the fact is, I must have somebody who will keep this house. Now, Marian, not a word!" as he saw symptoms of Mrs. Whitney's joining in the conversation. "You've been good; just as good as can be under the circumstances; but Mason will be home in the fall, and then I suppose you'll have to go with him. Now *I*," said the old gentleman, forgetting all about his head, and straightening himself up suddenly in the chair, "am going to get things into shape, so that the house will be kept for all of us; so that we can come or go. And how can I do it better than to have the Peppers—you, Mrs. Pepper, and all your children—come here and live, and ——"

"*Oh, father!*" cried Jasper, rushing up to him; and flinging his arms around his neck, he gave him such a hug as he hadn't received for many a day.

"Goodness me, Jasper!" cried his father, feeling of his throat. "How can you express your feelings so violently! And, besides, you interrupt."

"Beg pardon, sir," said Jasper, swallowing his excitement, and trying to control his eagerness.

"Do you say yes, Mrs. Pepper?" queried the old gentleman, impatiently. "I must get this thing fixed up to-day. I'm really too ill to be worried, ma'am."

"Why, sir," stammered Mrs. Pepper, "I don't know what to say. I couldn't think of imposing all my children on you, and ——"

"*Imposing!* Who's talking of *imposing!*" said Mr. King, in a loud key. "I want my house kept; will you live here and keep it? That is the question."

"But, sir," began Mrs. Pepper again, "you don't think ——"

"I *do* think; I tell you, ma'am, I *do* think," snapped the old gentleman. "It's just because I *have* thought that I've made up my mind. Will you do it, Mrs. Pepper?"

"What are you going to do, mamsie?" asked Joel, quickly.

"I don't know that I'm going to do anything yet," said poor Mrs. Pepper, who was almost stunned.

"To come here and live!" cried Jasper, unable to keep still any longer—and springing to the children. "Don't you want to, Joe?"

"*To live!*" screamed Joel. "O whickety, *yes!* Do, ma, do come here and live—do!"

"*To live?*" echoed Phronsie, over in the old gentleman's lap. "In this be-*you*-ti-ful place? Oh, *oh!*"

"Oh, *mamsie!*" that was all Polly could say.

And even Ben had his arms around his mother's neck, whispering "Do" into her ear, while little Davie got into her lap and teased her with all his might.

"What shall I do!" cried the poor woman. "Did ever anybody see the like?"

"It's the very best thing you could possibly do," cried the old gentleman. "Don't you see it's

for the children's advantage? They'll get such
educations, Mrs. Pepper, as you want for them.
And it accommodates me immensely. What ob-
stacle can there be to it?"

"If I was only sure 'twould be for the best?"
said Mrs. Pepper, doubtfully.

"Oh, dear Mrs. Pepper," said Mrs. Whitney,
laying her hand on hers. "Can you doubt it?"

"Then," said Mr. King, getting up, but still
holding on to Phronsie, "we'll consider it settled.
This is your home, children," he said, waving his
hand at the five little Peppers in a bunch. And
having thus summarily disposed of the whole
business, he marched out with Phronsie on his
shoulder.

XXIV

POLLY'S DISMAL MORNING

EVERYTHING had gone wrong with Polly that day. It began with her boots.

Of all things in the world that tried Polly's patience most were the troublesome little black buttons that originally adorned those useful parts of her clothing, and that were fondly supposed to be there when needed. But they never were. The little black things seemed to be invested with a special spite, for one by one they would hop off on the slightest provocation, and go rolling over the floor, just when she was in her most terrible hurry, compelling her to fly for needle and thread on the instant. For one thing Mrs. Pepper was very strict about—and that was, Polly should do nothing else till the buttons were all on again, and the boots buttoned up firm and snug.

" O dear! " said Polly, sitting down on the floor, and pulling on her stockings. " There, now, see that hateful old shoe, mamsie! " And she stuck out one foot in dismay.

"What's the matter with it?" asked Mrs. Pepper, straightening the things on the bureau. "You haven't worn it out already, Polly?"

"Oh, no," said Polly, with a little laugh. "I hope not yet, but it's these dreadful *hateful* old buttons!" And she twitched the boot off from her foot with such an impatient little pull, that three or four more went flying under the bed. "There, now—there's a lot more! I don't care! I wish they'd all go! they might as well!" she cried, tossing that boot on the floor in intense scorn, while she investigated the state of the other one.

"Are they *all* off?" asked Phronsie, pulling herself up out of a little heap in the middle of the bed, and leaning over the side, where she viewed Polly sorrowfully. "*Every* one, Polly?"

"No," said Polly, "but I wish they were, mean old things! when I was going down to play a duet with Jasper! We should have had a good long time before breakfast. Oh, mayn't I go just once, mamsie? Nobody'll see me if I tuck my foot under the piano; and I can sew them on afterwards—there'll be plenty of time. Do, just *once*, mamsie!"

"No." said Mrs. Pepper, firmly, "there isn't

any time but *now*. And piano-playing isn't very nice when you've got to stick your toes under it to keep your shoes on."

" Well, then," grumbled Polly, hopping around in her stocking-feet, " where *is* the work-basket, mamsie? Oh—here it is on the window-seat." A rattle of spools, scissors, and necessary utensils showed plainly that Polly had found it, followed by a jumble of words and despairing ejaculations as she groped hurriedly under chairs and tables to collect the scattered contents.

When she got back with a very red face, she found Phronsie, who had crawled out of bed, siting down on the floor in her little nightgown and examining the boot with profound interest.

" I can sew 'em, Polly," she said, holding up her hand for the big needle that Polly was trying to thread—" I can, now, truly; let me, Polly, do! "

" Goodness! " said Polly, with a little laugh, beginning to be very much ashamed. " What could you do with your little mites of hands pulling this big thread through that old leather? There, scamper into bed again; you'll catch cold out here."

" 'Tisn't *very* cold," said Phronsie, tucking up

her toes under the nightgown, but Polly hurried
her into bed, where she curled herself up under
the clothes, watching her make a big knot. But
the knot didn't stay; for when Polly drew up the
long thread triumphantly to the end—out it flew,
and away the button hopped again as if glad to be
released. And then the thread kinked horribly,
and got all twisted up in disagreeable little snarls
that took all Polly's patience to unravel.

"It's because you're in such a hurry," said Mrs.
Pepper, who was getting Phronsie's clothes. And
coming over across the room, she got down on one
knee, and looked over Polly's shoulder. " There,
now, let mother see what's the matter."

" O dear! " said Polly, resigning the needle with
a big sigh, and leaning back to take a good stretch,
followed by Phronsie's sympathizing eyes; " they
never'll be on! And there goes the first bell! "
as the loud sounds under Jane's vigorous ringing
pealed up over the stairs. " There won't be time,
anyway, now! I wish there wasn't such a thing
as shoes in the world! " And she gave a flounce
and sat up straight in front of her mother.

" *Polly!* " said Mrs. Pepper, sternly, deftly fast-
ening the little buttons tightly into place with
quick, firm stitches, " better be glad you've got

them to sew at all. There, now, here they are.
Those won't come off in a hurry! "

" Oh, mamsie! " cried Polly, ignoring for a moment the delights of the finished shoe to fling her
arms around her mother's neck and give her a
good hug. " You're just the splendidest, goodest
mamsie in all the world. And I'm a hateful, cross
old bear, so I am! " she cried, remorsefully, but-
toning herself into her boots. Which done, she
flew at the rest of her preparations, and tried to
make up for lost time.

But 'twas all of no use. The day seemed to be
always just racing ahead of her, and turning a
corner before she could catch up to it, and Ben
and the other boys only caught dissolving views
of her as she flitted through halls or over stairs.

" Where's Polly? " asked Percy at last, coming
with great dissatisfaction in his voice to the library door. " We've called her and called her, I
guess a million times, and she won't hurry."

" What do you want to have her do? " asked
Jasper, looking up from the sofa where he had
flung himself with a book.

" Why, she said she'd make Van and me our
sails, you know," said Percy, holding up a rather
forlorn-looking specimen of a boat, but which the

boys had carved with the greatest enthusiasm, " and we want her now."

" Can't you let her alone till she's ready to come? " said Jasper, quickly. " You're always teasing her to do something," he added.

" I didn't tease," said Percy, indignantly, coming up to the sofa, boat in hand, to enforce his words. " She said she'd love to do them, so there, Jasper King! "

" Coming! Coming! " sang Polly, over the stairs, and bobbing into the library. " Oh—here you are, Percy! I couldn't come before; mamsie wanted me. Now, says I, for the sails." And she began to flap out a long white piece of cotton cloth on the table to trim into just the desired shape.

" *That* isn't the way," said Percy, crowding up, the brightness that had flashed over his face at Polly's appearance beginning to fade. " Hoh! those won't be good for anything—those aren't sails."

" I haven't finished," said Polly, snipping away vigorously, and longing to get back to mamsie. " Wait till they're done; then they'll be good— as good as can be! "

" And it's bad enough to have to make them,"

put in Jasper, flinging aside his book and rolling over to watch them, "without having to be found fault with every second, Percy."

"They're too big," said Percy, surveying them critically, and then looking at his boat.

"Oh, that corner's coming off," cried Polly, cheerfully, giving it a sharp cut that sent it flying on the floor. "And they won't be too big when they're done, Percy, all hemmed and everything. There," as she held one up for inspection, "that's just the way I used to make Ben's and mine. when we sailed boats."

"Is it?" asked Percy, looking with more respect at the piece of cloth Polly was waving alluringly before him. "Just exactly like it, Polly?"

"Yes," said Polly, laying it down again for a pattern—"oh, how does this go—oh—that's it, there—yes, this is just *exactly* like Bensie's and mine—that was when I was ever so little; and then I used to make Joel's and Davie's afterwards and ——"

"And were theirs just like this?" asked Percy, laying his hand on the sail she had finished cutting out.

"*Pre*-cisely," said Polly, with a pin in her

mouth. " Just as like as two peas, Percy Whitney."

" Then I like them," cried Percy, veering round and regarding them with great satisfaction—as Van bounded in with a torrent of complaints, and great disappointment in every line of his face.

"Oh, now, that's too bad! " he cried, seeing Polly fold up the remaining bits of cloth, and pick up the scraps on the floor. " And you've gone and let her cut out every one of them, and never told me a word! You're a mean, old hateful thing, Percy Whitney! "

" Oh, *don't!* " exclaimed Polly, on her knees on the floor.

" I forgot ——" began Percy, " and she cut them so quick—and ——"

" And I've been waiting," said Van, in a loud, wrathful key, " and waiting—and *waiting!* "

"Never mind, Van," said Jasper, consolingly, getting off from the sofa and coming up to the table. " They're done, and done beautifully, aren't they? " he said, holding up one.

But this only proved fresh fuel for the fire of Van's indignation.

" And you sha'n't have them, so! " he cried,

making a lunge at the one on the table, " for I made most of the boat, *there!* "

" Oh, no, you didn't! " cried Percy, in the greatest alarm, hanging on to the boat in his hand. " I cut—all the keel—and the bow—and ——"

" Dear me! " cried Polly, in extreme dismay, looking at Jasper. " Come, I'll tell you what I'll do, boys."

" What? " asked Van, cooling off a little, and allowing Percy to edge into the corner with the beloved boat and one sail. " What will you, Polly? "

" I'll make you another pair of sails," said Polly, groaning within herself as she thought of the wasted minutes, " and then you can see me cut them, Van."

" Will you *really?* " he cried, delight showing all over his flushed face.

" Yes, I will," said Polly, " wait a minute till I get some more cloth." And she started for the door.

" Oh, now, that's too bad! " said Jasper. " To have to cut more of those tiresome old things! Van, let her off! "

" Oh, no, I won't! I won't! " he cried, in the greatest alarm, running up to her as she stood by the door. "You did say so, Polly! You *know* you did!"

"Of course I did, Vannie," said Polly, smiling down into his eager face, "and we'll have a splendid pair in just—one—minute!" she sang.

And so the sails were cut out, and the hems turned down and basted, and tucked away into Polly's little work-basket ready for the sewing on the morrow. And then Mr. King came in and took Jasper off with him; and the two Whitney boys went up to mamma for a story; and Polly sat down in mamsie's room to tackle her French exercise.

XXV

THE room was very quiet, but presently Phronsie strayed in, and seeing Polly studying, climbed up in a chair by the window to watch the birds hop over the verandah and pick up worms in the grass beside the carriage drive. And then came Mrs. Pepper with the big mending-basket, and ensconced herself opposite by the table; and nothing was to be heard but the " tick, tick " of the clock, and an occasional dropping of a spool of thread, or scissors, from the busy hands flying in and out among the stockings.

All of a sudden there was a great rustling in Cherry's cage that swung in the big window on the other side of the room. And then he set up a loud and angry chirping, flying up and down, and opening his mouth as if he wanted to express his mind, but couldn't, and otherwise acting in a very strange and unaccountable manner.

" Dear me! " said Mrs. Pepper, " what's that? "

" It's Cherry," said Polly, lifting up her head

from "Fasquelle," "and—O misery!" and flinging down the pile of books in her lap on a chair,
she rushed across the room, flew up to the cage,
and began to wildly gesticulate and explain and
shower down on the bird every endearing name
she could think of.

"What is the matter?" asked her mother, turning around in her chair in astonishment. "What
upon earth, Polly!"

"How *could* I!" cried Polly, in accents of despair, not heeding her mother's question. "Oh,
mamsie, will he die, do you think?"

"I guess not," said Mrs. Pepper, laying down
her work and coming up to the cage, while Phronsie scrambled off from her chair and hurried to
the scene. "Why, he does act queerly, doesn't
he? P'r'aps he's been eating too much?"

"*Eating!*" cried Polly, "oh, mamsie, he hasn't
had anything." And she pointed with shame and
remorse to the seed-cup with only a few dried
husks in the very bottom.

"Oh, Polly," began Mrs. Pepper; but seeing
the look on her face, she changed her tone for
one more cheerful. "Well, hurry and get him
some now; he'll be all right, poor little thing, in
a minute. There, there," she said, nodding per-

suasively at the cage, " you pretty creature, you! so you sha'n't be starved."

At the word " starved," Polly winced as though a pin had been thrust into her.

" There isn't any, mamsie, in the house," she stammered; " he had the last yesterday."

" And you forgot him to-day? " asked Mrs. Pepper, with a look in her black eyes Polly didn't like.

" Yes'm," said poor Polly, in a low voice.

" Well, he must have something right away, said Mrs. Pepper, decidedly. " That's certain."

" I'll run right down to Fletcher's and get it," cried Polly. " 'Twon't take me but a minute, mamsie; Jasper's gone, and Thomas, too, so I've got to go," she added, as she saw her mother hesitate.

" If you could wait till Ben gets home," said Mrs. Pepper, slowly. " I'm 'most afraid it will rain, Polly."

" Oh, no, mamsie," cried Polly, feeling as if she could fly to the ends of the earth to atone, and longing beside for the brisk walk down-town. Going up to the window she pointed triumphantly to the little bit of blue sky still visible. " There, now, see, it can't rain yet a while."

"Well," said Mrs. Pepper, while Phronsie, standing in a chair with her face pressed close to the cage, was telling Cherry through the bars "not to be hungry, please *don't!*" which he didn't seem to mind in the least, but went on screaming harder than ever! " And besides, 'tisn't much use to wait for Ben. Nobody knows where he'll get shoes to fit himself and Joe and Davie in one afternoon! But be sure, Polly, to hurry, for it's getting late, and I shall be worried about you."

"Oh, mamsie," said Polly, turning back just a minute, " I know the way to Fletcher's just as easy as anything. I couldn't get lost."

"I know you do," said Mrs. Pepper, "but it'll be dark early on account of the shower. Well," she said, pulling out her well-worn purse from her pocket, " if it does sprinkle, you get into a car, Polly, remember."

"Oh, yes, I will," she cried, taking the purse.

"And there's ten cents for your bird-seed in that pocket," said Mrs. Pepper, pointing to a coin racing away into a corner by itself.

"Yes'm," said Polly, wild to be off.

"And there's a five-cent piece in that one for you to ride up with," said her mother, tying up the purse carefully, " if it rains. Well, I guess you better ride up, *anyway,* Polly, come to think, and then you'll get home all the quicker."

" Where are you going? " asked Phronsie, who on seeing the purse knew there was some expedition on foot, and she began to clamber down out of the chair. " Oh, I want to go, too, I *do.* Take me, Polly! "

" Oh, no, Pet, I can't," cried Polly, " I've got to hurry like everything! "

" I can hurry, too," cried Phronsie, drawing her small figure to its utmost height, " oh, so fast, Polly! "

" And it's ever so far," cried Polly, in despair, as she saw the small under lip of the child begin to quiver. " O dear me, mamsie, what shall I do! "

" Run right along," said Mrs. Pepper, briskly. " Now, Phronsie, you and I must take care of Cherry, poor thing."

At this Phronsie turned and wiped away two big tears, while she gazed up at the cage in extreme commiseration.

" I guess I'll give him a piece of bread," said Mrs. Pepper to herself. At this word " bread," Polly, who was half-way down the hall, came running back.

" Oh, mamsie, don't," she said. " It made him sick before, don't you know it did—so fat and stuffy."

" Well, hurry along, then," said Mrs. Pepper, and Polly was off.

Over the ground she sped, only intent on reaching the bird-store, her speed heightened by the dark and rolling bank of cloud that seemed to shut down suddenly over her and envelop her warningly.

" It's good I have the money to ride up with," she thought to herself, hurrying along through the busy streets, filled now with anxious crowds homeward rushing to avoid the threatening shower. " Well, here I am," she said, with a sigh of relief, as she at last reached Mr. Fletcher's big bird-store.

Here she steadily resisted all temptations to stop and look at the new arrivals of birds, and to feed the carrier-pigeons, who seemed to be expecting her, and who turned their soft eyes up at her reproachfully when she failed to pay her respects to them. Even the cunning blandishments of a very attractive monkey that always had entertained the children on their numerous visits, failed to interest her now. Mamsie would be worrying, she knew; and besides, the sight of so many birds eating their suppers out of generously full seed-cups only filled her heart with remorse as she thought of poor Cherry and his empty one.

So she put down her ten cents silently on the counter, and took up the little package of seed, and went out.

But what a change! The cloud that had seemed but a cloud when she went in, was now fast descending in big, ominous sprinkles that told of a heavy shower to follow. Quick and fast they came, making everybody fly to the nearest shelter.

"I don't care," said Polly to herself, holding fast her little package. "I'll run and get in the car—then I'll be all right."

So she went on with nimble footsteps, dodging the crowd, and soon came to the corner. A car was just in sight—that was fine! Polly put her hand in her pocket for her purse, to have it all ready—but as quickly drew it out again and stared wildly at the car, which she allowed to pass by. Her pocket was empty!

"O dear!" she said to herself, as a sudden gust of wind blew around the corner, and warned her to move on, " now what *shall* I do! Well, I must hurry. Nothing for it but to run now! "

And secretly glad at the chance for a good hearty run along the hard pavements, a thing she had been longing to do ever since she came to the city, Polly gathered her bundle of seed up under her arm, and set out for a jolly race. She was enjoying it hugely, when—a sudden turn of the corner brought her up against a gentleman, who, having his umbrella down to protect his face, hadn't seen her till it was too late.

Polly never could tell how it was done; but the first thing she knew she was being helped up from the wet, slippery pavement by a kind hand; and a gentleman's voice said in the deepest concern:

" I beg your pardon; it was extremely careless in me."

" It's no matter," said Polly, hopping up with a little laugh, and straightening her hat. " Only—" and she began to look for her parcel that had been sent spinning.

" What is it? " asked the gentleman, bending down and beginning to explore, too, in the darkness.

" My bundle," began Polly. " O dear! "

No need to ask for it now! There lay the paper

wet and torn, down at their feet. The seed lay all over the pavement, scattered far and wide even out to the puddles in the street. And not a cent of money to get any more with! The rain that was falling around them as they stood there sent with the sound of every drop a flood of misery into Polly's heart!

"What was it, child?" asked the gentleman, peering sharply to find out what the little shiny things were.

"Bird-seed," gasped Polly.

"Is that all?" said the gentleman, with a happy laugh. "I'm very glad."

"*All!*" Polly's heart stood still as she thought of Cherry, stark and stiff in the bottom of his cage, if he didn't get it soon. "Now," said the kind tones, briskly, "come, little girl, we'll make this all right speedily. Let's see—here's a bird-store. Now, then."

"But, sir——" began Polly, holding back.

Even Cherry had better die than to do anything her mother wouldn't like. But the gentleman already had her in the shop, and was delighting the heart of the shopkeeper by ordering him to do up a big package of all kinds of seed. And then he added a cunning arrangement for birds to

swing in, and two or three other things that didn't
have anything to do with birds at all!   And then
they came out on the wet, slippery street again.

"Now, then, little girl," said the gentleman,
tucking the bundle under his arm, and opening
the umbrella; then he took hold of Polly's hand,
who by this time was glad of a protector.   "Where
do you live?   For I'm going to take you safely
home this time where umbrellas can't run into
you."

"Oh!" cried Polly, with a little skip.   "Thank
you, sir!   It's up to Mr. King's; and——"

"*What!*" exclaimed the gentleman, stopping
short in the midst of an immense puddle, and staring at her, "Mr. Jasper Horatio King's?"

"I don't know, sir," said Polly, "what his other
name is.   Yes, it must be Jasper; that's what
Jappy's is, anyway," she added, with a little
laugh, wishing very much that she could see
Jappy at that identical moment.

"*Jappy!*" exclaimed the stranger, still standing
as if petrified.   "Are there any little Whitney
children in the same house?"

"Oh, yes," said Polly, raising her clear brown
eyes up to him.   The gas-lighter was just beginning his rounds, and the flame from a neighboring

lamp flashed full on Polly's face as she spoke, showing just how clear and brown the eyes were. " There's Percy, and Van, and little Dick—oh, he's so cunning! " she cried, impulsively.

The gentleman's face looked very queer just then; but he merely said:

" Why, you must be Polly? "

" Yes, sir, I am," said Polly, pleased to think he knew her. And then she told him how she'd forgotten Cherry's seed, and all about it. " And oh, sir," she said, and her voice began to tremble, " mamsie'll be *so* frightened if I don't get there soon! "

" I'm going up there myself, so that it all happens very nicely," said the gentleman, commencing to start off briskly, and grasping her hand tighter. " Now then, Polly."

So off they went at a very fast pace; she, skipping through the puddles that his long, even strides carried him safely over, chattered away by his side under the umbrella, and answered his many questions, and altogether got so very well acquainted that by the time they turned in at the old stone gateway she felt as if she had known him for years.

And there, the first thing they either of them

saw, down in a little corner back of the tall ever-
greens, was a small heap that rose as they splashed
up the carriage-drive, and resolved itself into a
very red dress and a very white apron, as it rushed
impulsively up and flung itself into Polly's wet
arms.

"And I was so tired waiting, Polly!"

"The mischief, Phronsie!" cried Polly, hud-
dling her up from the dark, wet ground. "You'll
catch your death! What will mamsie say!"

The stranger, amazed at this new stage of the
proceedings, was vainly trying to hold the umbrella over both, till the procession could move on
again.

"Oh!" cried Phronsie, shaking her yellow head
decidedly, "they're all looking for you, Polly."
She pointed one finger solemnly up to the big
carved door as she spoke. At that, Polly gathered
her up close and began to walk with rapid footsteps up the path.

"Do let me carry you, little girl," said Polly's
kind friend, persuasively, bending down to the
little face on Polly's neck.

"Oh, no, no, no!" cried Phronsie, at each sylla-
ble grasping Polly around the throat in perfect
terror, and waving him off with a very crumpled,

mangy bit of paper, that had already done duty
to wipe off the copious tears during her anxious
watch. "Don't let him, Polly, *don't!*"

"There sha'n't anything hurt you," said Polly,
kissing her reassuringly, and stepping briskly off
with her burden, just as the door burst open, and
Joel flew out on the veranda steps, followed by
the rest of the troop in the greatest state of excitement.

"O whickety!   she's *come!*" he shouted,
bouncing up to her over the puddles, and cram-
ming under the umbrella.   "Where'd you get
Phronsie?" he asked, standing stock-still at sight
of the little feet tucked up to get out of the rain.
And without waiting for an answer he turned and
shot back into the house, proclaiming in sten-
torian tones, "Ma, Polly's come—and she's got
Phronsie—and an *awful* big man—and they're
out by the gate!"

"*Phronsie!*" exclaimed Mrs. Pepper, springing
to her feet, "why, I thought she was up-stairs
with Jane."

"Now, somebody," exclaimed old Mr. King,
who sat by the library table vainly trying to read
a newspaper, which he now threw down in extreme irritation as he rose quickly and went to the

door to welcome the wanderers, " ought to watch that poor child, whose business it is to *know* where she is! She's caught her death-cold, no doubt, no doubt! "

Outside, in the rain, the children revolved around Polly and Phronsie, hugging and kissing them, until nobody could do much more than breathe, not seeming to notice the stranger, who stood quietly waiting till such time as he could be heard.

At last, in a lull in the scramble, as they were dragging Polly and her burden up the steps, each wild for the honor of escorting her into the house, he cried out, in laughing tones:

" Isn't anybody going to kiss *me*, I wonder! "

The two little Whitneys, who were eagerly clutching Polly's arm, turned around; and Percy rubbed his eyes in a puzzled way, as Joel said, stopping a minute to look up at the tall figure:

" We don't ever kiss strangers—mamsie's told us not to."

" For shame, Joey! " cried Polly, feeling her face grow dreadfully red in the darkness, " the gentleman's been so kind to me! "

" You're right, my boy," said the stranger, laughing and bending down to Joel's upturned,

sturdy countenance, at the same instant that Mrs.
Pepper flung open the big door, and a bright,
warm light fell straight across his handsome face.
And then ——

Well, then Percy gave a violent bound, and upsetting Joel as he did so, wriggled his way down
the step—at the same time that Van, on Polly's
other side, rushed up to the gentleman.

"Papa—oh, *papa!*"

Polly, half-way up the steps, turned around,
and then, at the rush of feeling that gathered at
her heart, sat right down on the wet, slippery
step.

"Why, Polly Pepper!" exclaimed Joel, not
minding his own upset. "You're right in all the
slush—mother won't like it, I tell you!"

"Hush!" cried Polly, catching his arm, "he's
come—oh, Joel—he's *come!*"

"Who?" cried Joel, staring around blindly,
"who, Polly?"

Polly had just opened her lips to explain, when
Mr. King's portly, handsome figure appeared in
the doorway. "Do come in, children—why—good
gracious, Mason!"

"Yes," cried the stranger, lightly, dropping his
big bundle and umbrella as he passed in the door,

with his little sons clinging to him. " Where is Marian? "

" Why didn't you write? " asked the old gentleman, testily. " These surprises aren't the right sort of things," and he began to feel vigorously of his heart. " Here, Mrs. Pepper, be so good as to call Mrs. Whitney."

"*Pepper! Pepper!*" repeated Mr. Whitney, perplexedly.

' She's coming—I hear her up-stairs," cried Van Whitney. " Oh, let me tell her! " He struggled to get down from his father's arms as he said this.

" No, I shall—I heard her first! " cried Percy. " O dear me!   Grandpapa's going to! "

Mr. King advanced to the foot of the staircase as his daughter, all unconscious, ran down with a light step, and a smile on her face.

" Has Polly come? " she asked, seeing only her father.

" Yes," replied the old gentleman, shortly, " and she's brought a big bundle, Marian! "

" A big bundle? " she repeated, wonderingly, and gazing at him.

" A *very* big bundle," he said, and taking hold

of her shoulders he turned her around on—her husband.

So Polly and Phronsie crept in unnoticed after all.

" I wish Ben was here," said little Davie, capering around the Whitney group, " and Jappy, I do! "

" Where are they? " asked Polly.

" Don't know," said Joel, tugging at his shoe-string. " See—aren't these prime! " He held up a shining black shoe, fairly bristling with newness, for Polly to admire.

" Splendid," she cried, heartily; " but where are the boys? "

" They went after you," said Davie, " after we came home with our shoes."

" No, they didn't," contradicted Joel, flatly; and sitting down on the floor he began to tie and untie his new possessions. " When we came home Ben drew us pictures—lots of 'em—don't you know? "

" Oh, yes," said Davie, nodding his head, " so he did; that was when we all cried 'cause you weren't home, Polly."

" He drew me a be-*you*-tiful one," cried Phronsie, holding up her crumpled bit; " see, Polly, see! "

" That's the Little Brown House," said Davie,

looking over her shoulder as Phronsie put it carefully into Polly's hand.

"It's all washed out," said Polly, smoothing it
out, "when you stayed out in the rain."

Phronsie's face grew very grave at that.

"Bad, naughty old rain," she said, and then she
began to cry as hard as she could.

"The deary me!" cried Polly, in dismay, trying
her best to stop her, "oh, Phronsie, do stop!" she
implored, pointing into the next room whence the
sound of happy voices issued, "they'll all hear
you!"

But Phronsie in her grief didn't care, but wailed
on steadily.

"Who is it, anyway?" cried Joel, tired of admiring his precious shoes, and getting up to hear
them squeak, "that great big man, you know,
Polly, that came in with you!"

"Why, I thought I told you," said Polly, at her
wits' end over Phronsie. "It's Percy and Van's
father, Joey!"

"Whockey!" cried Joel, completely stunned,
"*really* and truly, Polly Pepper?"

"Really and truly," cried Polly, bundling
Phronsie up in her arms to lay the little wet
cheek against hers.

"Then I'm going to peek," cried Joel, squeaking across the floor to carry his threat into execution.

"Oh, you mustn't, Joe!" cried Polly, frightened lest he should. "Come right back, or I'll tell mamsie!"

"They're all coming in, anyway," cried little Davie, delightedly, and scuttling over to Polly's side.

"And here are the little friends I've heard so much about!" cried Mr. Whitney, coming in amongst them. "Oh, you needn't introduce me to Polly—she brought me home!"

"They're *all* Pepperses," said Percy, waving his hand, and doing the business up at one stroke.

"Only the best of them isn't here," observed Van, rather ungallantly, "*he* draws perfectly elegantly, papa!"

"*I* like Polly best, I do!" cried little Dick, tumbling after.

"*Peppers!*" again repeated Mr. Whitney, in a puzzled way.

"And here is Mrs. Pepper," said old Mr. King, pompously drawing her forward, "the children's mother, and——"

But here Mrs. Pepper began to act in a very

queer way, rubbing her eyes and twisting one
corner of her black apron in a decidedly nervous
manner that, as the old gentleman looked up, he
saw with astonishment presently communicated
itself to the gentleman opposite.

"Is it," asked Mr. Whitney, putting out his
hand and grasping the hard, toil-worn one in the
folds of the apron, "is it Cousin Mary?"

"And aren't you Cousin John?" she asked, the
tears in her bright black eyes.

"Of all things in this world!" cried the old
gentleman, waving his hand helplessly from one
to the other. "Will somebody have the extreme
goodness to tell us what all this means?"

At this the little Peppers crowded around their
mother, and into all the vacant places they could
find, to get near the fascinating scene.

"Well," said Mr. Whitney, sitting down and
drawing his wife to his side, "it's a long story.
You see, when I was a little youngster, and ——"

"You were *John* Whitney then," put in Mrs.
Pepper, slyly. "That's the reason I never knew
when they were all talking of Mason Whitney."

"John Whitney I was," said Mr. Whitney,
laughing, "or, rather, Johnny and Jack. But
Grandmother Mason, when I grew older, wanted

me called by my middle name to please grandfather. But to go back—when I was a little
shaver, about as big as Percy here ——"

"Oh, papa! " began Percy, deprecatingly. To
be called " a little shaver " before all the others!

"He means, dearie," said his mamma, reassuringly, " when he was a boy like you. Now hear
what papa is going to say."

"Well, I was sent up into Vermont to stay at
the old place. There was a little girl there, a
bright, black-eyed little girl. She was my cousin,
and her name was Mary Bartlett."

"Who's Mary Bartlett? " asked Joel, interrupt-
ing.

"There she is, sir," said Mr. Whitney, pointing
to Mrs. Pepper, who was laughing and crying together.

"Where? " said Joel, utterly bewildered. "I
don't see any Mary Bartlett. What does he mean,
Polly? "

"I don't know," said Polly. "Wait, Joey," she
whispered, " he's going to tell us all about it."

"Well, this little cousin and I went to the dis-
trict school, and had many good times together.
And then my parents sent for me, and I went to
Germany to school; and when I came back I lost

sight of her. All I could find out was that she had married an Englishman by the name of Pepper."

"*Oh!*" cried all the children together.

'And I always supposed she had gone to England; for in spite of all my efforts, I could find no trace of her. Ah, Mary," he said, reproachfully, "why didn't you let me know where you were?"

"I heard," said Mrs. Pepper, "that you'd grown very rich, and I couldn't."

"You always were a proud little thing," he said, laughing.

"Well, but," broke in Mr. King, unable to keep silence any longer, "I'd like to inquire, Mason, why you didn't find all this out before, in Marian's letters, when she mentioned Mrs. Pepper?"

"She didn't ever mention her," said Mr. Whitney, turning around to face his questioner, "not as *Mrs. Pepper*—never once by name. It was always either 'Polly's mother,' or 'Phronsie's mother.' Just like a woman," he added, with a mischievous glance at his wife, "not to be explicit."

"And just like a man," she retorted, with a happy little laugh, "not to ask for explanations."

"I hear Jappy," cried Polly, in a glad voice, "and Ben—oh, good!" as a sound of rushing footsteps was heard over the veranda steps, and down the long hall.

The door was thrown suddenly open, and Jasper plunged in, his face flushed with excitement, and after him Ben, looking a little as he did when Phronsie was lost, while Prince squeezed panting in between the two boys.

" Has Polly got —— " began Jasper.

" Oh, yes, I'm here," cried Polly, springing up to them; " oh, Ben! "

" She has," cried Joel, disentangling himself from the group, " don't you see, Jappy? "

" She's all home," echoed Phronsie, flying up. " Oh, Ben, do draw me another little house! "

" And see—see! " cried the little Whitneys, pointing with jubilant fingers to their papa, " see what she brought! "

Jasper turned around at that—and then rushed forward.

" Oh, Brother Mason! "

" Well, Jasper," said Mr. Whitney, a whole wealth of affection beaming on the boy, " how you have stretched up in six months! "

" Haven't I? " said Jasper, laughing, and drawing himself up to his fullest height.

" He's standing on tiptoe," said Joel, critically,

who was hovering near. "I 'most know he is!" and he bent down to examine the position of Jasper's heels.

"Not a bit of it, Joe!" cried Jasper, with a merry laugh, and setting both feet with a convincing thud on the floor.

"Well, anyway, I'll be just as big," cried Joel, "when I'm thirteen, so!"

Just then a loud and quick rap on the table made all the children skip, and stopped everybody's tongue. It came from Mr. King.

"Phronsie," said he, "come here, child. I can't do anything without you," and he held out his hand. Phronsie immediately left Ben, who was hanging over Polly as if he never meant to let her go out of his sight again, and went directly over to the old gentleman's side.

"Now, then!" He swung her upon his shoulder, where she perched like a little bird, gravely surveying the whole group. One little hand stole around the old gentleman's neck, and patted his cheek softly, which so pleased him that for a minute or two he stood perfectly still so that everybody might see it.

"Now, Phronsie, *you* must tell all these children so that they'll understand—say everything just as I tell you, mind! "

" I will," said Phronsie, shaking her small head wisely, " every single thing."

" Well, then, now begin ——"

" Well, then, now begin," said Phronsie, looking down on all the faces, and finishing up with two or three little nods.

" Oh, no, dear, that isn't it," cried the old gentleman, " I'll tell you. Say, Phronsie, 'You are all cousins—every one.' "

" You are all cousins—every one," repeated little Phronsie, simply, shaking her yellow head into the very middle of the group.

" Does she *mean* it, grandpapa? Does she *mean* it? " cried Percy, in the greatest excitement.

" As true as *everything?* " demanded Joel, squeezing in between them.

" As true as—truth! " said the old gentleman, solemnly, patting the child's little fat hand. " So make the most of it."

" *Oh!* " cried Polly, with a long sigh. And then Jasper and she took hold of hands and had a good spin!

Joel turned around with two big eyes on Percy.

" We're *cousins!* " he said.

"I know it," said Percy, "and so's Van!"

"Yes," said Van, flying up, "and I'm cousin to Polly, too—that's best!"

"Can't *I* be a cousin?" cried little Dick, crowding up, with two red cheeks. "Isn't anybody going to be a cousin to me, too?"

"Everybody but Jasper," said the old gentleman, laughing heartily at them. "You and I, my boy," he turned to his son, "are left out in the cold."

At this a scream, loud and terrible to hear, struck upon them all, as Joel flung himself flat on the floor.

"Isn't—Jappy—our—cousin? I—want Jappy!"

"Goodness!" exclaimed the old gentleman, in the greatest alarm, "what is the matter with the boy! Do somebody stop him!"

"Joel," said Jasper, leaning over him, and trying to help Polly lift him up. "I'll tell you how we'll fix it! I'll be your brother. That's best of all—brother to Polly, and Ben, and the whole of you—then we'll see!"

Joel bolted up at that, and began to smile through the tears running down the rosy face.

"Will you, *really?*" he cried, "just like Ben—and everything?"

"I can't be as good as Ben," said Jappy, laughing, "but I'll be a real brother like him."

"Phoo—phoo! Then I don't care!" cried Joel, wiping off the last tear on the back of his chubby hand. "Now I guess we're better'n *you*," he exclaimed, with a triumphant glance over at the little Whitneys, as he began to make the new shoes skip at a lively pace up and down the long room.

"O dear!" they both cried, in great distress.

"Now, papa, Jappy's going to be Joey's brother —and he isn't anything but *our* old uncle! Make him be ours more, papa, do?"

And then Polly sprang up.

"Oh! oh—misery!" And she rushed out into the hall and began to tug violently at the big bundle, tossed down in a corner. "Cherry'll die —Cherry'll die!" she cried, "do somebody help me off with the string!"

But Polly already had it off by the time Jasper's knife was half out of his pocket, and was kneeling down on the floor scooping out a big handful of the seed.

"Don't hurry so, Polly," said Jasper, as she jumped up and flew up-stairs. "He's had some a perfect age—he's all right."

"*What!*" exclaimed Polly, stopping so suddenly that two or three little seeds flew out of the outstretched hand and went dancing away to the foot of the stairs by themselves.

"Oh, I heard him scolding away there when I first came home," said Jasper, "so I just ran down a block or two, and got him some."

"Is that all there is in that big bundle?" cried Joel, in a disappointed tone, who had followed with extreme curiosity to see its contents. "Phoo! —that's no fun—old bird-seed!"

"I know," said Polly, with a gay little laugh, pointing with the handful of seed into the library, "but I shouldn't have met the other big bundle if it hadn't been for *this*, Joe!"

THE END